Your Or
(The Bennett Family, Book 8)

LAYLA HAGEN

Dear Reader,

If you want to receive news about my upcoming books and sales, you can sign up for my newsletter HERE: http://laylahagen.com/mailing-list-sign-up/

Chapter One

Caroline

"You missed me, huh?" I pat Bing's head, bending on one knee, hugging him. The golden retriever licks my face, wagging his tail. "I know you're alone all day, but Linda will be back soon. I'm gonna miss our walks."

At the word *walks*, he barks, raising one paw.

"Yes, yes. We're going out. Come on."

I'm dog sitting for my neighbor and good friend Linda, who's been in Hawaii for a week. Bing and I had a rocky start, but I slowly coaxed him out of his shell, one dog treat at a time. Yeah, I bribed him with goodies into loving me, but a girl's got to do what a girl's got to do.

I take Bing for a walk on our usual route around the block, stopping for him to bark at a squirrel, pulling him away from an overexcited pug with a shrill bark and a chronic tiny-dog syndrome.

My phone chirps in my purse, and while holding Bing's leash firmly in one hand, I clumsily extract my phone with the other, glancing at the text message from one of my best friends.

Summer: Proud aunt. Maddox is perfectly healthy.

She also sent me a picture, and I swear to God, my heart almost bursts. Red-faced and tiny, the newborn is absolutely adorable.

Caroline: He's sweet. Congratulations! Thanks for the pic. How are Clara and Blake doing?

Summer: Clara is tired but happy, and my brother is a little too excited. You know Blake...

A second picture comes through. Summer is holding the baby, and next to her is another brother of hers, my ex, Daniel. I wonder if there is an expiration date on calling someone an ex. Maybe it's time to use a more neutral label, such as acquaintance, or friend. After all, Daniel and I called it quits almost ten years ago, and I'm close to his mother and sisters.

A jolt in my arm nearly makes me lose my balance. I sway forward as Bing lurches after a stray cat.

"Bing, no! Stop. Sit. Bing!"

I break into a run to keep up with him, and by the time we're back in Linda's apartment, my arm feels like it's about to fall off. Bing raises both his front paws, standing on his back legs.

"I'll be back tomorrow, Bing."

Bing blinks, setting down one paw and then the other, then resting his snout on them, looking up at me with wide, accusatory eyes.

Lowering my voice to a conspiratorial whisper, I add, "I'll bring you beef jerky."

Well, damn. Not even the thought of beef

jerky cheers him up. I look around the neat, quiet apartment. I don't have the heart to leave him alone here.

"You know what we're gonna do? We're going to break the rules tonight." He lifts his head. "Yes, we are. How would you feel about spending the night in my apartment? Come on. Let's take the stairs. It's just one floor."

When I open the door, he springs up on all fours, wiggling his tail. Tightening my grip on his leash, I lead him down the stairs. Bing is psyched when I let him inside my apartment.

"House rules: don't chew the furniture. Or my shoes." He wiggles his tail some more, not a care in the world, eyeing the two pairs of flats on the floor with intent. Right, better safe than sorry. I stack the shoes in the closet next to the entrance door, then set Bing free. He runs straight to my living room, hops on the couch, and barks in excitement.

While eating dinner, I keep an eye on my canine guest, who is staring at one leg of my coffee table, possibly considering its merits as a tooth sharpener. Belly full, I chance a trip to my bedroom, changing into sweatpants and a baggy T-shirt. The outfit is my guilty pleasure, unattractive as it looks.

Another quick trip to the bathroom to brush my dark brown hair and pull it in a bun, then to remove my makeup. Not that I wear much, just some mascara and eye shadow to highlight my blue eyes, but I like my face clean when I'm home.

The legs of my coffee table are still intact

upon my return, and I sit next to Bing, opening my laptop and browsing Netflix. No better way to wind down after a long day than watching one of my favorite shows. But before I decide on a show, curiosity gets the better of me. I call Summer, intending to scoop out more details about the newest addition to the Bennett family.

She answers after several rings.

"Hey, Caroline!"

The voice doesn't belong to Summer, but to Daniel. My stomach tightens instantly, but I hope my voice sounds casual when I ask, "Hey, is this a bad time? I just wanted to get more details on your nephew."

From his end of the line, I can hear a mix of voices. As I imagined, his family is camping out at the hospital. The Bennett clan is tight.

"It's a little crazy around here. Summer's talking to Clara now."

"Okay, I'll just call her later, or tomorrow. I'll let you go back to your family."

"Wait, don't hang up. How are you? Haven't seen you in a while. Your toe okay?"

I laugh nervously. "It was nothing. I was good as new the next day."

We last saw each other at Blake and Clara's wedding two months ago. After drinking a little too much champagne and feeling far too comfortable around him, I challenged him to join me for a traditional Irish dance. My parents moved here from Ireland when I was ten, and despite having taken classes back home, I'm not much of a dancer, which I tend to forget at weddings. At this particular one, I stepped on my own toe, then could barely walk. It hurt like hell, but feeling Daniel's steely arms around me as he steadied me on my way to the cab sure was a great bonus. That's the problem with Daniel: I don't trust myself around him, not even after all this time.

"*Tell Caroline I need those black shoes back next week,*" Summer's voice resounds somewhere in his background.

"I heard everything," I say. "Tell her—"

I stop midsentence when I hear Summer talking in the background again. "*Actually, would you be the best brother in the world and meet her to get the shoes? My schedule is insane next week.*"

Daniel and I both laugh into the phone. Oh yeah, his sisters are relentless about pushing us together every chance they get—and if an opportunity doesn't present itself, they fabricate one. Daniel and I take this in stride, joking about it. We're so far past awkward when it comes to his sisters' matchmaking attempts that at this point we'd find it weird if they *didn't* try anything.

"Should have seen this coming," Daniel says. "Caroline, let's meet up next week since my sister's schedule is so *insane.*"

"And yours isn't?" I tease.

"Oh, it is. But I know better than to tell Summer no."

I tap my fingers on my belly, laughing again.

Summer has Daniel wrapped around her little finger. But the man also doesn't do anything he doesn't want, so there's that.

"Okay. Let's—Bing, no!" For the love of all that is holy! I sprint to the foyer to assess the damage. How did he manage to open the closet and take out a pair of shoes? And why didn't I notice?

"What?"

"Sorry, I was talking to the dog."

"You got a dog?"

"No, it's my friend's. Damn, I've got to go if I want to salvage my shoes. I'll text you, okay?"

"Sure."

I barely wrestle my shoe out of Bing's grip. After a quick assessment, I hand it back to him. It's damaged beyond repair anyway.

"Bing, we need to have a talk. You do *not* attack my possessions when I'm distracted. And talking to Daniel is a major distraction. I know it shouldn't be, okay? We're ancient history, but it is what it is." I waggle my finger at him. "And I need your full cooperation."

Bing chews happily on my shoe, and I pat him on the head with a sigh, returning to the couch. The photo of baby Maddox, Summer, and Daniel is still splashed on my screen. I sigh, taking in Daniel's dark, almond-shaped eyes, his charming smile.

Clearly, there's no expiration date on calling *him* an ex. He's still firmly in that category, with the label *dangerous* on it. *Charming, delicious, and dangerous.*

Chapter Two

Daniel

"I can't believe how much he looks like Blake," Summer says as we step inside the hospital's underground parking lot.

I bite back a laugh. I don't see any resemblance between the baby and my brother. All babies look the same to me, but I voiced that opinion half an hour ago, and my ears are still ringing with her explanation of eyebrow shapes, ear pointedness, and whatnot. I learn from my mistakes.

"Crap! I have a flat tire."

We come to a halt in front of her black Ford Focus, and her front tire looks as if it melted into the concrete.

"I'll change it for you. You have a spare?"

My sister beams. "Yes, yes I do. Thank you so much. You are the best brother in the world."

"I bet you say that to all our brothers." We have seven other siblings: two sisters and five brothers. Since Summer is the youngest, we've all spoiled her rotten. I was three when she was born, and fell right under her spell. Not much has changed in the twenty-seven years since.

"I will neither confirm, nor deny it." She

grins, opening her trunk. I take out her spare tire and bring it to the front.

"You did some damage. I'm surprised you didn't feel it on the way here."

"Wasn't paying too much attention. I was too excited to get here."

That I can understand. I practically flew out of a meeting when I got the call. It's not every day that my twin brother becomes a father.

Rolling up the sleeves of my shirt, I get to work on the tire. "By the way, the stunt with the shoes wasn't smooth."

"It wasn't a matchmaking attempt. I do need the shoes, but I leave for LA tomorrow for the gallery's workshop, remember? I'm coming back next Monday, and I need the shoes for an event on Tuesday."

"And you couldn't have asked Pippa?" Our oldest sister and Caroline are close friends. I don't mind an excuse to see Caroline, but it's important to call out my sisters on their matchmaking attempts; otherwise, things could escalate quickly.

"You're picking me up from the airport when I return. You can bring them then. Makes perfect sense." She smiles devilishly, clearly bursting to say more.

"Just say whatever you're dying to say."

"I'm going to be blunt about this."

I can't help a smile. "Because you've been so subtle until now?"

"You still have feelings for her. It's the way

you look at her. I saw you at Blake's wedding. *And* you've been helping her dad."

"I—how do you know about that?"

She shrugs one shoulder. "The Bennett rumor mill."

"Of course."

Talking to my family should come with a warning label: everything you say can and will be used against you.

"Exes don't usually stay involved with each other's families. Far be it from me to read too much into this—"

"Summer, here's some honest feedback: you always read too much into everything."

She holds up a finger as if saying "Pay attention."

"Even so, I have a theory. Hear me out, and I promise I won't say anything more on the topic today."

"Let's hear it."

"My theory is that you two have been in contact with the other's family because you want to be part of each other's lives any way you can."

Summer is one of the most romantic and optimistic people I know. Coupled with her tendency to read too much into everything, her theories are usually far-fetched. But this particular one hits surprisingly close to home.

Summer glances at me but doesn't break her promise.

"I'm almost done here. Do you have a cloth?

Something I can wipe my hands on? I have grease everywhere."

"I'll look for something." She disappears to the back of the car, returning with a cloth.

Handing it to me, she says, "By the way, rumor has it Simon Luther will be your client."

"It's true. And yes, I will get you his autograph."

"You really are the best brother. How did you guess that's what I was going to ask for?"

"Just a hunch." Summer had posters of the actor all over her walls growing up.

"I love your job. And I'm so happy you dropped the extreme adventures part."

"Me too."

My company offers everything that falls under the concepts of events, tours, adventures, and experiences, and it's attracting quite a famous clientele. When I started out, the big focus was on extreme adventures. I brushed aside my family's concerns, subscribing to the *It can never happen to me* mentality. Until it did happen to me. Out of sheer luck, I wasn't seriously injured, but at the next family dinner, it became clear that I couldn't put them through so much worry again.

"This is done." I rise to my feet, wiping my hands more vigorously on the cloth. The grease sticks.

"Thanks so much. I'll head straight home. You?"

"Need to stop by the office first."

She gives me a peck on the cheek, sighing. "I still can't believe Blake's a father. Next thing we know, it'll be your turn."

Summer's optimism in all its glory. That's not in the cards for me. Out of the nine of us, only Summer and I are single. I've watched my elder siblings and my twin fall in love and start families over the past few years. The connection each has to their spouse is so strong, I often feel like a third wheel when I'm in a room with just one of the couples.

I had that kind of connection with Caroline, years ago. But I have no claim on her anymore. Though I keep forgetting that detail whenever I'm around her; I can barely keep myself from flirting with her, touching her.

"Thanks for meeting with Caroline to take my shoes. Don't back out. I do need them."

"I'll get them for you, you little schemer."

"I love you too."

I kiss her forehead, opening the car door for her. She wiggles her eyebrows as she slides into the driver seat.

"Have fun in LA."

"Have fun picking up the shoes."

Smiling, I shake my head as I close her door. So much for my sister keeping her promise.

***

Traffic in San Francisco is usually bad, but

crossing the city at seven o'clock in the evening is a special kind of hell. I arrive at eight o'clock at the office, expecting to find the office empty, but Lena, our receptionist, is at the front desk.

"How did it go?" she asks.

"Nephew is perfectly healthy, and so is his mom. What are you still doing here?"

"The *Tour Company of the Year* award was delivered half an hour ago. Couldn't leave before adding it to our *Wall of Pride*."

Glancing at the wall in question, I immediately identify the newest addition. The award title is written in golden ink on a dark blue background, framed with a thin white rim. I'm not one to collect awards, but they motivate the employees big-time.

"The wall's gonna collapse soon," I remark with a grin.

"What a fantastic problem to have. Don't spoil our fun. Even Justin likes it, and he's the company grouch."

"Make sure you don't say that to his face." Justin Hamel was my first employee, though mentor might be a better word. He knows this business inside out, but his harsh way of dealing with the other employees isn't gaining him popularity points.

Lena snickers. "Of course not. How long will you be here? Do you need anything?"

"Just need to pick up the equipment for the group tomorrow. Go home."

"You sure?"

"Yeah."

"Okay, then I'm out of here." She slings her bag over her shoulder, waving to me on her way out.

As I'm about to head to my office, the frame with the award shifts sideways, and I stop to straighten it. With a surge of pride, I have to admit, my team is right in hanging up the awards. It's a nice reminder that hard work pays off.

My eldest siblings built an empire from the ground up—Bennett Enterprises is one of the largest jewelry producers. Joining the family company was always an option, but I knew it wasn't for me. If I spend too much time behind an office desk, I become restless. I like being outdoors, which is why I set up an adventure center, and I'm out in the field with groups as much as possible. My family cheered me on when I announced I'd strike out on my own. I want to make them proud.

I'm on my way to the basement of the building where we keep the equipment when I receive a message.

Caroline: Hey! I can bring you Summer's shoes on Monday if that's okay?

Daniel: I'm out with a group on Monday, but I'll be back in my office at six o'clock.

Caroline: Six works. Or I can just drop them with someone at your office.

Daniel: And risk Summer's wrath? :-) She set us up, the least she's expecting is a face-to-face meeting.

Caroline: One of these days we should

**make up a wild story, set her straight. I'll come
by at six, give you the shoes PERSONALLY :-)**

My imagination is already running amok. We
were wild... and so good together. So damn good
that I still beat myself up over letting her go.

Shoving the phone back in my pocket, I cook
up a plan. My sister might have set this up, but I plan
to take thorough advantage of my time with Caroline.

Chapter Three

Caroline

The next evening, I pull in front of Dad's house fifteen minutes too late for our dinner. He lives in the same modest two-bedroom unit where I grew up, in the Excelsior district. I've always loved my parents' house. When Mom was alive, the boxes under the bay windows were adorned with cranesbills. In their absence, an air of sadness hangs over the house, the chipping light-green paint standing out. It doesn't help that the sky is terribly gloomy, even for a late-September day.

The door swings open before I even ring. "Here's my girl. Everything okay?"

"Yeah. Sorry I'm late." Stepping inside, I hold up the bag of donuts. "Left the school too late and took forever to make these."

"I made stew," Dad informs me as we make our way to the dining room. He already set the table. Placing the donuts at one end, I fill both our plates with stew before sitting down.

"Followed your mother's recipe to a T," he says with pride.

Yeah... except Mom's had tasted delicious, and this one reminds me of the canned soups I ate in college. But I dutifully eat the entire plate. I offer to bring dinner as often as possible, but don't have the heart to tell him his talents don't lie in the kitchen. He already has a hard time looking after the house and running the bookstore by himself. I don't want to make him feel as if he can't even get this one little thing right.

"How are the renovations coming along, Dad?"

"We're ahead of schedule. I'll be able to open up much quicker than I thought."

Between the popularity of online shopping and the competition from large chains, my parents' bookstore has been struggling for some time. It didn't help that the place had looked new around the time when Bush senior was in office. A few months ago, Dad finally agreed it needed a thorough makeover. He's adding a small coffee shop too, the idea being to offer customers an *experience*, not just a point of transaction. We came up with this plan with the help of Dad's bank adviser.

"By the way, I've asked Daniel to look over the business plan."

"Daniel Bennett?"

Dad smiles. "Don't know any other Daniel. And the man's got a brilliant business mind. He made some good points. He says the improvements will turn things around, bring more of a profit."

Daniel is running a successful business. If anyone's advice counts, it's his. My talents lie in teaching little kids, not running a business, though this didn't keep me from committing most of my savings to the bookstore's renovation.

Daniel was close to my parents while we dated. He was always attentive—bringing flowers to Mom, chatting with Dad about his favorite soccer team. When Mom died last year, Daniel was here for us, and so was the rest of his family. I grew close to them again, especially his mother and sisters. I was friends with them back in college, but I pulled slightly away after we broke up. I had no idea he and Dad were still in contact.

Hmm… I could ask Dad more on the topic, but he's been channeling the Bennett sisters lately, throwing not-so-subtle hints about Daniel and me. I'll just ask the man himself when I see him.

We talk about my brother next. Niall lives in Dublin, practicing neurosurgery. He's the only family member who isn't Daniel's fan, *possibly* because he had a front seat at a few of my post breakup crying sessions.

I first met Daniel and Blake in our freshman year at college. The twins and I had an almost instant friendship over our dislike of the campus food and people who called San Francisco "Frisco." We bonded over endless talks about our families. The twins were sort of a substitute for my brother, who I missed like crazy. Blake at least. Daniel… eh, different story.

I wasn't immune to his charms from the very beginning. My pulse raced a little too frantically, my skin flushed too much when I was around him, and I put more stock in his compliments than anyone else's. In the beginning, I tried to convince myself it was a normal reaction, because well... Daniel was tall, strong, and exceptionally good-looking. But Blake was all those things too, and he'd never affected me that way.

I can remember exactly the moment things between Daniel and me shifted from the friendship zone. The three of us were headed to a party on campus at the beginning of our senior year, and the boys had come to pick me up. Neither of us had a date, but upon entering my apartment, Blake immediately started charming my new roommate, convincing her to join us.

Daniel and I waited in the doorway, sizing each other up.

"Looking sexy tonight," he said.

"You clean up well too."

We'd exchanged similar words maybe a million times before. But it was the millionth and first time that did it. Maybe it was the way Daniel had leaned in when he'd said it; maybe it was the way I'd drawn a sharp breath, bit my lip, Daniel's eyes following my every reaction. Then he'd leaned in even closer, so close I could smell him. Sandalwood and sea. It was the cologne I'd given him the previous Christmas.

"Maybe I should be your date tonight," he whispered, his hot breath landing on my cheek.

"Maybe I want you to." I said it in a playful tone and added a gentle jab with my elbow to his stomach. He winked, pulled away, but we both knew the game we were playing. We both pretended we were joking, but we both knew we were not.

He watched me dance the entire night, and there was no mistaking the heat in his eyes. But he didn't make a move, *not even when he walked me home at four o'clock in the morning. In front of my door, he kissed my cheek. He lingered with his lips on my skin, his fingers splayed on the side of my rib cage, digging slightly into my flesh. I burned with yearning for him the entire night.*

I was torn between wishing he made a move, and wishing he wouldn't. Torn, because I'd wanted Daniel for almost three years, but Daniel... well, he was like any other college-aged man surrounded by single women. He liked his variety, didn't want to be tied down, and I wasn't a big believer in changing people. I knew how to be Daniel's friend, but I didn't know how to be anything else. And I valued the twins' friendships, and his family's. I'd grown close to the Bennetts and wasn't sure that venturing into the shallow waters of nonfriendship was advisable.

My best intentions were blown to smoke when we returned from yet another party. It was November, and the air was chilly. Daniel gave me his jacket because mine was so flimsy it was like having no jacket at all. We had to cross the entire campus to get to my building, and that meant almost twenty-five minutes of walking.

Despite his jacket, I was shivering.

"You're still cold," he remarked.

"My feet are freezing."

I pointed to them. I was wearing flat shoes, but no socks. In November. Daniel stopped in his tracks. The lighting was dim, and at first I couldn't see exactly what he was doing, but then he was taking off his shoes and socks, handing the latter to me.

"Here. Put these socks on."

"I—thanks."

For some reason—possibly the three-year long crush and weeks of hot dreams about him—the gesture touched me deeply. When we reached my door, I wasn't ready to say good night. My roommate was gone for the weekend, and Daniel was shivering.

"Do you want to come in? I can make you some tea."

"Sure." He answered so quickly, it was clear he didn't want to say good night either. Two cups of tea later, he was still shivering. I regretfully gave him the socks back, scrambling for an excuse to make him stay longer. Resigned that I wouldn't come up with any smart ideas at four o'clock in the morning, I simply asked, "Do you want to sleep here? The couch is a pullout. Your apartment is a good distance away, and cabs aren't easy to find at this hour."

I'd said this all very fast, playing with the empty teacup in my hands. We were sitting side by side on the couch.

"If you want me to stay, I'll stay."

"Only if you want to as well."

I was really winning it, sounding like I was playing a game of chicken. The corner of his mouth quirked up.

"I'm staying."

"Okay. I'll find you some sheets."

When I returned with the sheets, Daniel was pacing around the small living room. He still looked frozen. I had to do something to make him more comfortable. I was the reason the cold had seeped into his bones after all. Monopolized the man's jacket and socks. I had brought him a blanket, but would that be enough? My imagination immediately supplied a more efficient solution. Skin-on-skin contact would warm him up in no time. I could use that as a pretext to snuggle against him on the couch, under the cover....

I shook my head, feeling silly, but my head pounded quicker just imagining touching his hard body, feeling his taut muscles against me. When I caught him sizing me up, heat crept up my cheeks. I looked away, afraid he could read my mind, but not before noticing his eyes were a little hooded.

"You don't mind if I sleep commando?" he asked.

The heat in my cheeks intensified. My brain went numb at the thought of a naked Daniel in my living room. "No, whatever makes you comfortable. You might be cold, though."

I gulped, not daring to look at him. But I could feel him watching me. The air around us seemed to have thickened with tension.

More to diffuse it than anything else, I asked, "Do you want a hot bath? It would warm you right up."

"That's right, you have a tub. Still can't believe it."

I grinned. "One of the reasons I moved in here. Small place, but it has a bathtub. I love it. Use it at least once a week. Want me to prepare one for you?"

"Only if you join me."

If I thought there was tension in the air before, I could hardly breathe through it now. He didn't try to pass it off as a joke, as we'd done so many times before when we were skirting too closely on the flirting line. In fact, he didn't say anything else, merely closed the distance to me, flattening me against the bathroom door. He looked down at me, brought his hand under my jaw, and traced the contour up my cheek to my ear. His other hand was on my shoulder, fingers on my sweater, thumb on my clavicle.

"Join me." It was a thinly veiled command, and my lower body reacted so strongly, I clenched my thighs. "You want

this. Me. Us. You want this as badly as I do."

"Yes."

He smiled. "Yes, what?"

"To all of that. The bath, wanting you. Especially the wanting you part."

It had been a memorable weekend. We'd made love in the tub, on the couch, in my bedroom, the kitchen. Many more similar weekends followed. We were inseparable. What I thought would be just fun in college turned into so much more. Daniel and I just clicked. We understood each other on all levels. I gave him my heart without any reservation. We were so good together.

Right until we weren't.

Things started to fall apart when it was time to decide about grad school. I had received a full scholarship from my first choice, the University of Washington. It was a two-year program, and the first one was in Dublin. I wanted to spend my time with my brother, who'd moved there five years before, and get to know the city I was born in better. Plus, the program was top-notch.

Daniel was going to Stanford for business school. The closer we came to the deadline for confirming our places, I was getting cold feet. I didn't want to be so far away from him. I'd only received a partial scholarship to Stanford, but I could swing it if I waitressed on the side. Daniel didn't like my idea at all.

"But Washington is your first choice. The one you want," he argued every time. "Don't settle for anything less than what's best for you."

I felt him pull away from me with every conversation. So, when he showed up at the bar where I was working, at the end of my shift, I knew that was it.

"Caroline, I thought about this a lot... and it won't work out. Long distance is so complicated, and you'd miss out on a lot of experiences if you spend half your time on a plane. Same for me. The best place for you is the University of Washington, with the year abroad. Don't settle for me."

We parted ways amicably. Our breakup conversation was very adult. No fighting, no shouting. Daniel did most of the talking. I just nodded and held my breath every time I felt like crying. I held my breath so often during that conversation I was half expecting to pass out. In theory, it all made sense; it was the best for both of us. But part of me knew we could have made it work. I was going to Dublin for a year, and spending the second one in Washington, not starting a colony on Mars.

Chapter Four

Caroline

"Hot date tonight?" Karla asks as we rise from our chairs. The school is empty except for the two of us, but we always stay later on Mondays to go over administrative issues.

"No, just meeting a friend."

She winks, shrugging. "A lot of effort for a friend."

I look down at my outift: dark blue dress tight around the waist, showing just a hint of cleavage, and a red jacket covering said cleavage.

"I like dressing up from time to time."

I could argue it's how I usually dress up when I go out with a friend, but the truth is, whenever I'm about to meet Daniel, I go out of my way to appear put together. Maybe it's a general rule that you don't want an old flame to see you looking anything but your best. Except it can't be too general because I couldn't care less what other exes think, but when I'm about to meet Daniel? *Ohhhh yeah, baby.* I bring out the big guns every single time.

We walk out together and I bid Karla goodbye, heading to the parking lot behind the school. Once I'm in my car, I kick off my shoes, curling and stretching my poor toes. Driving barefoot is frowned upon, but if a policeman stops me, I'll gladly ask him to drive wearing my five-inch heels. See how he does!

I arrive at the address Daniel texted me forty minutes later, pulling my car in front of a three-story building with the sign "Golden Escapes Adventure Center." I've never been to his office. Putting my heels back on, I climb out of the car and walk up the front steps. The sliding doors open when I approach and a friendly blonde greets me from behind a reception desk.

"Welcome to Golden Escapes. What can I do for you?"

"I just have to drop this off with Daniel." I hold up the paper bag containing Summer's shoes and a gift I bought for the youngest Bennett offspring.

"Miss Caroline Dunne, right?"

"Yes."

She points to the right. "His door is at the end of the corridor."

Nodding, I head in that direction, my palms growing a little sweatier as I approach the door. Shaking my head, I chastise myself. Still, I can't help the flutter in my stomach as I knock at his door, or the knot low in my body when he replies, "Come in."

Wow, his office is huge. Plenty of light comes in, and the large desk is positioned so he can look straight outside. At the moment, though, he's looking at me, and *hot, hot, hot damn.*

Stalking toward me, Daniel looks every bit as irresistible as usual. This mountain of a man is about six feet three. That he works out regularly is clearly visible by the way his black shirt hugs his torso. The contour of the muscles lacing his arms is visible on the upper part of the sleeve. He's rolled the lower part of the sleeves up to his elbow, and I have a clear view of the muscles and veins cording his forearms. Always been a sucker for strong forearms. And a dark stubble.

"Caroline, hey." Leaning forward, he kisses my cheek, grazing my skin lightly, one hand on my waist. He ignites my skin at every point of contact. As skillfully as possible, I step away and look around.

"I love the view. You don't spend a lot of time in here, though, do you?"

"No. I like being outdoors, in the middle of the action, but I do need an office for meetings and paperwork, so naturally I took the best room in the building."

I grin. "Naturally." Grinning, I hold up the bag. "Here's the delivery. Your sister's shoes and a gift for baby Maddox."

He takes the bag from me, rubbing the back of my hand with his thumb.

"How's dinner sound? Give us time to catch up, and I'm starving. There's a restaurant serving delicious enchiladas just around the corner."

My grin fades as I consider this. On the one hand, I love enchiladas. On the other hand, being around Daniel is *dangerous*.

Daniel leans in closer, bringing his hand to the small curve in my lower back. I wish he weren't so touchy-feely. And I wish I didn't enjoy it so much. "You love enchiladas."

"I do," I admit on a sigh, my mouth watering just at the thought of a juicy enchilada, and all those flavors exploding in my mouth.

"Perfect, that's a yes. Let's go."

"You'd twist anything I say into a yes."

The corners of his mouth twitch. "Summer is going to ask for a report on tonight, and there's a real risk I'll stop being her favorite brother if I don't even convince you to go to dinner with me."

I put both my hands over my chest theatrically. "I don't know what shocks me more: that you still live under the impression you're her favorite brother or that you fear her questionings so much."

"Well, if you've learned to shut my sister down, by all means, tell me how."

I drop my hands. "I just have evasive maneuvers, but those don't always work. Okay, lead the way."

After grabbing his jacket from the back of his chair, he leads me out of the room and the building.

"It's just around the corner."

Daniel's office building is on Hyde Street, and we pass the famously crooked section of Lombard Street with its hairpin turns, red brick paving, and bright green hedges. I love this city to no end. When I was in Europe for my year abroad, I traveled as much as I could afford. I went to London, Paris, Prague. Each city had a charm of its own, but I couldn't wait to return to San Francisco. Between the cable cars and the crooked Lombard Street, my hometown always seemed magical to me.

Not five minutes later, we arrive at the restaurant. There's a long line to the entrance, but Daniel walks with me right past it to the front.

"Mr. Bennett," the waiter greets him as if they are old friends. "Your table is ready."

"You made reservations?" I whisper. "What if I said no?"

He brings a hand at the small of my back, guiding me inside. "I was optimistic."

The waiter leads us to a table smack dab in the center of the room. Normally, I wouldn't mind it, but the tables are so close to each other, it feels claustrophobic.

Daniel doesn't miss a beat. "We want a more secluded table."

"Certainly!" the waiter says, leading us to a table in the back. As soon as we sit, I immerse myself in the menu, and my mouth waters just reading the offerings. Their *make-your-own-enchilada* option is particularly appealing. You can pimp it to your stomach's desire. The problem is that when I'm left to my own devices, and I have an empty stomach, I tend to take the pimping to a ridiculous level. Which is why I end up ordering an enchilada with twice as many ingredients as needed. A pang of guilt rears its head, but I push it away quickly. I was supposed to be on a diet, but between my dad's dinner and this… I'll start again next Monday.

"You come here often?" I ask.

"Often enough. It's a hit with many clients. Even the high-profile ones, and they're picky."

"You don't like working with them?"

He shrugs. "They're high maintenance. But they bring in a lot of business. It wasn't my focus when I first set up the business, but I did have a lot of contacts in the scene from my…."

"Wild years?" I supply because he seems to struggle with finding the right words.

"Yes."

"Well, smart of you to use those contacts."

His eldest siblings—Sebastian, Logan, and Pippa—founded Bennett Enterprises when Daniel and Blake were kids. By the time they were in college, the tremendous success of the company made the family a tabloids target. Daniel and Blake relished the attention in the first few years after college.

It wasn't uncommon for gossip sites to post pictures of them at high-profile parties, mingling with models and actors. I remember during my second year of the master's program perusing one such website—accidentally, of course, because I was absolutely *not* stalking Daniel—and marveling at how different our lives were becoming. We seemed to be like two perpendicular lines: coming from different directions, going in different directions, crossing paths once and then never again.

When the waiter arrives with our enchiladas,

we dig in right away. I am even hungrier than I thought. I only stop for a breather after I devoured half of the portion.

"Oh, this is divine," I inform him.

"Glad you approve. I've thought about bringing you here since I came the first time."

I lower my eyes to the plate, focusing on my food. *Don't read into this, Caroline. Don't read into this.*

Crap. I always read too much into everything when it comes to Daniel, which is ridiculous. We've been over for a long time, and we've both had relationships over the years. They didn't amount to anything, which is why we're both still single, but it's not like we've been pining over each other.

Ah, who am I kidding? I warm up all over every time he touches or compliments me, and my first instinct when he seems out of his depths is to soothe him. Those *are* signs of pining. But I like to lie to myself from time to time, pretend I'm immune to him. Everyone does this, right? Every woman has that ex she never quite got over, right? Here's to wishful thinking that I'm not a disgrace to the female population.

The most ridiculous of it all? I'm not actually hoping we'll make up. I have one cardinal rule: once I get my heart broken, I don't go back for more. Plus, I've gathered a lot of baggage over the years— the one weighing the most being my inability to have kids. But no point dwelling on that now, spoiling this beautiful evening.

"By the way, Dad said you've helped him with

the business plan for the bookstore. Thank you."

He waves his hand as if it's nothing. "My pleasure. I'm glad he's finally giving that place a makeover. And adding the coffee shop is a great idea. Any additional revenue stream helps. Helped him bring down the price they were asking him to pay for the furniture. Your dad is a great man, but…."

"Not a great businessman? Mom used to say the same thing. I miss her so much."

"I bet."

She never wanted me to become a teacher. She was hoping I'd follow in my brother's footsteps, become a doctor. When she wasn't trying to beat some sense into me, she'd give me a loving look while shaking her head in disapproval—yes, she could do both things at the same time—and say, "You're just like your father."

I knew exactly what she meant. Dad and I both like taking care of the people we love, making them happy. Unfortunately, those aren't marketable skills. Mom ran the bookstore with an iron fist because Dad's soft and trusting nature led to many mishaps with suppliers who overcharged him, and employees who stole from him.

"Thanks for helping him out, Daniel. I appreciate it."

"I've always liked your parents. Even though something must be done about your dad's cooking."

I burst out laughing. "Don't tell me he tried to poison you with his stew."

"Oh, he did, and that wasn't even the worst of

it. One time he made roast beef. Thing was so hard, I thought I'd break a tooth chewing on it."

"How often *do* you see my dad?"

"Now and again," he says vaguely.

I waggle a finger at him. "Not an answer. I know at least a dozen ways to lure information out of you. Just being fair and giving you a heads-up."

He leans over the table, a playful glint in his eyes. "I remember. Half of those ways involve no clothes. I much prefer those."

I open my mouth, then close it again, heat rushing to my cheeks. Yep, I dug my own hole here. No one to blame but myself. Daniel watches me intently, and I squirm in my seat, suddenly feeling warm. Moving on.

"I'd really like to know," I say eventually.

"After your mom passed away, I started stopping by a few times a month, whenever there was a soccer game on TV. He seemed lonely."

"Oh." His words reach someplace deep inside me. I shove the last bite of enchilada in my mouth, processing this. Dad *is* lonely, which is why I never miss our weekly dinner, and call him as often as I can. But he's *my* dad. Daniel is not related to him, and yet he's making more of an effort than my own brother. Visiting is hard, but Niall could call Dad more often.

"That's kind of you. He *is* lonely."

"And now you're getting sad. Let's change the subject. How is work at the new school?"

"How'd you know I changed workplaces?"

"I've always kept tabs on you."

His answer catches me off guard, filling me with all kinds of warmth. I laugh nervously, trying *again* not to read too much into this... and failing spectacularly.

"It's great. I love it. Much smaller groups, so we can focus on each kid. We're doing a lot of extracurricular activities with them too. I've only been there for a month, so I'm still on probation, but I'm doing a great job. No reason for them not to keep me. Next Monday we were supposed to take them to the Maritime Historical Park, but they called today to tell us they closed off a section, and I don't think it makes much sense to go. We'll have to find another idea for an outing because the kids are so psyched about going on a trip. Any ideas? You're the master of adventures."

"How old are they?"

"Nine."

"Whale-watching would be a hit. You can see humpback and blue whales around this time. They're still migrating."

"Great idea."

"I can set it up. Next Monday I'm taking a group out from Moss Landing. We're only going out in the afternoon, but I had to rent the boat for the entire day anyway. We could take the kids out in the morning."

"How are your prices?" I ask skeptically. "This is a private school, but... not your usual target market."

"I don't work just with celebrities. I'll send you an offer. I can give you a friend's discount." He flashes me a smile. *Oh hell no.* Not his wicked smile!

"That's not necessary. Send me the offer, and I'll pass it on to the principal and my colleagues."

I'm sure they'll be thrilled with it. I am too. For the kids' benefit, of course, *not* because I want to spend more time with Daniel.

For the remainder of our dinner, we chitchat about his family and their shenanigans, betting on how long it'll take for Summer to ask him how tonight went. We have our answer by the end of our evening when we're walking back to his office, since we both parked close to his building.

Daniel's phone chimes, and he chuckles as he glances at the screen, then turns it to me.

Summer: Got my shoes? How's Caroline?

"You're right, we should give her a taste of her own medicine, make up a wild story. I'm tempted to tell her we ended up having wild sex, just to see her reaction," he says.

Well, I don't know about Summer's reaction, but mine is *boom.*

My breath catches as my nipples turn to pebbles. The skin on my cheeks and neck feels on fire. So does my center. I try to laugh, but it comes out throaty and uneven. *Damn.* How can I react like this to a joke? Daniel watches me silently, and I hold his gaze, right up until the air between us becomes so charged I can't stand it. I need to break this tension, *stat.*

"Careful, say the wrong thing and she'll go into full matchmaker mode," I warn.

We come to a halt as we reach my car, and Daniel brings his hand to my face. For a brief second I think he'll pull me into a kiss, but then I realize he's just brushing off a leaf from my hair. His thumb touches my cheek in the process, and he lingers a little in his touch. *Danger alert!* Clearing my throat, I step back.

"Okay. Well, it was great catching up. I'll send you details about the trip. Have a nice evening."

"You too."

I climb into my car and rev the engine, which always needs a few minutes to warm up. Once I hit the road, I glance at the digital clock on my dashboard. It's nine o'clock. Plenty of time to sink in my tub. Hot water and my favorite caramel bath bomb are just what I need to relax... and figure out why I can't forget Daniel. On second thought, I'll also stop at Target. Hot water and a bath bomb are okay for relaxing, but they won't cut it for my late-night soul-searching.

This is a job for wine.

Chapter Five

Caroline

The next morning, I almost climb the flight of stairs to Linda's apartment before I remember she's back and I'm no longer on Bing duty. Dang, I'm going to miss that furball, chewed shoes and all.

I tell my colleagues and the principal about Daniel's offer as soon as I arrive at school. I don't even have to sell the idea to them; they fall for it hook, line, and sinker. We won't have disappointed kids and parents on our hands, and Moss Landing is just an hour and a half from San Francisco. Win-win for everyone.

After we leave the principal's office, Karla pulls me aside. "Girl, you know Daniel Bennett and didn't say anything? I need to become your best friend right now."

"He's an old friend."

"Friend? I've only seen him in photos, but friendship would be *so* wasted on that man. You've seen him in the flesh and didn't jump his bones?"

Something in my expression must betray me because Karla widens her eyes and adds, "Oh, but you have. He's the friend you wore the knockout dress for yesterday."

I need to work on my poker face. I don't want my colleagues to poke their nose in my private business, so I just say, "College sweetheart".

I work out the details of the trip with Daniel and one of his employees throughout the week, trying to ignore the flip in my stomach every time I talk to Daniel.

The following Monday, Karla and I are on a bus with twelve kids under ten years old, and they accost us with every version of "Are we there yet?" the entire journey.

"Wish Helen was here too," Karla says, referring to another colleague.

"We'll be fine," I assure her as the bus pulls into the parking lot of a hotel near the Marina Dunes Preserve. The boat will leave from here, heading out in the general direction of Moss Landing. As we descend from the bus, two of Daniel's coworkers, a man and a woman, approach us.

Shivering a little, I zip up my coat. *Brr.* It's the end of September, and I can already feel the temperature changing.

"Hi, I'm Marcel. We emailed," the man says as we shake hands. He's about my age, well-built, and tan. "This is Honor. We're both going to go out with you today."

I feel a pang of disappointment that Daniel won't head out with us too, even though I knew it already. He told me he has too much work to go through before he heads out with the group tonight.

I was still hoping, I suppose.

"The kids have to use the restrooms first," Karla says.

Honor motions to the hotel behind her. "You can use those at the hotel. The lunch boxes for the kids are at reception anyway. We have to pick them up too."

We head inside, the kids jumping up and down, talking incessantly. I love working with children. Their joy and excitement for every little thing is contagious. Sure, they turn into little devils when things don't go their way, but that comes with the territory.

The view here is breathtaking. The hotel lobby walls boast floor-to-ceiling windows, offering an almost unencumbered view of the ocean. There is nature as far as the eye can see. While Karla takes the kids to the bathroom, I take inventory of the lunch boxes.

"Hello, beautiful."

Looking up, I find Daniel right next to me. "Hey! I thought you'd only come in the evening with your group."

"Nah, I've been here since this morning. I've booked a room because I'm staying until tomorrow. I'm working from there. Do you need anything?"

"Is there anywhere I can buy a sandwich? I didn't have breakfast, and I don't want to eat my boxed lunch right now."

"The hotel has a breakfast buffet. Closes in twenty minutes. You still have time. Marcel wanted to grab a bite before you head out too."

Five minutes later, Marcel and I are loading our plates at top speed. I'm not even paying attention to the food; I just want to fill my stomach as quickly as possible. We sit at an empty table, and I wolf down my breakfast.

"Relax! Honor and Karla can handle the group. Daniel's with them too. Don't choke on something."

I smile sheepishly, swallowing. "You're right."

"Looking forward to the outing?"

"Yeah. I've been whale-watching once before, eons ago."

"It'll be a lot of fun, you'll see."

We chitchat about which type of whales we're most likely to see, and I'm impressed by his knowledge on the topic and his willingness to explain every detail.

"Say, Caroline, could I take you out to dinner sometime this week?"

I nearly choke on my bite. *Wow, way to be direct.* And here I thought he was just being polite, doing his job. My throat is itching as I swallow and consider the softest way to turn him down. He didn't do anything wrong, but well... he *is* Daniel's employee, and for some reason, this feels like I'd betray him. Silly, I know. I doubt Daniel would care.

Anyway, I'm not into dating right now. I haven't been into dating for the past three years. Still have to pluck up the courage to jump into it again, but I keep postponing it, even though I'm lonely as hell. But every time I remember my last two breakups, I conclude that maybe loneliness isn't so bad. Definitely not bad enough for me to risk another man making me feel small when I tell him I can't have children. Ever since the diagnosis five years ago, my romantic life turned into a game of chicken.

"I can't, Marcel. Sorry." My throat closes up, itching even worse than before. What the hell?

He nods curtly, smiling. "No problem. I had to try."

"Well, this is—" Talking past the itching in my throat is becoming more difficult. Grabbing the glass of water on the table, I take a sip, but don't manage to swallow. A hysterical fit of coughing overtakes me.

"Are you allergic to something?" Marcel asks.

Horrified, I lower my eyes to my plate, which I have cleaned. Did anything contain peanut sauce? Why the hell didn't I pay any attention?

Nodding, I manage to rasp out, "Peanut. EpiPen. Backpack."

Marcel jumps to his feet. There is a commotion all around me, but my eyes are fuzzy, burning from the effort of trying to breathe. My throat is closing up again. That's when I realize I don't have my backpack with me. I left it with the group outside. Oh God, I can feel my tongue swelling. My lips too, I think. Air, I need air. But the more I try to breathe, the less air seems to reach my lungs.

Heaving gasps reach my ears, and panic kicks in when I realize they belong to me. A sharp sting in my outer thigh alerts me that someone's using an EpiPen. Thank goodness.

"I'm taking her to the hospital," a familiar voice says. Daniel. He appears in my field of vision, which is very blurred.

"No hospital," I manage to slur. "Benadryl."

The next few minutes pass in a haze. Someone forces me to swallow a liquid—probably Benadryl—and then I'm lifted from my seat, warm, strong arms carrying me. I close my eyes because my vision is so blurry that the effort to make out my surroundings makes me dizzy.

When I blink them open again, I'm lying on a bed, and Daniel is shoving more Benadryl into my mouth. Laying my head on the pillow, I close my eyes again, focusing on my breath, which slowly returns to normal. My throat isn't itching anymore. Tongue appears to be normal-sized too.

I don't know how much time passes before I hear Daniel whisper, "Caroline, let me take you to a hospital."

I shake my head, which turns out to be a big mistake—it makes me even dizzier. "No, I'm fine. I can breathe normally. Need to get back to the group."

"You're not going anywhere like this. They already left, anyway."

I blink my eyes open. "What? When?"

"An hour ago."

"Shit! I've been out of it for an hour? I need to—"

"Caroline, relax. Marcel and Honor are with Karla and the kids. They'll manage fine. You can't go out right now. Rest for a while. You can always head out later."

"Okay." Truthfully, I'm not up to boarding on a boat. Hell, I'm not even up to getting out of this bed.

"How do you feel?"

"Very tired. A bit dizzy."

Daniel leans forward until his face is level with mine, his chest pressing to my side. "Bad sign."

"Nah, just side effects of Benadryl."

He rubs a hand up and down my arm. The gesture is so tender, I swear my heart bursts with hope. *Oh no, no, no!* I have a hard time keeping myself in check around him even when I'm sober, but when I'm high on Benadryl....

"Are you sure you're okay?"

I nod, but Daniel still seems unconvinced. He scoots even closer to me until his chest squishes the side of my right boob. I can feel the ridges of his trained abs pressing against the length of my arm.

"Watch it, Daniel. Pressing the deliciousness that is your body against an under-sexed woman is a dangerous endeavor." His sharp intake of breath alerts me that my words are so far beyond inappropriate, they deserve a category of their own. "This is the Benadryl talking, by the way." Ah, brilliant. Brilliant. I couldn't have found a better scapegoat if I tried. Whatever happens while I'm under its influence cannot be held against me. Considering I'm seeing Daniel as if there's a foggy window between us, I'm not even making this up.

"Don't worry about anything, okay? The kids are in good hands. Honor and Marcel are pros."

"He asked me out," I find myself saying. "At breakfast, he asked me out."

"Marcel?"

"Yeah."

"What did you say?"

I blink twice, trying to clear my vision. No such luck. "Why does it matter?"

Is it my imagination, or has Daniel gone rigid next to me?

"Don't go out with him. Please! I know I have no right, but please don't go out with an employee of mine." He's gone very still. "I'm close to them, and when we go out after work they bring their spouses or significant others, and I couldn't watch you with him."

My heart hammers so wildly, I feel like it will jump out of my chest any second now. My mind spins, and it's not just from the Benadryl. At least I don't think so. My vision is so foggy I can't see past the tip of my nose, but my mind is clear. I'm not imagining this, or projecting. First he took care of my father, now this....

Gathering my courage around me, I ask in a small voice, "You care?"

"Of course I care. I've always cared."

He cradles me in his arms, and 1 feel something warm on my forehead—his lips. Then sleep pulls me under.

Chapter Six

Daniel

Pushing myself on an elbow, I watch her drift to sleep. Her breathing pattern seems normal, but I'm still worried. She scared me down in the restaurant: the way she slurred her words, lost her balance. She shifts her position, tossing and turning until her head is dangling off the pillow at such a weird angle, she'll get a neck strain if she sleeps like that. As carefully as possible, I shove the pillow back under her head, but then Caroline shifts again, turning on one side, grabbing my hand and placing it between the pillow and her head.

I smile. She used to do this all the time when we were together: monopolize my hand, then my entire body, sleeping on me, claiming I was the best pillow. I gladly endured the hardship of her climbing me in her sleep. I'd loved feeling her soft breath on my skin. When she wasn't hogging me, she was thrashing in the bed. She'd been a messy sleeper. I wonder if she still is.

I contemplate the best way to free my hand without waking her, but when she sighs and lays a hand on my wrist, I give up. I'll stay just a little longer. Just a few more seconds.

She shifts even closer to me. I can't move away because I'm right on the edge of the bed. A whiff of her perfume reaches me, something floral, but not jasmine, which was what she'd worn when we were together.

But jasmine or no jasmine, she's still the same sweet woman I fell for in college. She's still the one person who spends as much time hovering around her family as I do around mine. She still loves the same simple things she did then: great food, great books. I bet she still binge-watches TV shows in the evenings.

Seeing her in my bed brings back so many memories. A truth I haven't allowed myself to think hits me hard. *I miss her.*

But the only sensible thing to do at the moment is to climb out of this bed, which I do, extracting my hand from under her head carefully.

Standing at the end of the bed, I ponder what to do next. I knew she was allergic to peanuts, but I haven't seen the allergy in action before on her. She looks all right, but I don't want to leave her unsupervised. What if she gets worse?

I debate for all of two seconds before reaching a decision. I step out of the room to call Honor and Marcel and inform them of the next steps.

"Wait, I'll put you on loudspeaker so Marcel can hear you too," Honor says. "How is Caroline feeling?"

"Better, but she's asleep, so she won't join

you for now at least."

"No problem," Marcel says. I grip the phone harder, remembering he had the guts to ask her out.

"I'm staying with her until she wakes up. If that doesn't happen until the next clients arrive, you take care of everything."

There is silence for a few seconds, and then Honor asks hesitantly, "Are you sure?"

"They're looking forward to meeting you," Marcel puts in.

"Then do your best to represent me." My tone allows for no argument, and none comes. Excellent. I'm not in the mood for negotiations.

"Sure. Call us if you or Caroline needs anything," Marcel adds. I barely keep myself from lashing at Marcel. Damn it, I have no right to be jealous.

"Keep me posted." I click off and return to the room. I smile at the sight of Caroline on her belly, spread-eagled. She messed up half the bed in the span of minutes.

I have my laptop here, but the sound of my clicking on the keyboard could wake her up. Sitting in the armchair, I pull out my smartphone and start typing on the touchscreen, which makes no sound at all. Halfway through answering my emails, I come across one that chills me.

Subject: How the hell did this happen?

Message: This was my daughter's birthday!!!! I don't want her exposed to the fucking paparazzi and you promised 100%

privacy. I'm never giving you my business again.

Inside the email are leaked photographs from the event I hosted yesterday for the drummer of a rock band. They made it onto all the major gossip sites.

I lean back in the armchair, dragging a hand down my face. My unique selling proposition for my famous clients *is* 100% privacy.

When it comes to the media, I've had years to cut my teeth.

Right after college, I did small consultancy projects, but I spent a lot of time enjoying the fame the Bennett name brought me, even though I hadn't earned a lick of it. I'm not proud of it. Bennett Enterprises was such a draw for the media that the press hadn't minded which Bennett they got a snapshot of. Sebastian, Logan, and Pippa, and even Christopher and Max, who joined the company later, stayed out of the limelight. But Blake and I were young, and the pull was far too tempting for both of us.

Eventually, the press wasn't satisfied with reporting on the success of Bennett Enterprises. They started digging for dirt, anything to tear my siblings down from the pedestal. That was when Blake and I pulled out of the limelight, but when the media gets no stories, they fabricate them.

Blake and I made it a point to kill fake stories before they hit the media. Our siblings had enough on their hands; they didn't have to deal with this kind of crap too. We were successful most of the time, and the exercise brought me invaluable media contacts.

Something good came out of that chaotic time. In my business, I had my first famous clients via the contacts I made in those years when I rubbed elbows with models, TV presenters, even actors and actresses. I have enough experience with the press to know how to avoid it and offer utmost privacy. Word of mouth from satisfied clients brings me an insane amount of business. Negative word of mouth can just as well disrupt everything.

And I hate not delivering on my promise. This was a kid's tenth birthday, for God's sake. The client has every right to be livid. If this had been one of my nieces or nephews, I'd be livid too.

How did these photos leak? There were no paparazzi inside the venue, and I made sure the surroundings were clear as well. The guests were close friends only, and those know the drill.

My mind is spinning as I set to work and do some damage control. I check on Caroline periodically and chuckle every time because she tosses and turns in the strangest positions. She's exactly as messy a sleeper as I remember.

My bed will smell like her tonight. That's something to look forward to.

Chapter Seven

Caroline

The room is dark when I wake up, with a small beacon of light at the far end. Pushing myself up on my elbows, I pat the nightstand until I find the light switch for the lamp and flick it on.

"You're up." The beacon of light was Daniel's phone. He's sitting in the armchair at the foot of the bed, watching me with a smile. My backpack is on the floor next to him.

"Yeah." My voice is rough, the inside of my mouth gummy. "What time is it?"

"A little past ten."

"Wow, I slept the entire day?"

"You woke up in between but fell right back asleep." Something in his stiff position clues me in that he's been sitting for a long while.

"Have you... were you here the entire time?"

"Yeah. I was afraid you'd get worse."

And cue the swooning.

"But your activity this evening—"

"Marcel and Honor took care of it, don't worry about it. You're more important."

Oh! I'm not equipped to deal with this level of swooning right after getting up.

"The kids and Karla—"

"Left for San Francisco this afternoon on the bus. The hotel has a shuttle service. I can arrange that for you. I'd drive you myself, but I'm staying here tonight. I've got another group here tomorrow."

I nod, still feeling out of sorts. "I need a shower first. Some food would also be good."

"You can order room service."

"Did you have dinner?" I ask. If he's been here the entire time, I guess he didn't.

"No."

I swallow, grabbing the menu for room service from the nightstand, perusing it. Usually, purely as a defense mechanism, I would avoid being alone for too long with Daniel. That goes double considering we're in a hotel room. Also, I have a feeling I said some things I shouldn't have before falling asleep.

But the man carried me to my room and forfeited his day and clients for me, so the least I can do is buy him dinner. As soon as I shower, I'll be perfectly equipped to deal with his charm.

"What do you want?" I ask.

"Do they have pizza?"

"They do. Capricciosa?"

"Yeah." I can practically hear the smile in his voice. I still remember his favorite. Without glancing his way, I dial room service, ordering pizza for both of us.

"How are you feeling?" Daniel asks after I hang up.

"Perfect. Can't believe I was so stupid, not paying attention to the food. I'm sorry you wasted your day on me, though. And I've rumpled your bed."

"You always were a messy sleeper, hogging all the space."

"The affliction got worse with age, I'm afraid." I laugh nervously, racking my mind for another topic, and end up rambling about which whales the kids might have seen until there is a knock at the door. "Wow, that was fast."

Several minutes later, Daniel and I are sitting at the edge of the bed, practically inhaling our food, even though it's still so hot I can't feel the roof of my mouth after the first few bites.

Daniel is apparently immune to the heat because he's already finished his pizza and is currently rumbling through the minibar, returning with two cans of Coke. I immediately take a swig from mine, cooling my mouth, pizza slice still in one hand.

I barely swallow the cool liquid when Daniel takes a mouthful from my slice.

Setting my Coke on the floor, I point a warning finger at him. "You ate your own pizza. No stealing mine."

"Or what?" Daniel fixes me with his dark eyes. His molten gaze is a little playful, a lot intense. I avert my gaze because I've never been able to think straight when he looked at me like that.

"I'll cook up an appropriate revenge plan. Just

as soon as I finish my pizza so you can't use it as leverage."

"Carried you all the way from the restaurant up here. I deserve at least one slice for the effort."

I tap my chin, pretending to be thinking hard. All the while, my heart thumps erratically in my chest because Daniel's moved so close to me that I can feel the warmth of his body.

"And you watched me for hours. You deserve a bonus. Another half slice."

He laughs throatily, and every shaky breath of his lands on my cheekbone, that's how close he is.

"I thought you'd put up more of a fight. It's more fun stealing it."

"Fine, suit yourself. You're not getting anything."

I half expect him to fight me for it. Instead, Daniel simply watches me. I focus on my food as heat rises to my cheeks, intensifying by the second. When I can't bear it anymore, I chance a glance at him. Yep, he's still watching me.

Drawing in a deep breath, I focus on the last slice. What on earth is wrong with me tonight? I seem to be even more responsive to all things Daniel than usual, and I can't blame it on the lingering effects of Benadryl. I'm usually better at propping up my defenses... but how am I supposed to keep them in place when he's been shooting holes in them the entire day? Truth be told, he shot the first hole when he told me he's been stopping by to watch soccer games with Dad. It's only been getting bigger since.

"I'm going to shower," I announce once I swallow the last bit, rising from the bed.

"Sure. There are towels in the bathroom."

The warm spray of the water is soothing, as is the ginger-scented shower gel, which I rub vigorously into my skin before washing it off. Perching one foot at the edge of the tub, I intend to hop off on the other side. Instead, the foot I'm standing on slides to one side.

"Aaaaargh."

I collapse on the floor of the bathtub, my left leg and arm squished underneath me, but I narrowly manage to avoid bumping my head too. The door swings open the next second.

"Get out, I'm naked!" I exclaim at the same time Daniel asks, "What happened? Are you hurt?"

"I slipped. I'm fine. Get out."

Except I'm not fine. When I try to push myself up, I discover my left leg hurts too much to be reliable, and I nearly collapse again. Daniel catches me midfall. Hooking an arm around my waist, he hoists me up against him. My entire body is shaking. After about ten seconds or so, I become aware that I'm wet, naked, and both my breasts are pressing against his chest.

"I'm naked," I repeat, not daring to look up at him.

"I've seen it all before."

"You're not helping," I inform him on a groan.

"Can you stand on your foot?"

I test it out, shifting my weight onto it. It hurts less than before, but still enough for me to doubt its reliability. "I don't think so."

"Okay, up you go." He makes a motion as if to lower himself and hoist me up, and panic flares inside me.

"Daniel, no! I mean, can you give me a towel first, please?"

Smiling, he reaches to the rack, still holding my hand firmly. When he hands me the towel, I wrap it around me as quickly as I can. Daniel makes no effort to look away the entire time, his gaze not just appraising but downright hungry. Despite the mortification and the throbbing leg, pride surges inside me, because... priorities. Unable to help myself, I drink him in too. I soaked the front of his shirt, so the sinewy lines and ridges of his abdomen are clearly visible. Good God, his six-pack is as delicious as ever, not to mention the V-shaped dents leading down to his jeans. Biting down on my lips, I raise my gaze, which crisscrosses with Daniel's. Heat jolts through me, and an undercurrent of awareness passes between us.

Wordlessly, Daniel picks me up, carrying me to the bedroom. How did I end up in his arms for the second time today? After breakfast, I was too sick to take it all in, but now... *oh my,* am I making up for that.

Every nerve ending where my bare skin presses against Daniel is perking up. The bits covered by the towel aren't faring much better. A light shudder passes through me when Daniel lays me on the bed. To my dismay, he sits on the edge, pulling my left ankle in his lap, inspecting it.

"Does it hurt?"

"No." I flex it a little, testing it out. "Definitely no sprain, but I'm going to have bruises tomorrow all over my left side. I think you bring me bad luck. I seem to have all sorts of accidents when I'm around you. First I nearly sprained my ankle at Blake and Clara's wedding, and today——"

"You scared ten years off my life today." Daniel shakes his head, putting my foot back on the mattress.

He's frowning as he shifts his weight until he sits right next to my hips. I don't like that frown one bit, but then I remember Daniel isn't mine to make happy. Still, I can lighten up the situation.

"Hmm, now that you mention it, I can see two white hairs. Weren't there before. Must have sprouted while I was asleep."

Reaching out, I'm aiming to touch a random spot on his scalp, but somehow end up running my hand through his hair. *Damn it, he's not mine to touch.* Why do I keep forgetting this?

My heart thumps wildly when I realize Daniel's leaning into my hand as if… as if he's been yearning for my touch as much as I've yearned for his. Has he missed me just as much?

I barely formulate the thought when he grabs my hand, kissing the inside of my wrist. I feel the contact reverberate through my entire body until my center is on fire. Goose bumps erupt everywhere on my skin, and I have no way to hide them. Daniel's pupils dilate. I'm not the only one who is aroused.

"You look even more beautiful than I remember, Caroline."

I shake my head. "I've put on weight."

"You're perfect. You're—"

Daniel doesn't finish the sentence. Instead, he leans over, sealing his lips against mine. *Oh God, his lips.* They're so warm and feel *so, so good* against mine that I fist his shirt without thinking, pulling him even closer, scooting over to one side, making space for him.

Chapter Eight

Daniel

She sighs against my mouth, and it's as if my brain short-circuits, leaving only one thought to stand out: I want this woman. I need her.

Pulling away, I bring her hand to my lips again, kissing her knuckles, then the back of her hand, up her forearm. Goose bumps form where my lips touch her. She's as responsive to me as she's always been. I kiss up her arm, her bare shoulder, inching closer toward her neck. I pause in the act of feathering my lips over her clavicle, the tip of my nose nearly touching her neck. I wait, holding my breath, until she finally tilts her head up, giving me access.

I lavish her neck with kisses, especially at the crease where her neck meets her shoulder. She shudders in my arms, fisting the pillow. That's still a sweet spot for her.

I'm overcome by the primal need of touching and licking every morsel of her skin. Is her earlobe still a sweet spot? Would she still come just from feeling my tongue inside her and my thumb pressing on her clit?

Her body has changed since we've last been

together. In college, she'd been slender, but now her hips and ass are filled out; she's all luscious curves and firm muscle. I worshiped her shape then, and now I want to rediscover every inch of her skin, want to discover every new way in which I can bring her pleasure. I want to do so many things to her that one night will never be enough.

Grazing her earlobe with my teeth, I skim my hand down her thigh, from the apex down to her knee, my fingers brushing the towel until I find bare skin. Instantly she presses her thighs together, nestling my hand in the space just above her knees.

I'm dying to touch her pussy, taste her, but I still have a long way to go until I'll be there. There is so much of Caroline to touch and enjoy.

I inch with my mouth from her earlobe down to her cheek, stopping when the corners of our lips touch. She's still holding my hand hostage between her legs, and as I rub my middle finger in a slight circular motion on the skin, I feel her break out into goose bumps again. On her legs, her arms. If I touched her pussy now, she'd have goose bumps there too. The thought sends a shot from my balls right to the tip. My fingers instantly curl, digging into her skin.

Caroline exhales sharply. I've been so lost in rediscovering her that I haven't been paying attention to her fingers unbuttoning my shirt. I stop any movement for a second, my hand hovering over her thigh, my lips at the corner of her mouth. I just want to feel her for a moment, bask in the knowledge that she's here with me, opening herself to me once more. Her scent overwhelms my senses—not her perfume, but the scent of her skin. It's just as I remember it.

I can't hold back anymore. I capture her mouth. She parts her lips at the same time she opens her thighs in a silent invitation, and I'm so hard, the zipper of my jeans might burst.

Without interrupting the kiss, I move us both until we're lying side by side on the bed, facing each other. Our pelvises are touching, but it's not enough. I need her skin on mine. I have to get us both naked.

When I hook my thumb into the towel, Caroline stills. Her body is tight with tension. I kiss her deeper, coaxing her tongue into a wild dance. I kiss her until I feel the tension ebb away from her, shudders replacing it. And then she hooks her thumb alongside mine into the towel, and we unfasten it together. The fabric slips off her, leaving her completely naked. My shirt, jeans, and boxers go next.

We're still both on our sides, facing each other when I palm one breast, twisting the nipple, and her whole body arches in response, her hips bucking forward, her pussy slamming right into my bent leg. *Oh, fuck me.* She's dripping wet and coats my skin in her arousal too. All my plans to prolong the foreplay fly out the window. I'm blind with need.

"Caroline, you're so sexy. So beautiful. I'm dying to be inside you. Oh, fuck. I have no condoms with me."

"Don't worry. I'm—just don't worry about

it."

I inch so close to her until I can feel the skin of her pelvis on the length of my erection. She perches her upper leg on top of mine. Gripping myself at the base, I rub the tip just above her navel, then slide it farther down to her pubic bone, and lower still, pressing it against her clit. She grazes my chest with her nails.

"Look at me."

She lifts her gaze just as I position myself at her entrance and slide inside her.

"This feels so good. So good," she chants. Gripping the back of her head, I bring her closer until our foreheads touch.

"Say my name."

"Daniel."

"Say it the way you used to."

"Dan."

Energy coils through me, a bolt of heat searing me from the point of our connection right to the nerve endings between my shoulder blades and the tips of my ears. She's so tight around me I can barely take it. *This* is everything. The scent of her skin mixing with the scent of her arousal, her breath on my lips.

She opens up beautifully, thrusting her chest to me, the leg she hooked around me clenching slightly. Leveling myself on my forearm, I kiss her, bracing my free hand on her hip. I can't pace myself anymore. I drive into her wildly, using my hand to steady her, to pull her up and down my cock. She squeezes me so good and so tight…. Pulling out slowly, I slam against her again, filling her up, but I know I can go even deeper. First I have to make sure she's at that point too.

"Caroline, can you take me deeper?"

She nods, and I hook my elbow under the knee of the leg she swung around me, lifting it higher, pushing it toward her torso. As the angle changes, I pull out, then slam back in, taking her so deep that my balls slap against her ass crack. I nearly black out at the intensity of the feeling.

"Oh God, I forgot how this feels." She bites her bottom lip as her face contorts, pleasure etched on every feature.

"That's it, beautiful. Give me your pleasure. All of it. Touch yourself while I'm inside you."

She doesn't hesitate and lowers her hand. I look between us, watching myself slide in and out of her while she circles her clit. I increase the rhythm when she starts clenching and spasming around me and then go completely still inside her as she explodes. The muscles in the leg I'm pressing up to her torso string tight. She's so snug around me, it makes my eyes roll into my head.

I nearly climax too but I hold it off, watching her, feeling her come all around me. While she's still quivering, I pull out of her.

***

Caroline

I can't ground myself, hard as I try. Just as I think I can ride out my orgasm, another wave of pleasure hits. My eyes are unfocused, so I feel rather than see what happens next. Daniel pushes me on my back, shifting his weight on top of me. I part my thighs, cradling him between them, but he doesn't enter me again. Instead, he kisses me, slowly and gently, his hands finding mine at the side of my head and he intertwines our fingers. I want to soak up every detail about this moment: the heat radiating from his skin, the way his body trembles lightly.

I feel his hard erection pressed between our bodies. His control is hanging on a very thin thread. I'm going to make him lose it.

"Dan," I whisper softly when he pulls away.

He's everywhere. His lips are on my breasts, teeth grazing my nipples, tongue swirling around the areola. His palms glide up the sensitive skin on my arms, then drift down on my rib cage, my waist. His thighs are spreading mine apart. My body is tight with tension, my senses overwhelmed by everything he's doing to me. When he skims his fingers over my clit, as if the bundle of nerves is a harp, I nearly come again.

"Oh God, Dan. I want you inside me. I need—"

But before I can make more demands, he turns me over on my stomach, kissing and touching my back as thoroughly as he did my front.

"I want to make this last all night. And I don't want this night to end."

His confession stirs something deep inside me. His hot mouth flows down my spine, over one ass cheek. Then I feel him shift his weight, spread my legs wide apart, and lift me up on all fours. The mattress shifts again, and then I feel his hot breath caress one ass cheek. He gives me no warning; I have no way to brace myself—

He plunges his tongue deep inside me, knocking the breath out of me. He's out just as fast and then pulls my clit between his lips.

I scream his name into the pillow. I'm not a screamer, but *this*. Oh God, *this* is something else. I need... oh God, I need my release right away. Desperate for it, I touch myself the moment Daniel takes his lips away.

"Oh, fuck, Caroline. You're sexy."

His control snaps the next second and he slams into me, filling me up until I think he'll split me in two. My knees quiver, and then the quiver turns into a full-body shake from the intensity of a building orgasm. My calves are burning, muscles protesting.

My knees give out.

With one powerful thrust, Daniel pushes me off my knees and flat on my stomach. Pinning me against the mattress, he intertwines our fingers and slides in and out of me relentlessly until we're both spent.

Chapter Nine

Caroline

"You gave us a scare yesterday," Karla says the next morning. We're in the staff room, preparing for the day. The kids will arrive any second now.

"I'm perfectly fine, don't worry. Good as new."

"When did you get back to San Francisco?"

"Late last night. With the hotel's shuttle service."

Truthfully, I arrived this morning. I'm lucky I arrived in time at all. I woke up with a start at six o'clock in the morning and nearly had a panic attack when I realized Daniel was sleeping next to me, and I'd be late for work. He was still sleeping soundly when I left the room.

The hotel staff was kind enough to arrange my transport, but I still arrived at the school in the nick of time.

Last night was reckless on so many levels that I can't even wrap my mind around it. The moment he kissed me, my common sense flew out of the window. Nothing existed except him. It was wild, unexpected, and my pulse spikes just remembering it.

When the kids arrive, they bombard me with

questions. "Where were you yesterday? Why did you get sick? Are you going to be sick again?" I spend more than half an hour calming them down, then distract them from the incident by asking them to tell me about their adventures. And while they talk my ear off, I can't help remembering my own adventure. Daniel pops in my mind, and then memories of last night rush in: the sinfully delicious touches, the bliss of feeling him inside me again... the way my heart thumped when he said he didn't want the night to end.

Damn heart! It always longs for what it can't have—or worse, for what it shouldn't want, no matter how perfect it felt to be in Daniel's arms again. It felt like home, like I belonged there. But this was a one-time thing, a night of weakness. Nothing more.

I can barely concentrate on our lesson—the life cycle of a butterfly—and during the first break I walk into the staff room determined to do better for the rest of the day.

Helen's already inside, motioning to my bag, which I forgot here. Well, am I not a complete scatterbrain today?

"Your phone rang a few times."

"Thanks."

Walking over to my bag, I take out my phone. I have two missed calls from Daniel, and a message.

Daniel: Sorry I slept like the dead. Didn't hear you leave. I'll be back in San Francisco in the afternoon. Can I take you out for a ristretto?

Still your favorite coffee, right?

My face instantly breaks into a smile, my heart skips a beat, *and* I'm tingling in the most sensitive places covered by my silk underwear. Yep, the whole package... all because he remembers my favorite coffee.

We're both creatures of habit. When we're eighty, his favorite pizza will probably still be capricciosa, and my favorite coffee ristretto macchiato. And he *remembers*.

The longer I linger on that thought, the more excitement builds inside me, filling me with an almost jittery energy.

"Caroline? Everything all right?" Helen points to my hands.

"Oh, yeah. Had a strong coffee this morning."

"Are you sure you don't need to take the day off? Karla told me about what happened yesterday."

"No, no. I'm fine." The last thing I need is for Helen to think I can't do my job. She's the principal's daughter, and while she seems to like me well enough, I can't be too careful. Allergy or not, I forfeited my responsibilities yesterday.

"Okay."

I head out in the yard, intending to stretch my legs, walk off some of this energy. I also need to eat my sandwich, or my stomach will start growling midway through the second lesson since I skipped breakfast.

Halfway through eating my sandwich, I've almost calmed down completely, but then my phone rings, Daniel's name appearing on the screen. I'm tempted to mute it and call him back after my workday is over, but that wouldn't do much good. If I don't talk to him, I'll spend half my time wondering what he had to say. Besides, I'm a strong, independent woman. I will not fall back in love with Daniel over a hot night, or because he remembers my favorite coffee.

Sandwich in one hand, I lift the phone to my ear with the other.

"Hey," I greet him.

"Hello, Caroline."

Ah, two words into the conversation and my skin is already humming. To my defense, my name in his mouth sounds just as sinful as it did last night.

"You didn't reply to my text."

"Ristretto is still my favorite," I say playfully, knowing full well this isn't the answer he was looking for. I'm just a chicken, always have been. Between blaming my loose tongue yesterday on the Benadryl, and my vagueness now, I'm taking my tendency to chicken out to a whole new level.

"I want to take you out. For coffee, or dinner."

"We have after-school activities until six, and I already have plans after."

"We need to talk about last night."

"What?" I ask in alarm, accidentally brushing my sandwich against my top, smearing mayonnaise just over my left boob. Fantastic. Sighing, I carefully weigh my words. "There's no need to talk about anything, Daniel."

"I disagree."

"I'm shocked," I mutter, and he chuckles. "But I can't tonight, really. Already have plans."

"Tomorrow?"

Well damn, he's persistent. "I have plans every evening after work this week."

"What plans do you have on Saturday, birthday girl?"

He remembers my birthday!

"Ironically, not so many. I'm having lunch with Dad, but we can meet in the evening."

I can't ignore him forever, nor do I want to. At the latest, I'll see him at some Bennett event, and it's best to get the awkward out of the way before. Why did I have to complicate things and sleep with him? After our breakup, I pulled away from his family, because the whole thing was too awkward. But after Mom died last year, I grew closer to Jenna Bennett—Dan's mom—again. I rekindled my friendship with Summer and Pippa. I don't want to give that up, and I want Daniel in my life too, but in a *safe* way—in a platonic way.

"Excellent. See you on Saturday. And look out for my gift."

"You don't have to buy me anything," I say quickly, but my voice sounds unconvincing even to my own ears. I *love* presents in any way, shape, and form.

"Oh, I do. Making up for falling asleep and all that."

"You're going to milk this for all it's worth, won't you?"

"You bet. Plus, I know how happy presents make you."

Oh man, here come the butterflies in my stomach. There might be a bit of toe curling involved too. How on earth am I supposed to keep things platonic?

Chapter Ten

Caroline

On Saturday, I wake up with a smile on my face. My thirty-first birthday. Picking up my phone from the nightstand, my face breaks into a grin. I have a dozen unread messages from friends wishing me happy birthday. Niall is the first to call me. It's already lunchtime in Dublin.

"Happy birthday, baby sis. What are your plans for today?"

"Lunch with Dad and dinner with Daniel."

"Bennett?"

"Yeah."

"You're not starting again with him, are you?" The disapproval rolls off his tongue like acid.

"Niall—"

"He's not good for you. Not what you need."

I roll over on one side in the bed, wondering why on earth I brought this up. "I'm a grown woman, Niall. I can make my own decisions. But thank you for your concern."

"He hurt you once."

Now I'm getting pissed. "We were kids. We made mistakes. Did you know he helped Dad with the business plan? And negotiating with the furniture supplier?"

A pause and then, "I had no idea. Still doesn't mean he's good for you."

"Stop it. You're ruining my birthday mojo."

He laughs softly. "Sorry, wasn't my intention. I'm about to make it up to you, though."

"Aw, what did you get me as a present?"

"You're going to see it when you meet Dad. But I meant something else. Guess who will be in San Francisco in two weekends?"

"You're flying here? Niall, are you serious? Oh my God. Oh my God. Did you tell Dad? I bet he was excited."

"Didn't tell him yet."

"How long are you staying?"

"Just for the weekend. I'm coming to a conference. They invited me as a speaker last minute."

"Wow. Congratulations." I do my best to hide how gutted I am that he'll only be here for such a short time. "Oooh, I just had the best idea. We can move the reopening party of the bookstore to that weekend, so you can be here too."

"Sure, I have a few hours on Saturday afternoon."

"Can you stay for dinner too?"

"Nah, have to be with the other conference attendants for dinner."

"Oh, okay. Would Sunday be better? Or Friday?"

"Schedule's too tight on those days with the

flight and some keynote talks."

"So, we'll only see you for a few hours?" I pout like a baby, even though he can't see me.

"It's the best I can do. My schedule is insane."

"A few hours is better than nothing, anyway. So happy to see you."

"Me too. Have to go, sis. Happy birthday again."

I grin as the call ends, excited to be seeing my brother in two weeks. It's been almost nine months since I last saw him, at Mom's funeral. Today of all days, I miss her fiercely.

Jenna Bennett calls to wish me happy birthday just as I'm getting out of bed, and after talking to her for half an hour, I barely bring myself to end the call. Hour-long talks with her every now and then have become the norm in the past nine months. I'm becoming a stage-one clinger, and I really have to stop while I'm ahead. I'm not a kid, for God's sake.

But is there an age at which people stop needing their mothers? Their advice, their warmth, their love?

I hop in the shower but stop midway, shampoo still in my hair, when the doorbell rings. Did I order something online and forgot? After rinsing quickly, I step out, fasten a robe around myself, and head to the front door. I peek through the peephole and see a gigantic bouquet of roses.

"Good morning. If you'll sign here, please," the deliveryman says when I swing the door open.

I sign the sheet he's holding, then take the

flowers back inside. There are thirty-one of them, and there is an envelope there too. My fingers prickle with excitement as I open it. Inside is a birthday card.

Dear Caroline,

Happy birthday. I have left my credit card at Macy's—ask for Christa. It's my gift for you.

Daniel

Holding the card to my chest, I do a happy dance in my living room, grinning ear to ear. Then I reread the card a few times to make sure I'm not imagining it. I can't *believe* him. But then again, Daniel always had his own style of doing things. Still, reining in my excitement, I pick up my phone, dialing his number. My insides warm just at the thought of hearing his voice. Other parts warm too, damn it. I pause just before pressing the last digit.

Should we clear the air about what happened that night first? Yeah, right. No way am I bringing it up. It's too early in the morning to face that level of awkwardness. Biting the inside of my cheek, I resume dialing.

"Morning, birthday girl."

"Hi!"

"I take it you got the flowers?"

"Yes. And the card. But I can't possibly accept this gift, Daniel."

It kills me to refuse this, but it's not right. A present would be one thing, but free rein with his credit card? That's the sort of thing a girlfriend would do, and I'm not his *anything*. Common decency dictates that I can't accept it.

"Oh, you will. I want you to accept it. Go wild, Caroline."

I lick my lips, pressing my free hand to my cheek, which suddenly feels on fire. Images of us together in the hotel bed sweep into my mind, of Daniel asking me to call him Dan, asking me if I could take him in deeper.

Aw, shucks. My imagination escalated quickly, and he hasn't even been flirting. Clearing my throat, I try to gather my wits around me.

"Daniel, this is not—"

"Stop trying so hard to do what you think is right. You're dying to go shopping."

I can hear the smile in his voice, and my decency is melting away by the second. Why does he have to know me this well? I love shopping, but a teacher's salary requires a lot of self-restraint. I love my job, working with kids. I'm not good at much else, but I'm really good at this one thing. The slight downside is the salary, but I've built my life so I don't need a lot. For some, it would seem like a small or restrictive life, but I like it.

I have a strict no takeout policy, only eating out when the situation requires it. I often invite friends over instead of going out, and I cook for them. I only buy the clothes I need, and try to keep to timeless pieces—jeans, little black dresses—so they won't go out of style quickly. Some things I even buy from thrift stores. There's an excellent one nearby, and I came across unexpected gems there.

But what Daniel is offering is insane. I'll make one last attempt to dissuade him. Just to have a clear conscience.

"It's just not right."

"I already bought you some presents, so you'll have to pick them up anyway."

"Wow."

"Thought you might need extra convincing. Pick them up, and buy anything else you want."

"What did you buy me?" I ask, despite myself.

"You'll see."

"Okay." Energy courses through me as I pace the living room.

"Have fun, and I'll see you tonight at seven."

We agreed on dinner in a restaurant in the Presidio to celebrate my birthday and talk about *that night*, but now I'm losing my nerve about the latter.

"Let's talk about the elephant in the room now," Daniel suggests. *Shit, shit, shit.*

"No elephant here," I say with an awkward laugh, heading to the kitchen. I can't face this without caffeine. While brewing coffee, I whip myself up a sandwich, keeping the phone between my shoulder and my ear.

"Okay, let's leave it for the evening, then. Unless you'd rather we talk about it another day?"

"You wouldn't mind?"

"You're the birthday girl. Don't want to spoil your day. But I still want my dinner this evening."

"Sure. Dinner's on. No conversation about elephants."

To be honest, I don't see how a conversation would help anyway. We both had a slip in our control; that was all. No need to beat a dead horse. Do I crave his touch, miss how safe and cherished it made me feel? Sure I do, but that doesn't mean I should act on it. Some things are not for me, and Daniel is one of them.

"See you at seven. Have fun shopping. Promise me you'll go wild."

Laughing, I try to focus on my sandwich and not the way my pulse skitters. My poor sandwich doesn't stand a chance of distracting me.

"I will."

***

Lunch with my dad is a rather melancholic affair. We don't talk about Mom, but we both feel her absence. He gives me Niall's present, a cotton throw with a Celtic motif. My brother is *the best*, seriously. I told him I was looking for a new throw, something to cozy up with on my couch, and this is beautiful.

"Niall's outdone himself," I exclaim. "By the way, he's coming to San Francisco." I share with him all the details, suggesting we move the opening party to include him.

"Of course we'll move the reopening party early. Ah, it's good to see that boy."

The weather is pleasantly cool for early October, so we head to Pier 39, carving our way through the flocks of tourists who're watching the seals roast lazily in the sun, talking about the bookstore and Niall, indulging in old memories. After I part ways with Dad, I head straight inside Macy's, more excited than guilty. I go to the nearest vendor, reading the name tag. Allyson.

"Hi, miss. How may I help you?"

"I'm looking for a colleague of yours, Christa."

She nods, surveying the floor. "Look, she's right there by the cardigans. The blonde with the pink ends."

"Thanks."

I practically fly toward Christa, my excitement now drowning out my guilt completely. She looks up at me as I approach.

"Hi, Christa. I'm Caroline."

Her face breaks into a grin. "Yay! Follow me. Wow, you're so lucky. This is so romantic, my goodness. I wish my boyfriend would do something like this, but I'm lucky if he remembers to make dinner reservations for my birthday."

"Daniel's not my boyfriend," I explain as I follow her up the rolling staircase.

Her eyes widen. "Then he's trying very hard to be, isn't he? Well, I wouldn't put up much of a fight. You won't either. Wait to see what he got you."

Alarm flares inside me. What exactly did Daniel buy me?

"You know him long?" Christa continues. "Sorry, not my business. It's just… well, this is so unusual."

"For about ten years." I offer her a small smile, choosing to stop there. Up and up we go on the escalator, coming to a halt on the next to the last floor. My eyes scan the information table right next to the staircase. *Domestics* and *lingerie*.

My knees go weak because I have an inkling of which of the categories Daniel was interested in. Sure enough, two minutes later, Christa leads me into the lingerie section. Ah, damn, everything here looks exquisite. I'm so lost in the delicate and sexy offerings around me that I nearly forget Christa is with me until she shows me three sets lying on the wooden table next to the cash register, where vendors usually pack the purchases.

"Oh, they're beautiful." One is a matching set of red lace panties and a demi-cup bra. The second set is white silk, with an embroidered pattern on the strapless bra. The third is black, made of satin and cotton by the looks of it. "Daniel chose these for me?" I whisper. "Personally?"

"Yes. Shall I bring them to the changing room for you to try them on?"

Even though I'm one hundred percent sure they will fit, I nod. Truth is, I'm dying to try them on.

Once she hangs the three sets on the hanger, she arranges the curtain so no one can see me from outside, leaving me alone. I undress at top speed, not bothering to hide my grin as I put on the black set first. I keep my thong on, though, merely sliding the black one over it. It's an ironclad rule, I never try on panties on bare skin.

I love what I see in the mirror. The black silk has a subtle elegance. Some would say it's too simple, but I disagree. The way it molds against my skin, the softness of the fabric… every detail is perfect. I try on the white one next. It looks a little subdued against my pale skin and I decide to get out in the sun as soon as I have the chance. I touch the intricate pattern of the lace on the bra, the ribbon clasp between the cups. With a smile, I remember Daniel much prefers bras with the clasp in front. In a flash, sinful images fill my mind of Daniel unfastening the bra, touching my breasts.

I break out in a sweat, then shimmy out of the white set, trying on the last one. I saved the best for last. The red lace is downright sinful perfection. The bra pushes my breasts together. The panties are wider over my hips than regular thongs. At the back, a smooth line covers the crack between my ass cheeks. I much prefer these types of thongs to strings. They give me an air of wicked playfulness.

And I was right. Daniel guessed my size correctly, even though I've gone from a size four when we were together to a size eight. I'm still not used to the size of my thighs, not to mention my ass. The only positive part of them growing is that they've kept the same proportion to my waistline, which has also expanded.

Still, looking at myself right now, I've never felt sexier. The skin on my chest and neck becomes almost as red as the lace as a flush spreads over that area. I haven't felt this sexy, or *wanted*, in a long time.

Releasing a shaky laugh, I chastise myself for reading so much into all of this. But then I realize the man bought me *lingerie* for my birthday. What does this even mean?

"They fit?" Christa's voice reaches me from beyond the curtain.

"Yeah. Perfectly." Quickly I change back into my own bra, then put on my clothes. When I pull back the curtain, Christa grins at me, taking the three sets of lingerie.

"Excellent. I'll pack these, and then we can go see what else you like. Credit card's open. No limit."

Oh snap. I'd forgotten. "This is more than enough."

"Tsk, tsk, tsk. I have my orders to pester you if you don't go wild."

"He said that?"

"Exactly like that. So, ready to go wild?"

"Not even close to ready."

I get the hang of it quite quickly, though. In the beginning, I exercise every ounce of self-restraint, going for small things: new moon-shaped earrings, a pair of gloves. But Christa is a little devil, tempting me like nobody's business, and I'm a weak woman when it comes to pretty things.

She flaunts a knee-length floral dress with white straps and a wide belt around the waist, and I'm a goner. I try it on and it fits perfectly, but when I look at the price tag, my stomach plummets. This is

Daniel's card, but there's a difference between wild and taking advantage.

"Only dresses on sale," I tell Christa firmly.

"Daniel didn't tell me anything of that sort."

"I'm telling you. Please. I have half a mind to leave with what I got up to now anyway."

That sets her straight, and she only tempts me with items on sale next. I end up buying a knee-length, thick sweater dress that molds to my body nicely and red ballerina shoes. Neither breaks the bank, but I draw the line here. While I watch Christa pack everything, my phone vibrates in my purse. Taking it out, I discover a message from Daniel.

Daniel: How's project wild going?

Caroline: Well under way.

Daniel: Picture or it didn't happen.

If he thinks he's going to get pics of me in my underwear, he's got another think coming.

Caroline: Cheeky bastard.

He calls me, of course. I step a few feet away from the counter.

"Whatever you say won't convince me to send you pics in my underwear. Buy a swimwear magazine."

"I just want to see you, Caroline. Just you."

"You've got some nerve, mister. And you're still not getting pictures."

"Did you have fun?"

"Yeah. Lots of fun."

"Good. Wear something you bought tonight."

The not-so-subtle command in his tone sends

heat low in my body.

"I can do that. Have to go now, I'm holding up the line."

After clicking off, I shove the phone back in my purse, smiling devilishly. I can definitely do that.

Chapter Eleven

Caroline

The shopping trip took so long that I only have time to hop in the shower and then dress fast before having to bolt back out the door. I put on my new sweater dress but don't inspect my appearance in the mirror until I have my flats on too. Judging an outfit without shoes is like asking how the Thanksgiving turkey is without the gravy.

I assess the outfit critically. It's great for a chill night out between friends, conveys exactly the message I want, which is "I look put together," not "I can't wait to put out again."

Briefly, I wonder if I should bring up our night together after all, clear the air. Even in my mind, the conversation would sound awkward.

Daniel, even though this was the best night—

Even though you gave me two orgasms and they were by far—

Hmm... maybe I shouldn't lead with that. I can see how I might give off the wrong impression if I do. Best not to bring the subject up after all.

I leave my building with a pep in my step, taking in the beautiful October evening surrounding me. Clutching my matching red purse under my arm, I stride with purpose. I live in a rather crowded section of the Richmond district, with residential units so close to one another it's borderline claustrophobic. But I'm just a few blocks away from the Presidio, or if I'm in the mood for a long walk, I can hike up to Golden Gate Park to the north.

Some twenty minutes later, I arrive at the 14th Avenue gate entrance and find Daniel already there, pacing, hands in his pockets. He doesn't see me approach, and I take advantage of this to study him. He appears lost in thought, a frown creasing his forehead, his five o'clock shadow more pronounced than usual. The impulse to replace that frown with a smile hits me hard. *He's not mine to make happy. Not mine.*

"Hi!" I announce myself, stopping right next to him. Daniel snaps out of his thoughts, turning to me. His handsome face breaks into a wide smile, all traces of the frown gone. Excellent.

My heart skips a beat as he bends to kiss my cheek, lingering with his lips on my skin. He presses a hand at the small of my back. An electric charge jolts right through me. Oh, God. The touch isn't intimate at all, but maybe the details of our night together are still too fresh in my mind. I swear every nerve ending springs to life. When we pull apart, my entire body is buzzing. *Way to go, Caroline.* I was not expecting this assault on my senses.

I do a full turn, sashaying my hips playfully.

"Both the dress and the shoes are courtesy of your credit card and Christa's impeccable taste."

He assesses my appearance, a playful twinkle in his eye...

The twinkle just turned scorching hot. I can almost read the question on his lips. *How about the lingerie?*

Better get that out of the way. "Not wearing the lingerie you bought me. I never wear new lingerie without washing it first. Too many germs."

There. Nothing unsexier than germs.

If I thought that would turn him off, man, was I wrong. The corner of his lips twitch. Right, moving on.

"Let's go before our reservation expires."

We hike on a trail with towering trees on either sides. The smell of eucalyptus hangs in the evening air, energetic and fresh. The restaurant is chock-full when we arrive, but thankfully the wall opposite the entrance is lined with floor-to-ceiling windows, which are all open.

Feeling optimistic about the weather, I request to be seated at a table nearest to the door. Daniel is wearing a suit, so he should be fine, and I stashed a jacket in my purse.

"How was lunch with your dad?" he asks after we order.

"Nice. We're both psyched that Niall will be here in two weekends. We're moving the opening party of the bookstore to that Saturday, by the way."

"Good to know." Leaning slightly over the table, he narrows his eyes. "I'm still invited, right?"

"My dad invited you, so I can't revoke it," I say playfully." Besides, you're his top adviser. You're basically a guest of honor. But I understand if you can't make it. The change is very last minute."

"I wouldn't miss it."

"Thanks. I'm so happy Niall will join us too. It's been so long since we saw him."

"He doesn't call often, does he?"

I shrug, trying to downplay this. "He's busy. Works like a hundred hours a week."

"You can always make time for family."

Well, dang. What can I say? He's perfectly right.

The waiter arrives with the food, and damn the aromas are killing me. I ordered roasted chicken salad with sweet potato fries, and Daniel ordered a steak. Sighing, I dig into my sweet potato fries, and we spend the next fifteen minutes or so in companionable silence as we wolf down our food. When my plate is empty, I still feel like voicing one more thought. I didn't say anything today to Dad or Niall because I didn't want to make them sad, but I need to say it out loud.

"I miss Mom so much."

"Tough thing, losing your mom. Lucky you've got mine, who fusses over you just like my sisters. She was all over me this week. 'Don't forget to call her. Buy her a nice present. Cheer her up. It's her first birthday without her mom.'" He mimics his mother's tone, and I can't help but laugh.

"Ah, so that's why you bought me presents," I say playfully, touched at Jenna's thoughtfulness.

He wiggles his eyebrows. "The lingerie was all my idea."

"I bet." I shift a little in my chair, feeling heat heading low in my body like an arrow. Suddenly, the table feels tiny. Is there really less than a foot between us?

Under the table, Daniel cradles my legs between his. There are two layers of fabric between us—his pants and my pantyhose—but the contact electrifies me as if it were skin-on-skin.

I change the subject before we head into dangerous territory, turning the tables on him.

"How are *you* doing?" I inquire. "Troubles at work? You looked worried when I arrived."

"You got that?"

"Yeah." A gust of wind rustles the trees around us, and I retrieve the flimsy jacket from my purse, shrugging into it. Doesn't help much, unfortunately.

"You're the birthday girl, so no talking about me."

"Not fair. I can't go on talking about me the entire night."

"Oh, this is going to be an all-night event?" He flashes me his best grin, the one that sends my senses into overdrive.

"Not what I meant. Came out wrong."

His grin becomes even wider. "Freudian slip?"

"Daniel!"

As another gust of wind rushes past us, I shudder. My flimsy jacket is useless. I run my hands up and down my arms to warm myself up, but it's not working. Then Daniel rises from his seat, draping his own jacket over my shoulders.

"It's not so chilly," I protest, but oh boy, is the jacket cozy. Smells like him too, which is a bonus.

"It is, and you're cold," Daniel says in a tone that allows no argument. "You still don't know how to dress weather-appropriate, I see."

As my gaze meets his, I am certain he's rehashing the same memory I am. Our first night together, the walk home where he gave me his jacket and his socks. The hot shower, the even hotter sex.

"Don't worry. I won't invite myself into your shower. Unless you want me to."

I let out a nervous laugh, averting my gaze. "This escalated quickly." My own fault, I suppose, for thinking we could keep this platonic. Squaring my shoulders, I gather my wits around me and look straight at him. "I'm the birthday girl, remember? You're not allowed to make me uncomfortable."

"Whatever the birthday girl wishes." A smile is playing on his lips, and I instantly become suspicious. He's letting me off the hook too easily, but I'm not about to look a gift horse in the mouth.

Since neither of us wants dessert and the walk to the edge of the park will take a while, we decide to call it a night.

"I'm walking you home," Daniel announces

as we reach the exit of the Presidio. Maybe not the best idea, but I'm not ready to say good night yet.

"It's seven blocks away. We can walk or take a cab. Unless you came with your car?"

"Nah, cab. Let's take one."

On the way home, I talk his ear off about the neighborhood, then point out my school, which is halfway between the park and my apartment. By the time we climb out of the cab in front of my building, I'm still not ready to say good night. But it's the smart thing to do.

I shrug out of his jacket, hand it back to him.

"Thank you for the jacket and the evening. And the presents, of course. It was a fantastic birthday. I didn't have much time to be melancholic about Mom, thanks to you."

Daniel smiles warmly. "That was the point."

"Wow, so you did have a master plan behind the shopping spree idea. And here I thought you were just hoping to see me in sexy lingerie."

"I was. Still am." He steps so close our chests almost touch. A shiver runs through me, and I'd love to blame the chilly wind for it, but it's Daniel's fault. It's all Daniel. He rubs my arms with his hands, resting one on my shoulder, feathering his thumb in the crook of my neck. My mouth goes dry... unlike other parts of me. My pulse quickens. *Oh God, can he feel it?*

***

Daniel

I remember the first time I realized the connection between Caroline and me was more than friendship. Blake had been in a minor accident because of a fraternity dare. I was outside the campus infirmary, and the waiting was turning me insane. Caroline joined me the second I told her what happened, and just having her with me made everything so much easier. She said the right things to put me at ease, even made me laugh. She knew exactly what I needed, and I realized she was more than a friend.

After Blake came out, with a bandaged arm and a shit-happens attitude, Caroline came with us to the apartment I shared with Blake. It was late, so I suggested she sleep in my bed. In the second it took me to add that I'd sleep on the couch in my room, her cheeks were red.

Just like now.

There are two things I love about Caroline's Irish heritage. One, her clumsy attempts to perform traditional Irish dances at weddings. She's hopeless at it, but adorable to watch. Two, she blushes like a redhead. Even though she inherited her father's dark hair, her mom was a redhead, and Caroline inherited her light skin. Right now, even her scalp has a reddish hue.

"Which one's your favorite?" I ask.

"What do you mean?"

"The lingerie. Which set is your favorite?"

She clears her throat, fiddles with her thumb. "The black one."

"My favorite is the white set."

Exerting self-restraint while choosing her presents wasn't easy. I wanted to buy the entire damn floor. I saw the white set first and knew it was perfect for her. I can easily imagine her wearing it. My favorite part is the bra clasp in the front. I'd flick it open, and her breasts would spill right into my mouth.

"I was sure. You were always a fan of clasps in the front."

When our gazes cross, she makes a small noise at the back of her throat. *Fuck me.* She's thinking the exact same thing.

"I bet the red one looks sexy as hell. All that lace," I continue, brushing a strand of hair from her face. Her breathing becomes more labored when my thumb brushes her neck. "Is it comfortable? Or does it… graze your skin?"

I trace a small line up her neck, and she presses her thighs together as if she felt my touch straight there. *Oh fuck, fuck, fuck.* It was a light reaction, but I saw it, and she knows I did.

"It's comfortable. There's no lace on the inside. Just cotton."

"Everywhere?"

She swallows hard, avoiding my eyes and laughing nervously. "Everywhere."

A few drops of rain splatter on the asphalt. One lands straight on her nose, making her jump.

"Head inside before you catch a cold," I say.

Her eyes widen in surprise. I bet she was expecting me to push more, ask her to invite me upstairs. Any other time I would, but this has been an emotional day for her, and I won't take advantage. She's so responsive to me that I know how easy this night could end between the sheets. But that's not what I want, or what she deserves. Our connection is still here, always has been, we just fought hard to ignore it. It's how I knew she needed a distraction today, how she could tell I'm worried without even asking. We've had another incident with photos leaking, and I'm coming to a conclusion I don't like at all.

"Yeah, sure. Okay. Have a nice evening."

"Any other plans for tonight?"

She grins. "Oh yeah, I have a date. Really hot dude. Potty mouth, six-pack, hypnotic blue eyes. Pity he's on screen and doesn't even know I exist."

"You still binge-watch TV shows?"

"Of course. Once a TV junkie, always a TV junkie."

"I'll leave you to your date."

Taking her hand, I kiss her knuckles, then watch her enter her building.

We need to have *that* conversation, but I promised I wouldn't bring it up today, and she's still the birthday girl. For a few more hours.

Chapter Twelve

Caroline

A few minutes later, I slip between the sheets with my laptop and switch on my favorite streaming service. I have four brand-new episodes to watch. Rubbing my hands in excitement, I press Play.

I am midway through the third episode and my second glass of wine when my phone beeps. Someone who probably just remembered it was my birthday. I reach out for my phone without taking my eyes off the screen. The leads are just about to kiss for the first time, and it looks like the ten-episode wait will be worth it.

But then I forget all about the kiss as I read the message.

Daniel: 12:01, birthday day is officially over. Time to tackle that elephant.

I should have known he wouldn't let me off the hook so easily. Pressing Pause on the screen, I sit up straight on the bed, my heart thumping in my throat. I can do this. It's best to clear the air, and it's easier to do it via text or on the phone than face-to-face.

Caroline: Tell me what you were worried about today.

Daniel: ????

Caroline: Don't be cruel, ease me into this.

Daniel: Had two incidents with leaked photos from celebrity events to the press. The problem is I suspect someone from my team did it. On purpose.

I read through his text twice, my neurons a tad befuddled by the wine. But the second his meaning sinks in, my stomach coils. I call him right away.

"What do you mean, on purpose? Why?" I ask instead of saying hello.

"Money. Gossip magazines pay a good buck."

"Let me get this straight. These are pictures of events you did for your famous clients?"

"Yeah."

"And you're sure some other attendees didn't leak the pics?"

"Not one hundred percent sure, but everyone attending wants privacy. And it happened at two different events, no common attendees."

I hug my knees to my chest, resting my chin on them. "What are you going to do?"

"Do a bit of detective work. I like my team. I trust them. Not looking forward to it."

"I bet not."

"So, time to bring up the elephant."

Damn! I'd almost forgotten about it. Carrying out this conversation after I had two glasses of wine isn't the smartest thing. I might let slip things I don't mean… or worse, things I do mean but don't want him to know. *Breathe in, breathe out. I can do this.* Time to rip off the Band-Aid.

"It was a one-time thing, Daniel. Let's forget about it. These things happen, right? Wouldn't be the first time two exes fall in bed with each other."

A brief pause, and then he talks in a low, smooth voice. "It wasn't just sex."

His words wrap around me like a blanket of comfort. Knowing it meant more than sex to him too reaches somewhere deep inside me. Still, it doesn't change things.

"No, it wasn't, but it was still a one-time thing."

More silence, which unnerves me. Daniel usually has no problem filling silences of any kind. My stomach twists and turns in anticipation.

"Why did you give up on me so easily, Caroline?"

Huh? Not what I was expecting at all. Tension gathers between my shoulder blades, but I try to keep my calm. "What do you mean?"

"When I told you it was best to break things off, you didn't say anything."

Right, out the window goes my determination to remain calm. "You'd broken my heart, what was I supposed to say?"

I climb out of the bed, suddenly filled with too much energy. Needing to walk it off, I just pace my bedroom.

"Something. Anything. Fight me on it. You

accepted it so easily, as if it was what you'd wanted too."

"Is this what you told yourself to feel better about being an ass?"

"Partly," he admits. "But it did feel like you accepted it all too quickly."

"I can't believe this. I was twenty-one, and hurt, and it was clear you didn't want me anymore. What was I supposed to do? Beg?"

"No, just... I don't know, Caroline. I've been thinking about it many times, about how it could have gone differently."

This catches me off guard. "Different how?"

"No idea, any way I got to keep you."

Is he saying what I think he's saying? No, it can't be. Must be all that wine, and I'm reading into things. But not even I can read too many things in "any way I got to keep you." Still, I gather the courage to ask for clarification.

"Dan, what are you saying?" I whisper.

"Of my top five regrets, losing you is right at the head of the list. I should have told you that a long time ago. I'm sorry I didn't."

Ah, but even hearing it now is more than I was hoping for. Time to put his mind at rest too.

"I *didn't* want to break up, Daniel. I just didn't know how to fight you, or fight for you. I thought pushing back would be humiliating."

"And I'd just broken your heart."

Despite myself, I laugh. "Yeah."

More silence follows, but it's not

uncomfortable this time.

"You know what the second thing on that regret list is?"

"What?"

"Not getting my act together sooner and pursuing you again. I never stopped caring."

Oh God, make him stop. Is he aware that this is every woman's dream? Well, my dream at least. To find out that I still mean something to the man I could never forget? Who still means so much to me....

"I didn't stop either. Caring, I mean."

He lets out a long breath into the phone. Sounds like a *relieved* breath.

"Summer *was* right," he says with a chuckle.

"You told Summer about our night? Aw, come on. The girls have been dropping hints about us for a long time. What are they planning? Setup lunches? Impromptu get-togethers where we somehow end up alone? Something even worse? I need to start preparing my defenses."

I only stop because I'm out of breath. I even stopped pacing to concentrate on remembering the girls' techniques, but I'm not naive enough to believe I remember them all. And regardless, they can whip up plans faster than I can come up with defensive techniques.

"Slow down, woman. Take a deep breath. Good to know I'm not the only one they've been pestering. And no, I haven't told them. I've learned to keep my mouth shut unless I want everyone in my business. Come to think of it, I wouldn't mind that right now."

What does this even mean?

"But Summer said you and I have been involved with each other's families because we didn't want to let go."

"Ah, and here I was thinking you watched games with my dad out of the goodness of your heart," I tease.

"I do like spending time with your dad, but I won't lie. I was half hoping you'd drop by whenever I was there."

"Can't say my mind wasn't on the same track when I was helping your mom and sisters plan Blake and Clara's wedding. Though I love the bunch of them as if we're related."

"You're adorable."

"No, no, you don't get to charm me." I'm *so* proud that I'm still hanging on to my defenses. By my fingertips, but still. "Clearing the air was good, but that's all this was. We're in the past."

"Except the still caring bit."

"We can handle it. We're adults, and I'm not the girl you fell in love with anymore." I don't volunteer more information because that'd be one confession too many. And he doesn't need to know, anyway.

"I changed too. It's been ten years for both of us." After a brief pause, he adds, "Remember the night I told you I loved you?"

I smile. Oh, I only remember every detail

about it. "Yes. You were so nervous that evening at the restaurant. And then when you said it I teared up and tried to hide my face, and you were so sweet. God, you were so sweet. You held me and said it again, and again."

"I haven't felt that way about anyone since."

Boom! Straight through my defenses. This would be a good moment for my heart to pull up those walls, remember all the crying I did after we broke up. Instead, all I can remember are the good times. Sort of like biting into a delicious but hot s'mores and burning your tongue. All you remember later is how good it tasted, not how badly your tongue burned.

"Neither have I, Dan."

Rubbing a hand over my face, I decide it's time to end this call. I've had too much wine, and he's way too good with words. If we take a walk down memory lane, I might not come out unscathed.

"I...I don't know what else to say. We should call this a night," I say firmly. "It's late."

"Yeah, you're right. I have to wake up early anyway."

"On a Sunday?"

"I'm leaving with a group to go to the Adirondack Mountains. Hiking trip until Thursday. We're leaving at five o'clock, so I'd better go to sleep. But Caroline? What happened in the marina hotel wasn't a mistake. There's a reason neither of us moved on. Good night."

"Good night."

After we hang up, I feel a little shaken and a lot flummoxed, a single thought circling in my mind. How will the dynamic between us change after our midnight confessions?

Chapter Thirteen

Caroline

"One more time before the break. Three, two, one. Go."

The chorus starts again, and I fight with all my might to keep a straight face. We're currently rehearsing the songs for the Halloween celebration, and I swear each of the fifteen kids is singing to their own tune. They put so much heart and soul into it, bless them, that I don't have the heart to keep correcting them.

"Lovely," I announce when they're done. "I'll see you after the break."

They skitter around, their laughter and chatter filling the air. I head straight to the staff room. Karla and Rita slip in right behind me, talking about their plans this evening. I join the conversation, grateful for the distraction. *I will not check the weather report in the Adirondack Mountains. I will not check it.*

Ever since Daniel told me he's taking a group there this week, I've been refreshing the page with the weather forecast about a dozen times a day. Monday there was just an alert about windy conditions. Tuesday they announced there was a mild risk of a blizzard. As of this morning, the risk was mild too, but they said there is a real possibility the warning will change to red around noon. It's eleven o'clock now. Midway through the break, I break down and check the weather report. My stomach clenches. There is now a high risk of a blizzard.

Is Daniel still there with his group? He has been reckless in the past, though I can't imagine him endangering his life and that of his clients this way. Still, if I just *knew* for sure, I could breathe more easily. I've been sleeping like shit since Monday, worrying. Wondering. Tapping my fingers on my phone, I briefly considering texting Summer or Jenna, asking them if they've heard from Daniel, but that would open a can of worms.

I only have one option left: calling Daniel himself. Excusing myself from the staff room, I head to my empty classroom and dial his number. It rings for so long, I almost give up, but then he answers.

"Hey, Caroline."

I swear my very bones liquefy as the tension melts from my body. I hadn't even realized I was so tense.

"Hey! How are you? Everything all right?"

"Sure. Why wouldn't it be?"

With a jolt, I realize how awkward I'm coming across, calling out of the blue to ask if he's okay. Sitting on my desk, I dangle my legs, carefully considering my words.

"I saw they announced a blizzard in the Adirondacks, and I…."

"You were worried about me."

No point denying it. "Yes."

"Don't. We canceled the hiking trip yesterday. Too dangerous. We're improvising other activities for the rest of the week."

"When are you returning to San Francisco?"

"Next Thursday. I'm going to another group in the Rocky Mountains after I finish here. Can't wait to be back home. It's not sunny, but at least it's not as cold. Almost forgot how it feels to be warm."

"Drink some hot chocolate and you'll be golden," I encourage. The second the words are out of my mouth, I can't stop a vision forming in my mind, of me heading to Daniel's when he returns on Friday, helping him warm up, take care of him. I make a mean cup of hot chocolate. Shaking my head, I inwardly laugh at myself. I have no claim on Daniel. He's not mine to make happy. Except... friends cheer each other up. I could go over as his friend. Ah, who am I kidding? By the way my body hummed at his proximity last Saturday, I'd fall right back in his bed.

"There are better ways of getting warm." The subtle change in his tone alerts me that his thoughts aren't on the straight and narrow path either. "Hot wine, a hot shower. Skin-on-skin contact. What d'you think? Asking for a friend."

I grin from ear to ear, but try to work in as much severity as possible in my tone. "You're insufferable."

He laughs. "You sound *so* convincing. For your information, your voice sounds different when you smile."

Clearing my throat, I force my facial muscles in a serious expression, but they put up a good fight. "Oh, Dan, I can never win against you. I just called to make sure you're okay. Let's leave it at that."

He's silent for a few seconds, then finally says, "I'm sorry you were worried about me. I would've texted if I knew."

"My own fault for checking the weather report so often. But you're okay, so I can go about my day."

"And you won't give me another thought?"

I'm the one who can hear the smile in *his* voice now. "Not one single thought. I have to go, by the way. Break will be over soon."

"Sure. Enjoy your day." A few seconds pass, but I'm still holding on to the call. "You can hang up anytime."

"You hang up." I smile, remembering we used to play this game eons ago.

"I'm not the one who has to go."

"Fine, I'll hang up. Bye, Daniel." I click off the next second, feeling a little light-headed.

The feeling persists the entire day, right until I receive another phone call, from my brother, just as I'm on my way out of the school.

"Hey, sis, I'll be quick. I have some bad news. I'll only be able to make it to the opening party for half an hour or so when I'm in town."

My stomach sinks. "Oh?"

"One of the keynote speakers dropped out,

and they asked me to fill in for him. The keynotes are back to back, and I only get one break, which is when I'll swing by at the store."

"And you can't say no? They have time to find someone else."

"This is a fantastic opportunity to get my name out there."

"I know, it's just... I wish you could stay longer. We'll only see you for half an hour? We could drive you to the airport."

"That's a drag. How about an early breakfast on Sunday morning? You can show me everything we don't have time for on Saturday."

"Yes! Thank you, thank you, thank you!"

Just like that, my good mood is back.

***

Daniel

On Friday morning, I pace around the meeting room, waiting for my team to arrive. Our weekly meetings are usually on Tuesdays, but we had to reschedule since I was in the Adirondacks last week and the Rocky Mountains this week. We used to do them Monday, but since many weekend events last until Monday, part of the team was always missing.

I usually look forward to the weekly meeting. Everyone presents the highlights of the past week, the plans for this one. We strategize and brainstorm.

If there are any problems, we tackle them together. Damn it, I trust every single person on my team. But those leaked pictures were too clear to be taken by paparazzi from outside with a long-lens camera.

And the only ones attending both events were the four people from my team: Marcel and Honor, who spearhead all events of this type; Justin, who's an excellent organizational talent and has been with the company almost from the beginning; and our intern, Colbert. It's too early to point fingers, but I'm going to keep a closer eye on Colbert. He's been with us for only four months, and is the most likely to be tempted by the money gossip magazines offer for insider pics.

My assistant, Jennifer, arrives first, sitting in her usual chair. "Morning."

"Morning, Jen."

One by one, the rest of the team filters in, all twenty-five of them. I pace the room even after everyone sits. I decide to open up with the unpleasant subject, get it out of the way, though I won't share my concern about the culprit being part of the team.

"As you all know, we had a second case of leaked photos last week. We can't let it happen again."

"We'll secure the perimeter outside better," Honor suggests at once.

Marcel taps his fingers on the table, frowning. "Maybe as a precaution, we should ask the guests to leave their phones with us for the duration of the event."

Justin shakes his head. "These are heavyweights in the entertainment industry, not kids going to a concert. You bring that up, you'll piss them off. Any more bright ideas like this, and soon we won't have customers left."

Justin's experience is worth its weight in gold because he's absolutely right. As the most senior member of the team, I respect him. He's like a mentor to me, but he lacks tact. His tone is so cutting that Honor almost recoils. Marcel sets his jaw. Colbert doesn't say anything, but he rarely does. He's a doer, not a talker. One of the reasons I gave him the internship.

"No restrictions on the guests," I say. "We need them happy. Happy guests come back for more."

"Honor and I will work on a list of measures to implement," Marcel says. Looking around the table, he adds, "Everyone around here is welcome to send me suggestions. I'll go through them with Daniel. No point discussing them now, or we'll spend the entire meeting doing just that."

"Let's move on," I agree. "Anyone have any issues which are not on the agenda?"

Chelsea, our activities coordinator, clears her throat. "We're getting more and more inquiries about indoor activities—team sports, individual training, maybe even indoor rock climbing."

"You want us to add a gym," I say, finally sitting too. We've had this conversation a few times, and I wasn't sold on the idea. Doesn't fit under our umbrella of *experiences* too well, but I might just be too subjective because I like being outdoors so much.

"It's not exactly our jam, but why not give people what they want?" As if reading my mind, she adds, "Everything can be an *experience*. Depends how we sell it. I've compiled a list of the activities that keep popping up in the requests."

"Okay. Come to my office after the meeting, and we'll go through them."

"I've had some requests too. I'll gladly pass them on," Marcel says with a look at Chelsea, who nods appreciatively.

Unlike Justin, Marcel has the right qualities to lead a team. He commands respect without fear, keeps calm even in a crisis. But suspicion nags at me today. Was his suggestion to move on from the topic of the photos just tact, or is he hiding something? Was Honor's idea to secure the perimeter outside quick thinking, or an attempt to keep the focus on outsiders?

***

"Friday is my favorite day of the week," Summer exclaims, hopping on a barstool, stretching.

"Sounds like you need a drink," Blake says. He's behind the counter, mixing a cocktail. His bar is my favorite place to come to relax after a long week. A few other Bennetts should filter in too at some point. Friday is the unofficial family day. Blake's at the bar anyway, and whoever has time stops by.

"Or five," my sister counters.

Blake shakes his head. "Cutoff is at three."

Summer leans over the bar, poking him in the ribs. "Oi, I wasn't asking for permission."

I laugh. "He's just doing his brotherly duty."

She sits back on her chair, waggling her finger from Blake to me. "I'm twenty-seven."

Leaning closer to her, I put an arm around her shoulders. "Yeah, but see, we're always going to be three years older than you, so you'll always be our little sister. That's how it works. No escaping it."

Summer sighs dramatically. "Brothers! Can't live with them, can't live without them."

"So, what happened this week to make you need five drinks?" I inquire, wondering if she's having any troubles at the gallery.

"Oh, nothing bad happened. I'm just feeling feisty."

She attacks her drink as soon as Blake shoves it in front of her. Sebastian and Logan arrive shortly afterward, making their way to the counter through the crowd.

"Just the five of us tonight," Sebastian says. "Max and Christopher are still in a meeting, and they're going straight to their homes afterward. Pippa has gone shopping with Julie."

Logan points at the draft. "I'll have a beer, please."

"In a second. Let's move the party to the table I reserved. Easier to talk," Blake says, motioning with his head to the right. "My bartenders will take care of the bar."

Taking our drinks, we head to the table. Since it's in a corner, it's marginally quieter than the rest of the venue.

"So, who's got any news?" Sebastian asks after we sit.

I consider bringing up the issue with the photos, then dismiss the idea. No reason to involve my siblings in my mess, least of all a mess involving the media. When it comes to the media, I have their backs, not the other way around.

I listen to each of my brothers in turn, but something about Summer's expression tips me off that she's hiding something. No one is more terrible than my baby sister at keeping secrets.

Blake seems to be thinking along the same lines because he points at our sister, saying, "Summer, you're bursting to say something."

"This isn't my news to tell, but I guess she'll tell you soon enough anyway."

Sebastian frowns. "She? Who are you talking about?"

Summer grins. "Alice is coming back."

"You mean *moving* back?" Logan asks.

She nods decisively. Alice moved with her husband, Nate, to London because he was directing a famous British TV show there. Alice co-owns three restaurants with Blake and has been handling the marketing and strategic planning from a distance, flying in every two to three weeks.

"Are you sure?" Blake asks.

"She and Nate talked about it, and he wants to be back here too. He found a directing job he's happy with here. They both want to be closer to the family. They're planning to move back after New Year's."

Fantastic news. Finally, all the Bennetts will be in the same city again. Some were in and out over the years. I never had wanderlust. I traveled a lot, but never had the impulse to move anywhere else. I love this city and being close to my family.

We toast to Alice's return, and afterward I take out my phone, intending to call her. A Facebook notification distracts me, from Caroline and Martin's opening party tomorrow. Frowning, I open the app.

I read the top announcement on the event page.

Don't forget, the opening party is tomorrow instead of next week! An all-day event! Coffee and cake will be on the house.

I check the details of the event. A lot of people canceled after the date was changed. Moving the event on such short-notice wasn't the best business move, but Caroline tends to decide with her heart most of the time. It's one of the things I've always loved about her, but that won't pay the bills.

I glance up at my siblings, weighing the pros and the cons of spilling the beans on this. No way will I be able to pass this up as just a casual favor I'm doing for a friend. They know me well enough. Telling them will mean having everyone in my business. But a dozen Bennetts would make that coffee shop/bookstore appear fuller, which would attract customers more than an empty shop. First rule of business: fake it until you make it.

"What are you all doing tomorrow?" I ask.

"Taking Ava and the kids out on the ocean in the morning. Logan and his troop are coming too," Sebastian says.

Summer shrugs. "I'm going shopping."

"Clara and I are doing a baby photo shoot in the morning. Why?" Blake asks.

Here goes nothing. "Anyone up for an afternoon snack at a coffee shop that's opening tomorrow? Well, technically it's a bookstore—"

"Yes!" Summer claps her hands. "I—this is Martin's bookstore, right?"

Sebastian holds up a hand. "Wait... Martin Dunne? Caroline's dad?"

"Yes," I clarify.

"Are you and Caroline—" Logan begins, but Blake interrupts.

"Look at Summer. She looks like you just told her sales season is here early. All signs point to yes."

"They renovated the bookstore, integrated a coffee shop, and are reopening tomorrow. It'd be nice if they had a full house, or at least some company," I say.

Blake lifts a brow. "Nine years and now you finally make a move? What happened?"

"Yeah, Daniel. What happened?" Summer props her chin on her palms, grinning. "The shoe delivery escalated quickly, huh?"

"What?" Sebastian and Logan ask at the same time.

"Never mind. Can you drop by?"

Sebastian nods. "I'll check with Ava, but I'm sure we can. As long as we can bring the kids."

"You can. They have a kids' corner with games and stuff."

"We'll drop by too," Logan says. "And I'll spread the word to the rest of the family."

Blake chimes in next. "Baby naps in the afternoon, and Clara tries to nap at the same time, but I'll be there."

"Excellent, now that everyone answered your question…" Summer drums her fingers on her cheeks. "Details, please. No dirty ones, just the romantic stuff."

I groan, glance around at my brothers. "Help!"

"Men don't talk about this stuff, Summer," Logan says patiently.

"I'm just saying, if I don't get some facts, I'm going to construct my own scenarios. My mind is a dangerous place."

"Jesus, Summer, slow down!"

She bats her eyelashes at me, but I just shake my head, fully aware of how bad my track record is when it comes to giving in to Summer.

Logan smirks. "He doesn't need questioning, Summer. He needs advice."

"I don't," I say automatically, but resign

myself to listening anyway. Just as Summer will always be the family baby, and we're going to be protective of her, Logan will never step out of his older brother role either. He loves giving advice. I rarely admit it out loud, because I'd never hear the end of it, but it's usually damn good advice.

"You're the only unmarried brother here," Blake points out with a grin. "If I were you, I'd be taking notes."

Chapter Fourteen

Caroline

On Saturday morning, I'm at the bookstore at six o'clock, helping Dad and his one employee, Ailish. She's in charge of the coffee shop's kitchen, and she's a whiz, having worked at Starbucks for a year.

"Caroline! I've got all this," she assures me. "Go finish the inventory."

"I'm going, I'm going."

At ten o'clock, we have our first customers— well, *customers* is perhaps not the right word. They are old friends of Mom and Dad's who are here for company and gossip, not to buy anything, but at this point, I'm grateful for anyone coming in. An empty store is unnerving.

Later today, I'm hoping some of my school contacts will show up. I spent the entire week spamming the parents at pickup, talking their ear off about the bookstore. The problem is that most of them live near the school, and the bookstore is literally at the other end of the city, but here's to hoping some will show up anyway.

Niall arrives shortly before lunch, and I greet him with a hug so tight, I almost suffocate him. God, how I missed my brother.

"Wow, you did a great job," he says once I step back. He sweeps his eyes around the room as Dad gives him a shorter and manlier hug. "Great job. Looks even better than in the pictures."

"Want a coffee?" Dad asks.

"Sure. I'll drink it while you give me the tour." Niall runs his hand through his hair, ruffling it a bit. Though my brother's hair is as dark as mine, he has reddish hues because Niall favors our mother more than I do.

While Dad makes him coffee, Niall pulls me a little farther away. "How are the finances on this? Was the money enough?"

Niall and I both chimed in with an equal amount of money for the renovation.

"Yeah, it was just about right."

"If he needs anything else, tell me. Dad doesn't always tell me if he's in trouble."

Shifting my weight from one leg to the other, I say, "Could you call him more often? He misses you."

Niall nods, swallowing. "I'll try to. I don't mean not to call him, but my schedule is insane. But I'll try more. I promise."

"Okay."

As Dad hands him the coffee cup, we begin the tour, which ends all too quickly because Niall has to return to the conference.

I head to the back once he's gone, going through the boxes containing the latest batches of books we ordered. I might finish in the back today, and tomorrow morning I'll arrange the new merchandise on the shelves inside.

Several hours later, I'm neck-deep in lists and boxes, double-checking everything on my computer.

"Caroline, how are you doing in there?" Dad asks, poking in his head.

"My eyes will cross soon," I answer honestly.

"Take a break, come out to the front."

"Okay." Stretching, I follow him out. "Whoa."

The back door opens into the coffee shop area, and there are more people than I expected milling around, some sitting at the tables, others inspecting the shelves lining the walls. It takes me a few seconds to realize quite a few are named Bennett. *How the...?* I specifically didn't invite them because I didn't want them to feel obligated to come. But man, am I happy to see them. Daniel must have told them.

"Wait a second. I'll go shut down my computer and join everyone for an extended break."

Heading back inside the storage room, I barely pick up my computer when I hear Daniel's voice through the open door, sounding as if he's heading this way. "Martin, you did a great job."

"Thank you, son."

"Where's Caroline?"

I jump at the sound of my name.

"In the back."

Since I have my back to the door, I don't see but rather *feel* him stepping inside the room. The air seems to charge instantly, the fine hairs on the back of my neck stand on end. A current of awareness shakes my entire body as I spin around to face him.

"Hey! I was just finishing up here. Thanks for stopping by and bringing your family."

"My pleasure." He smiles, leaning in to kiss my cheek. Heat zings through me. *Oh boy!* My entire body reacts to his presence. The memory of our night together is still too fresh in my mind, the feeling of his touch imprinted on my body. Not to mention our midnight confessions; I'm not likely to forget those anytime soon. Between the memory of his touch, and his words, he's pulling me in like a magnet.

"When's Niall arriving?" he asks, instantly cutting the tension.

"He was here before lunch, but he couldn't stay longer. We'll see him tomorrow for breakfast again."

"Come out in the front, you two," Dad calls from outside the room. "Ailish just finished a fresh batch of cookies."

I head out of the room, Daniel hot on my heels.

To my delight, the Bennetts even brought some of the little ones. Pippa's twins, Mia and Elena, Sebastian's kids, Will and Audrey, and Logan's son, Silas, are all here, and I've got just the thing to entertain them.

I do an inventory of the adults too. Ava and Sebastian, Logan and Nadine, and Pippa and Eric are on one side of the room. On the other side of the room are Blake and Summer. Their parents, Jenna and Richard Bennett, are a few feet away.

I greet everyone fast, tripping over my own feet as I inquire what they want to drink.

After they're all set up, I turn my attention to the kids.

"I've got some coloring books for you," I tell the younger ones, who seem to be hanging on to my every word. "Come on."

"Kids are well entertained," I announce to no one in particular when I join the Bennetts again. God, it's so good to have all of them here. I'm beyond thankful. That's when I realize I haven't thanked them. I've been so beside myself, I forgot to say it out loud.

"Thank you all for being here."

Blake puts a hand on my shoulder. "Anytime. Besides, we were all waiting for the day Daniel would come to his senses. Made a bet with Summer on when that would happen. I lost by about three years."

This isn't awkward at all....

"What... no, we're friends," I mumble, feeling my face go up in flames. At least Daniel is not within earshot, but at the other end of the room, inspecting the middle shelf of the Travel section. Thank heavens for small mercies.

Summer steps closer. "Yeah, you're blushing worse than ever. Friends, my ass."

Oh boy.

If I thought my face was hot before, now I'm expecting steam to come out of my ears. Between Blake and Summer, I'm toast. I'm out of practice fending off curious Bennetts, but I need to polish those skills until they shine like silver.

Summer grins, giving me a knowing look. Pippa, on the other hand, appears to be surprisingly *uninterested* in the topic, perusing the Lifestyle shelves. This is so unlike her that I instantly realize she's up to something.

Ah, man. If any of the Bennett women get wind of what happened in the marina hotel, I'm a dead woman. And I'm not being dramatic. It's the honest-to-God truth.

I don't have time to dwell on this alarming idea because Ailish brings everyone cookies, and we dig in. My eyes sweep around the room, and I'm pleasantly surprised to see a set of parents from my school.

I immediately rush over to thank them, giving them a tour of the bookstore.

"Nice place," the woman comments. "Pity it's so far away from where we live."

"It was nice of you to come by. Can I tempt you with another coffee on the house?"

They smile. "Won't say no to free coffee."

Once I've set them up with steamy cups, I retreat in the corner between the Lifestyle and Healthy Living sections, surveying the room. If at least ten percent become paying customers... I start to mentally crunch numbers and am so absorbed in it, I startle when Daniel walks up to me.

"Everything okay?" he asks.

"I hope the cafe addition will work out," I confide. I feel like I'm going to implode if I don't voice my concerns soon, and Daniel has a sharp business acumen. "We already lost out on the back-to-school sales because we weren't open. I hope we'll make some decent sales centered around Halloween items."

"You'll do great. Just make sure you have a system in place so people can't stay in the coffee shop for hours just paying for one drink."

"What do you mean?" I ask in alarm. "I don't want to be one of those places hazing customers to order something every half hour."

Daniel strokes his chin, seeming to carefully weigh his words. "It's not hazing—it's not letting people take advantage of you."

Protest rises in my throat. "But this is a place for people to come and relax."

"Yeah, but relaxation shouldn't come for free. You have twenty seats here. If you get ten people who come in regularly to buy two drinks and spend six hours, half of your shop is gone. No way can you turn a profit."

My protest turns to panic. "But won't people hate the nagging?"

"Those worth your time won't, trust me. The customers who value what you have to offer won't mind paying for it. You don't need the rest."

"That's something Mom would say," I admit.

"Your mother was a great businesswoman."

I slash the air with my finger. "I know what you mean... how Dad and I are lousy at business."

"You're not lousy, but you're not exactly profit-oriented either. You care about people's experience, which is great. That's how it should be, customer first and everything. But you still need to fend off the moochers. Don't be afraid to demand what you're worth."

I nod. In theory, he makes sense, but I'm not sure how this translates into practice.

"Can I run a few ideas by you?" I ask.

"Sure. You can run *anything* you want by me."

I laugh, warmth spreading through me. "There are plenty other Bennetts I can ask for advice."

"Yet you chose me. I have plenty of evidence that I'm your favorite Bennett."

"Like what?" I challenge. God, it's so easy to get caught in his banter, his playfulness.

He trails his fingers up and down my spine as if it's only natural for him to touch me. I'm playing right into his illusion, though, by not moving away.

"One word: marina."

"I was on Benadryl," I counter, but the argument is weak. Daniel wastes no time pointing it out.

"Not when we made love."

No, no, no! He can't go there again. He won't. This shameless, merciless man. I had a few hours of weakness, and he's using them against me like a weapon.

"Daniel... can we just forget about that?"

He pushes a strand of hair behind my ear, tilting his head to one side. "I don't want to. And you don't either. You were kissing me like you never wanted me to stop."

"Of course I didn't want you to stop. You were giving me fabulous orgasms." I wink, keeping my tone light and casual. Maybe if I can keep this focused on the sexy part, I'll convince him that it was nothing more than a blip in my control.

"I remember every detail, every sound you made, and fuck, I want to hear them again. Just remembering how you felt in my arms, how you opened up for me, brings me to my knees, Caroline. Tell me you don't think about that night."

"I do. Every night... and day. Basically all the time."

Daniel cups the right side of my face in his hand, resting his thumb at the corner of my mouth. A memory flashes in my mind, when he touched me the exact same way. The memory is so vivid that I instantly ache on the inside.

Right, I need him to stop touching me. Otherwise, I'll never whip my thoughts into a coherent sentence. I swear the spell this man has on me should be illegal. Everything about him is just too intense. Too overwhelming. I step back, sizing him up.

"But we'll get over it eventually."

I do a mental fist pump because my voice sounded strong, and firm. It wavered a teeny tiny little bit, but I'm sure only I could tell that. Except Daniel is *smiling*.

"Why are you smiling?" I ask.

"Never mind, go on. I'm listening."

"Well, I—for the love of God, *stop smiling*. It makes me feel like you know something I don't."

"Maybe I do."

I poke his ribs with my finger. "You're infuriating."

"Can't disagree there."

"Wanna share what's got you smiling so much?"

"You're so fucking adorable trying to convince yourself, it makes me want to kiss you right now."

I take a giant step back, hold up a finger menacingly. "Don't you dare!"

Daniel smiles even more broadly. "I'd believe you don't want it if you weren't licking your lips."

Whoops.

I open my mouth, close it again, unsure what to say. Do I want to feel the warmth of his body again, hear him murmur sweet nothings in my ear? Of course I do. But the failure of our last rendezvous still looms over me. Besides, I'm not a catch. I'm not whole anymore, and there's no way around that. No point deluding myself... or him.

"Let's go back to your family," I say.

For a split second, he looks like he's going to

call me out on the change of subject, then nods. I take that as a sign he's going to drop this. Grudgingly, but will drop it.

But as the day goes on, I'm not so sure anymore. Every time we're next to each other, he touches me relentlessly: my hand, the small of my back, my shoulder.

The Bennetts spend the entire afternoon with us, right up until we close at six o'clock. Afterward, Dad insists on inviting the family for dinner. I use all my cunning to convince him to order pizza, instead of him "whipping up something quickly." It would be a poor repayment to the Bennetts to torture them with one of my father's cooking attempts.

"It's good to have the house full again," he comments excitedly. "Feels like when you kids were little."

Guilt gnaws at me. Dad is lonely, and I have no clue how to remedy it. I can always stop by for dinner more often, but I suspect he needs company of his own age.

The dining room in Dad's house is far too small for so many people, so we decide to host dinner in the newly built coffee shop. We push the small tables together to form a long one, arranging the chairs around.

"Here you go," Daniel says, and I nearly jump out of my skin. My arms are full of pizza cartons. They were taking up too much space, so I decided to take them to the trash cans outside before eating.

Daniel is carrying the boxes I couldn't fit in my arms. I was so lost in thought, I didn't realize he was right next to me, opening the back door.

"By the way, I had an idea," I say as we step outside. "I could talk to nearby schools and preschools, tell them about our kids' corner, invite them to do readings."

"Excellent idea."

"It just occurred to me because I told the parents at my school, but obviously no one's gonna cross the city from Richmond to Excelsior for this. But this is a family-friendly neighborhood. Lots of kids. Parents can bring them and enjoy a coffee while the kids play in their corner."

Daniel nods thoughtfully as we walk the distance to the trashcans. "That's the best way to position yourself—as a meeting point for your local community."

"I'll think about more activities we can organize here. How do you come up with ideas for new stuff to add in your business?"

"In the beginning, it was just in-house brainstorming, but now we have a large pool of customers, and we listen to their feedback and ideas. Right now I'm looking into opening a gym because so many of our clients want to do indoor activities."

Unfortunately the trash cans are almost full, so stuffing the cartons inside takes a bit of creativity and a lot of brute force. I hold the lid open while Daniel does his best to press the boxes over the existing mountain of garbage. After a few ridiculous

LAYLA HAGEN

tries, we finally manage to close the lid on the cans again.

"What kind of activities?" I ask on our way back.

"Everything from climbing to team sports."

"How about kickboxing?"

He shakes his head. "Not on the list, but Krav Maga is. Why?"

"A friend of mine is a trainer. He does kickboxing, maybe Summer told you."

"Yeah, she did mention you roped her into this."

"He offers Krav Maga too. If you need a trainer, I could introduce you to him. He owns a small studio, but he moonlights at other studios too. I'm training with him tomorrow. Would you like to come?"

"What time? I'm working in the morning."

"Seven o'clock in the evening."

"Works for me. I'll bring my equipment too, test it out myself. I don't like offering activities I've never done."

Swallowing, I tell myself this is a good thing. This would be beneficial for both Daniel and Theo.

But seeing Daniel training is a dangerous temptation. All those muscles flexing, all that sweat, the manly sounds. Not to mention seeing him in his training clothes.

"I'll text you the address," I tell him. "My friend will be over the moon at the chance of having a new customer."

That's right. I'm inviting him along because it would benefit both of their businesses, *not* because I want a front row seat at seeing Daniel flex his muscles.

Liar, liar, pants on fire.

Chapter Fifteen

Caroline

"So, Dad told me the Bennett clan was here yesterday," Niall says the next morning during breakfast. We're at the coffee shop, enjoying some of Ailish's delicious cake and cookie leftovers. The tips of my ears feel hot as I sip from my coffee. I wish Dad would hurry from the back. He went to get a book for Niall, and I have a feeling my brother is about to grill me on the topic of Daniel.

"Yeah, it was great of them to show up here."

"They're a friendly bunch. Daniel was here too?" He winks at me, biting into a cookie.

"Of course. Dad invited him. I told you he helped with the business plan."

He sighs. "Caroline, be careful."

"I am. Don't go into overprotective brother mode."

"It's in my genes. Can't help it. I remember how sad you were when you came to Dublin. I just don't want you to be so sad again. Ever."

"It was a long time ago. I'm a big girl now."

"I know you are. If you need anyone to give him the talk, hit me up. Dad's too soft."

I poke his forearm. "Niall! I absolutely don't

need that."

He smiles sheepishly. "I'll keep an eye out."

Once Dad returns, there is no more talk of Daniel, and we focus on the bookstore and Niall's conference instead.

After he leaves, we start arranging the new merchandise on the shelves. We haven't even gotten around to unpacking it. I'm in charge of the fiction books since that's the most straightforward part. All I have to do is arrange them alphabetically according to their genre. Dad's in charge of everything else, from nonfiction books to miscellaneous items such as puzzles and society games.

By ten o'clock, I'm done with the Action & Adventure, Classics, and Crime fiction sections. Panic shoots through me when I realize I'm not even a third through. I open the first box labeled "Mysteries." Just as I'm about to unload the first batch, my phone vibrates on the shelf in front of me. A message pops up with a photo of a pelican attached.

Daniel: Morning sighting from Fort Funston. Are pelicans part of those birds that only have one mate for life?

Caroline: Nope, they are faithful to their partner just for the mating season.

Setting the phone back on the shelf, I focus on the box, but I only manage to unload one stack of books when my phone chirps again, this time with an incoming call from Daniel.

"You're bad for my work ethic," I inform him

the second I pick up. "I'm working on unloading the same box of books since you texted."

"Bad influence, am I?"

"Absolutely. So, I assume you want to ask which birds have just one mate?" Holding the phone between my ear and my shoulder, I start arranging the stack I unloaded on the shelf.

"Nah, I just wanted to hear your voice."

Oh, wow.

"Daniel, what are we doing here?"

"Finding our way back to each other?"

I clasp the book tighter, an unnerving energy coursing through me.

"Tell me you haven't thought about it. Tell me and I'll hang up."

My breath catches. "Don't hang up."

He laughs softly, and I feel his relief in my bones.

"So, why are you at Fort Funston, anyway?"

"Hang gliding. With Freeda and some of her friends."

I nearly drop the book. "The famous singer? She's your client?"

"Yeah."

"Wow, you sure keep famous company."

"Dan, come on. I want to be up in the air." The voice calling him in his background belongs unmistakably to Freeda.

"Did she just call you Dan?"

He chuckles. "Asked her not to, but she does whatever she wants. Jealous?"

Yes, yes I am. But I'm not ready to own up to that. How on earth did I back myself into a corner ten seconds into this conversation?

"No, just surprised. I know you don't like it when people call you Dan."

"I love it when you do it. Can't wait to see you later. It's been a long day. Woke up at five."

"Wow, what a hell of a day. Are you sure you're up for Krav Maga? We can always do it another day."

"I just got you to admit you've thought about us getting back together. I *will* see you tonight."

"I didn't admit anything," I say with a smile. "I just didn't deny it. And you're underestimating Theo if you think we'll talk much tonight. One round with him and all I'm up for is a glass of cabernet on my couch. You should try it too."

"It'll be my pleasure. It's a date."

Laughter bubbles out of me, unrestrained and unapologetic. "I can't believe you just tricked me into inviting you to my place."

"I'll make it worth your while, Caroline. That's a promise."

***

Daniel

I arrive at the address Caroline texted me at seven o'clock in the evening. Christ, she's a sight, with her training clothes molding to her every curve.

Her hair is up in a messy bun, and I have a vision of pulling the elastic band out of her hair, sinking my hands in it while she wraps her legs around me.

I stand there, watching, not making any sound as she starts exercising, performing a string of kickboxing moves. Her body moves swiftly, the swell of her curves, the tightening of her muscles a goddamn vision. She's beautiful, strong, fierce.

The sharp determination on her expression shows me a new side of her. Every protective instinct springs to life, making me want to keep her out of harm's way. It's great that she can defend herself, but I don't want her to *have* to.

A side door opens and a man comes in, heading straight to Caroline. I can't hear their exchange from here, but soon enough he starts touching her waist, her arms. Sliding behind her and correcting her pose. I swear, if he touches her ass….

"Daniel, I didn't see you there," Caroline exclaims, snapping me out of my murderous thoughts.

"Just arrived."

I head to them, shake hands with the instructor.

"This is Theo," Caroline explains.

"Figured as much."

"Caroline tells me you want to offer Krav Maga at your gym," Theo says.

"It's something I'm looking into, yes. And I want to test it out first."

He nods, assessing me and the bag over my

shoulder where I stuffed my gear, and points me to the changing rooms. For the next half hour, he shows me the basics while Caroline performs postworkout stretches, then busies herself around the studio, cleaning up, rearranging the mattresses on the floor.

"Focus!"

I barely block Theo's next punch. If I keep looking at Caroline, I'll leave here with a black eye.

"Why are self-defense classes all the rage?" I ask once we're done.

"It's a great way of getting the tension out of your system," Theo explains. "My guess is this is what most are looking for."

"Makes sense. I figured it wasn't just everyone fearing they'll be attacked all of a sudden."

"So, what's the verdict? Is this interesting enough for your clients?"

"It's definitely one of the more popular wishes. It'll take a few months to set everything up, but let's keep in touch. How flexible are you?"

Theo shrugs. "I can work around anything."

Caroline walks up to us, beaming. "You boys worked everything out?"

"We'll keep in touch," Theo says. "And I saw you clean up. You weren't supposed to do that."

"I had time on my hands, and you're tired. You've been here since eight o'clock. You should go upstairs, relax for the night. I can close up here, throw the key in your mailbox."

The way she talks to him sets me on edge: too

personal, too much warmth. I have no right, but I'm jealous as fuck.

"Don't say that twice or I'll take you up on it," Theo replies.

"Well, this is me saying it twice. Come on, go rest."

Theo doesn't wait for her to say it a third time. He marches out, leaving Caroline and me alone.

The second he's gone, she beams widely, clasping her hands together. "He's great, right?"

"You dated him?"

She blinks, her smile fading. "It's not your concern, but I don't want this costing Theo business. He's just a friend. A dear friend. Nothing more."

"When I came in, he had his hands all over you, and just now you seemed so… familiar."

She presses her lips together. Another telltale sign I should back off, but I can't. Plus, she looks gorgeous all worked up, the skin on her cheeks flushing.

"As I said, not your concern."

I step closer to her, smelling her feminine scent—vanilla and something edgy. "In case you can't tell, it concerns me whether I want it to or not."

She presses her hands at the sides of her neck, studying me. "You're not a jackass usually. Something's up with you. "

How the hell does she read me so well?

"Sorry, I'm… you're right. Remember the leaked photos issue?"

"Yes."

"I have some suspicions about who on my team is behind it, and we have other events tonight."

I wanted to press pause on the celebrity events until I figure this out, but it was too short notice for the four events tonight. I split the dream team into four, so Honor, Marcel, Justin, and Colbert are each attending one. I don't expect any leaks tonight unless Colbert is really thick, or greedy. Any leaks would immediately identify the culprit, but it's worth a try. If greed wins, it will save me more detective work. After I explain all this to Caroline, she huffs out a breath.

"Sounds like you still have a lot of pent-up tension. How about another round of training before we head out to my place for that glass of wine?"

"You do Krav Maga too?"

"Not well, but you're a beginner."

"Yeah, but I've got about thirty pounds on you."

"Theo's bigger than me too, and I can hold my own."

Yes, but Theo's an instructor. He probably knows how to go easy when needed. How hard can it be to go easy, though?

Turns out it's hard as hell. At least, if one wants to do it without the other party catching on.

"Come on, Daniel. Don't go easy on me just because I'm a woman."

She aims and I block her, which is all I've been doing for the past few minutes. I'm in defensive mode because I suspect that, if I throw a punch, she might hurt herself by blocking it.

"I'm not going easy because you're a woman. Just because you weigh about half what I do."

"Come on." She continues her attack, and between her heavy pants and beads of sweat trickling down her chest, I'm falling under her spell. Throw her Lycra-clad thighs into the mix, and my brain conjures up images of her legs wrapped around me, and—

Wham.

Punch straight to my gut. Literally. I buckle, the air knocked out of my lungs. I lose my balance and bump into her, knocking us both off our feet. As we fall, she makes a desperate swing with her arms, which earns me an elbow to the side of my head. *Fucking hell, it hurts.* I barrel on top of her, no grace, no softening the impact. Then we dissolve into laughter.

"That's what you get for handling me like a damsel. Next time, go hard on me so we don't go down like fools."

Caroline wipes her tears of laughter. I could move off her to the side, but this is too good. Feeling her breasts pressed against my chest, one of her legs cradled between mine, the other bent by my side.

Sustaining myself on one forearm, I run my hand up and down the thigh that's by my side.

"Oh, love, you know I like going hard on you, but not on the fighting mat. Remember last time? I went so hard on you, your thighs gave out."

Her hips give a slight jerk under me. Her

thigh quivers under my hand. *Oh yeah, she remembers.* Turning her head to the side, she breaks eye contact, giving me a full view of her sweaty neck, the vein pulsing in it. I barely hold back from leaning in, licking her, tasting her.

"Caroline, I want the right to be jealous back. The right to call you mine."

She snaps her head right back to me, her eyes wide, a mix of emotions staring back at me. She moves a hand to my cheek and I lean into her touch, wanting more. Needing more. Tension gathers between my shoulders as I wait for her answer.

"Dan…," she whispers softly. Some of the tension bleeds away because she's not saying no. She's not saying yes either, but that twinkle in her eyes? It's hope. Uncertainty too, but I'll focus on the hope. "How's your head? I hit you with my elbow."

The second she mentions it, I become aware of the thumping in the right side of my head. Pushing myself off her at last and sitting on the mattress, I touch the sore spot.

"Just needs some ice and it'll be fine. You hurt?"

She shakes her head, and we push ourselves up to our feet. "My ankle's a bit sore, so walking back will be fun."

"Walking?"

"My building's just three blocks away, so I walked."

"I'm here with my car."

"Thank God. Let's go, then. We did enough

damage tonight, and I have a bottle of wine in the fridge for us. Do you want to shower here? Or you can use the one in my apartment. If you want."

"Oh, I want to."

A strand of hair dislodges from her bun, dangling over her eye and cheek. Leaning in, I blow it away.

She laughs nervously. "Okay, let's go. I'll take care of your head, ice it for you."

"I'll return the favor and ice your ankle."

Placing my hand on the small of her back, I guide her out of the room, keeping my hand there while she locks up and leaves the key in Theo's mailbox.

Tonight, I'm going for broke.

Chapter Sixteen

Caroline

It's official. I'm a magnet for accidents when I'm around Daniel. Though this time, he was the one causing the mishap. At least there's that. He wasn't only being chivalrous, that wasn't why he didn't block the last punch. He was also distracted, his eyes glued to *certain* parts of my anatomy. Men.

Still, I can't be a hypocrite. I was distracted myself. Couldn't help it with all the contours of those fine muscles showing through his shirt. The stubble on his cheeks wasn't any less distracting. I kept wondering how it would feel against my skin. Well, haven't I gotten myself on a slippery slope?

"I've got ice in the freezer," I tell him as soon as we enter the kitchen. "Could you get it while I pour us wine?"

"Sure."

Five minutes later, we walk together to the living room. I'm carrying the glasses of wine, Daniel the ice and a kitchen towel. When we both slump on the couch, he wraps the ice cubes in the towel

"It's more comfortable for the skin if it's wrapped in something."

"You're a pro at icing, I see."

He smiles ruefully. "We get the odd ankle sprain or minor injury on our tours. Learned a few tricks."

Sitting at the opposite edge of the couch, he takes my foot into his lap. It feels like heaven when he sets the towel-wrapped ice on my ankle.

"You've got a nice place here."

"Thanks. I love it. Can walk to work too, which is a plus. Why aren't you putting ice on your head too?"

"I'm fine. It doesn't hurt."

I raise a brow because I remember smacking him pretty hard.

He shakes his head, concentrating on my ankle. *Men.* For the love of God! Do they think their balls will fall off or something if they admit to feeling pain?

I scoot closer until my ass is almost brushing his thigh, touch the spot where I hit him. "This is swollen."

He winces, and I immediately take the ice from his hands and my ankle, then bring it to his head.

"I can hold this," he argues.

"I'll do it. Let me take care of you." In a softer tone, I add, "That's the right I want back."

His gaze snaps up to me, searching my face in surprise, as if he can't believe what I'm saying. If I'm honest, I can't believe I'm saying it either.

"Better?"

Eyes shut, he nods, relaxing even more, a

smile playing on his lips. Suddenly, I become aware of how close we are. My foot is still on his lap, my knee and leg propped against his stomach. My other leg is bent at an odd angle between my crotch and his thigh. Awkwardly I try to shimmy around, stand up a bit, but I only manage to make it more awkward. Great, now I look like I'm straddling him. Just as I'm about to pull away, he cuffs my ankle in one hand, blinking his eyes open.

"Stay. It feels good. It feels right. Let's talk about us."

I forgot how direct he can be. I wish he'd have eased us into the conversation, give me time to warm up a little. On second thought, if I warm up more, I might end up on fire.

"Caroline, I want a second chance for us. I've wanted this for years."

"Oh, Dan, I want it too." My hands are shaking slightly, and I grip the ice tighter in one, resting the other on my belly. "I just don't know if we should."

"I never said it would be easy." He pulls me flush against him, knocking the breath out of my lungs. Our bodies aligned, I can feel the ridge of his obliques pushing against my pelvis. Or maybe that's just my dirty imagination at work. Jesus, I'm going down fast. Daniel seems to be thinking along the same lines.

"Look at you. You're blushing and panting."

I don't miss a beat. "Because you're warm and I nearly lost my balance when you pulled me."

Daniel chuckles, but then the sound fades as he brings my hand to his lips, kissing the back of it, then my palm.

"Caroline, I miss you. Us. This is our chance."

A soft thumping starts in my ears, intensifying by the second. My right knee weakens, then the left. Worst case of swooning if I ever had one.

"I miss all of it too," I murmur. He straightens up, looking directly at me. His eyes are full of their usual smolder (which adds a healthy dose of desire to the swooning), but also tenderness and emotion (which doesn't help the swooning in the slightest).

This man, I swear! He thinks he can just waltz back in my life, take over like this. I wish I could say his delicious promise or the heat in his eyes doesn't sway me, but why pretend? I'm hanging on to his every word, but I need to make something clear.

"We can't just pick up where we left," I say weakly.

"That's not my intention. We'll start fresh, and it'll be so much better than last time."

"Was pretty good last time too, except for the end."

His smile fades. "I can't promise you forever before we even begin. It would be an empty promise. What I *can* promise is that I know how special this thing between us is. I didn't last time, even though I suspected as soon as I lost it. But now I don't suspect. I'm sure."

"I know too," I assure him, heart pounding

hard. Being here in his arms feels so good, so warm and perfect.

He seals his lips to mine in a hot, hard kiss. Over my shirt and sports bra, he feathers his fingers around my nipples, turning them into tight, sensitive buds without even touching them. His gaze is molten, his breath rushed. Palming one ass cheek, he brings me flush against him. He's hard already. Oh, I want this man. I want him so badly, my entire body is shaking. Daniel is all I see. All I want.

Sliding out of his grasp, I hook my fingers in the waistband of his pants, pushing them down, then do the same with his boxers.

Moving from the couch down on my knees, I stop when my mouth is right in front of his erection. I don't attack him right away but tease him first, dragging my thumb from the base up to his tip, following the blue vein. The way he exhales between his teeth gives me immense satisfaction. I follow the same vein with my tongue, using just the tip. Daniel jerks his hips, fisting my hair with one hand. When I flatten my tongue against his heated skin, licking right up to the crease under his crown, circling it once, he tightens his grip. I love that I can make him lose control so fast.

Greedy for more, I finally lower my mouth onto him slowly, watching his expression out of the corner of my eyes. With every inch I take in, his nostrils flare. He tastes so good. A little sweaty, a lot masculine.

"You're so good, baby. So, so good!"

While I slide up and down, I bring one hand to the base, clasping what I can't take in, squeezing tightly and then releasing, moving my hand lower, cupping the soft skin on his balls, sliding a finger down his perineum. He releases a loud, guttural groan that makes his entire chest quiver. To know I can undo this mountain of a man with one touch....

"Oh, fuck. Caroline, you're—"

He never finishes that sentence. Instead, he pulls back, and before I realize what's going on, he slides off the couch and onto the floor, shifting me until we're both lying on the carpet, on our sides, my mouth in licking distance of his erection, his head level with my crotch.

When he slides one palm between my thighs, I open up, desire soaking my thong. Any second now, he'll lower my Lycra pants and thong—

Rrrrrrrip. He rips the pants right at my crotch. My thong is a thing of the past too.

"Daniel!"

"I'll buy you new ones. I'll buy you ten. But I want to lick you right now."

I'm sweaty, I want to protest, but the words die on my lips. We look at each other between our tangled limbs, and this moment holds so much tension and anticipation, I feel myself dripping.

"I want to eat you out while you suck me off."

His dirty words fuel me like nothing else. I take him in my mouth as deep as I can.

"I will make you come hard, Caroline. So hard

your head will spin."

He buries his mouth between my legs, and I nearly bite him when I feel the lash of his tongue against my clit. He's relentless and wild, and I match him every step of the way. Then he slips two fingers inside me, and I moan loudly around his erection. This is an assault on my senses. I've never opened myself intimately this way.

Feeling his fingers inside me, his lips pulling my clit between them while I'm tasting him, is too much. I take him in deeper, feeling him at the back of my throat. Wetness rushes between my thighs when he starts moving his hips lightly, taking control, making love to my mouth at the same time his tongue draws maddening circles around my clit. Around and around he goes, coaxing pleasure from deep inside me until I explode.

I pinch my eyes shut as we both climax, rocking and thrashing, lost in each other.

Daniel shifts around until his eyes are level with mine.

"You okay?" He smiles, pushing a few loose strands out of my face.

"Thoroughly satisfied," I inform him, returning the smile.

"Oh, baby, but I'm not done with you tonight."

Even though my body is limp with pleasure, tingles of anticipation run through me. Daniel helps me to my feet, his hand warm and steady. Something feathers along my inner thigh. One look down and I want to hide my face in my hands. My ripped panties dangle down my inner thigh, the ripped pants leaving nothing to the imagination.

"I need to shower," I say.

"That's where we're going. And stop overthinking. I loved your taste."

"I was sweaty!"

"I loved it."

I lead him to my bathroom, still self-conscious of the thong hanging between my legs, the ripped pants. On the plus side, my ankle doesn't hurt anymore. We drop our clothes on the tiled floor and step into my shower stall, which isn't big enough for two. But my tub isn't either, and we'd splash water everywhere if we used it because I don't have a protective curtain. I only use it for lazy baths.

"Cozy in here," Daniel remarks as the spray of water rains down on us. We do a quick job of cleaning ourselves, but feeling him right behind me is distracting. Ah, what this man does to me. It should be illegal for him to be able to turn me on without even touching me.

"Tonight I will take my time with you," he whispers.

"You did that in the marina hotel too."

"No. At the hotel I loved you like it would be the last time. This, tonight, is a new beginning."

I shudder in his arms, his words traveling over me like a caress. He pushes my hair to one side, kissing the the back of my neck, turning my knees weak.

"Put your hands up and hold them there."

I immediately do as instructed.

He trails kisses down my spine, skimming his fingers at my sides, over the roundness of my breasts, my rib cage, and waist. By the time he is touching the curve of my hips, wetness rushes through my center. I press my hands on the tiles, clenching my teeth. He's turning every inch of my skin into an erogenous zone.

He kisses down one of my thighs, until he reaches the back of my knee, moving his tongue in small circles. I suck in a breath, dearly hoping my legs won't give out again.

When I feel his fingers trailing up my inner thighs, I open my legs wide without any shame or restraint, bracing myself.

He lets out a rush of hot air right against my ass cheek as he slides one finger inside me.

"Fuck, I love your sweet ass." He gives it a little smack, then palms a cheek. I press my palms against the wall, but they skid a little on the wet tiles. My glutes are tensing. "Your pussy." He slides in a second finger, and I lick my lips. "Every part of you."

He parts his fingers, forming a small V inside of me.

"Daniel, oh…. Oh!" I pinch my eyes shut, biting my lower lip. He's stretching me, getting me ready for him. I can't stand it for one second longer. I need to kiss him, now that he's mine again. Mine to touch, to love, to hold.

As if reading my mind, he pulls his fingers out

and commands, "Turn around."

I do just that. He's on his knees on the shower floor, his head level with my navel. As I begin to lower my hands, itching to touch him, he shakes his head.

"Put your hands above your head, against the tiles."

I pout. "But I want to touch you. Your hair is so damn sexy. Practically begs me to run my fingers through it, tug at it a little."

Daniel merely watches me, gaze hard and unflinching, as if saying, "I'm in charge here." Wordlessly, I raise my hands. Daniel lifts one of my legs, hooking it on his shoulder, then pushes me against the cold tiles, kissing me intimately. Feeling the cold tiles against my back and his hot mouth on me at the same time is too much. And he's just getting started. He licks and nips at my clit, using his fingers to spread open my folds, then push them together, driving me crazy. My vision clouds as pleasure ripples through me, starting from where his lips work on me and spreading everywhere. I'm so close to the edge. So close.

"I want you to keep your hands there when you come. Do you understand?"

Keep… what? Is he insane? I need to touch him *right now*. More than that, I need to ground myself, to hold on to something. I can't protest, though. Words fail me as an orgasm blindsides me, sweeping through me with such force that the leg I'm standing on gives away. I feel Daniel's hands, strong and steady, holding me up, keeping me from crumbling right onto his face.

This isn't just an orgasm. It's a Danielgasm—the full-body kind of pleasure that leaves your skin zinging, your teeth clattering, and your mind spinning.

He leaves me no time to breathe or recover. I barely make out his shape as he rises to his feet, palms each ass cheek in one hand, and lifts me off my feet. Instinctively, I wrap my legs around his middle, crossing them on the upper part of his ass.

He lowers me onto his erection in a single, desperate thrust that knocks the breath out of my lungs. The size of him, *fuck*. I blink once, twice, trying to clear my vision. And Christ, what a vision this is. Now I can touch him. I run my hands over his shoulders, descending, feeling the way the muscles corded around his arms tense with the effort of lifting me up and down onto him.

My breasts jolt on every thrust, my nipples grazing his chest as he leans in to pepper my face with kisses in between. Feeling him pull away and then fill me again so utterly and completely is so intense I can barely keep myself from falling apart. I want to wait for him to reach the cusp too, so we'll fall off the edge together.

"You're beautiful. So perfect. So sexy," he murmurs. "Oh, God, Caroline. You feel—"

A crease appears on his brow, and the set of his mouth is tight. I come the moment I feel him widen inside of me. I cry out, my inner muscles clenching so tight, I'm afraid I'll pass out.

"Oh, fuck. That's it. Come around my cock, beautiful."

Tremors ripple through my body, my orgasm intensifying as I feel him finish too, feel his pleasure spread throughout me. He tucks me into him as we rock against each other.

Once we come back from cloud nine, he lowers me until my feet are on the shower floor. My thighs are quivering slightly. I'll be sore tomorrow.

"Are you okay?" he inquires, his eyes searching me. I swallow twice, clearing my throat and finally finding my voice.

"Perfect."

Chapter Seventeen

Daniel

She looks like a vision, walking around the kitchen in the early morning light wearing my shirt, unbuttoned. It reaches just below her ass, hiding it. I'll remedy that in a second, but for now, I just want to enjoy this moment. She's here. She's mine.

"Holy crap," she exclaims, whirling around. "I didn't see you. You scared me. Sorry, I didn't mean to wake you."

Closing the distance to her, I wrap an arm around her waist, pulling her flush against me. Her thighs rub against my jeans, her breasts against my bare chest. Her nipples feel like pebbles. I lean into her, intending to kiss her, but she turns her head, offering me her cheek. "Caroline?"

"I have morning breath. I came straight to the kitchen to start the coffee machine. Didn't shower or brush. You can't kiss me like this."

"You're fucking adorable." I kiss down her neck, push the shirt off one shoulder, nip at her skin.

"Dan… what are you doing?"

"Kissing every other inch of you, since your mouth is off-limits."

She groans. "We can't. Don't tempt me. I

have to leave for work in half an hour."

"Call in sick."

"I can't take the day off. You can't either. You run a company, remember? Go run one of 'the most successful companies in the Bay.'"

The words sound familiar. "You've read that article?"

"Yeah, I did. Kept the magazine too. Though I found the article lacking. They didn't mention your IQ, or that you were the best in our class, and at Stanford too. Blake told me. You're the smartest person I've met."

Knowing she thinks so highly of me is the best damn way to start the day.

"So go run your company. Go boss people around."

"Today I just want to boss you around." I give her ass a little smack, and she shudders against me.

With a shrug, she says, sounding a little nervous, "So you want to come by tonight? If you don't have plans. Only if you want to. You don't have to."

"I want to." I tilt her chin up and cup her face with one hand. "I want to see you every night. Don't be so nervous around me."

"I'm sorry. I guess... I'm just afraid of doing or saying the wrong thing." A deep breath, another shy shrug. "I can't believe you're here, in my kitchen. That this is happening. That we're happening." She drops her head in her hands. "I'll stop talking now.

I'm embarrassing both of us."

I run my nose from the crook of her neck to her ear, bite at her earlobe. "We are happening. And I want to spend as much time with you as possible. Caroline, whatever you need, just say it, ask for it. I'll do the same. We'll work everything out."

"One awkward moment at a time." She moans softly while I kiss back down her neck. "Dan, I need to go shower."

Instead of letting go, I wrap my arms around her.

"In a minute. I just want to hold you for a minute."

She melts against me as I bury my nose in her hair, enjoying our togetherness as much as I do.

***

Caroline

Ten minutes later, I step out of my bedroom fully dressed. Hurrying back to the kitchen, I discover Daniel's made sandwiches. I want to memorize everything about this moment: Daniel walking around my kitchen, wearing nothing but jeans. I've left his shirt here, but he didn't put it on.

"Looked through your fridge, hope you don't mind."

"Not at all. I'm starving. Thanks for making these."

"Dig in."

I don't wait to be told twice; I grab a sandwich and bite into it. It's delicious. When I down the last mouthful, two strong arms come around my waist, washboard abs pressing against my back.

"For a second there, I thought you'd run off again when I woke up and you weren't there."

I laugh. "Where would I run off to? It's my apartment."

"So, you would have left if we weren't at your place?"

"No, no. Sorry, that came out wrong. Not what I meant."

He flips me around, placing his palms at the edge of the counter at my sides, caging me in. "You sure?"

I nod, startled at the doubt in his eyes. "One hundred percent." Standing on my toes, I place a quick kiss on his lips. Correction—I meant it to be quick. But Daniel takes charge the next second, slinging a hand at the back of my head, the other on my waist. He kisses me so hard and so hot that all my lady parts quiver. When he palms one of my breasts over the fabric of my blouse, I moan against his mouth. I smile ear to ear as we pull apart.

"What's with that smile?" he asks.

"Nothing," I answer quickly. He levels me with his gaze. I stubbornly hold it, and hold it… and lose. I never could win a staring contest against Daniel. In my defense, though, the man holds so much heat in his gaze, I'm sure he could melt glaciers. If ice doesn't stand a chance against him, what chance does poor little me have?

"Fine, if you must know, I was thinking that it was almost worth it to get you all worked up for that kiss. There, I said it."

I jut my chin forward in a challenge. Daniel's lips curl in a smile, but his gaze loses none of the intensity. The disheveled morning hair and five o'clock shadow on his cheeks look good on him.

"Want to put your shirt on?" I ask.

"Why? Am I too distracting?"

"Damn right, you are. When do you have to be at work?"

"In two hours."

"So how come you woke up so early?"

"The bed was cold. I needed you."

Wham! Shot straight to the heart. *I needed you.* Three simple words are all I need to feel like I'm walking on a cloud. Leaning forward, he traces the contour of my lips with the tip of his tongue. I feel every lick straight between my thighs.

Gathering my wits, I push him away. "Stop tempting me or I won't leave the house in time."

"Sounds right up my alley."

"Daniel Bennett, don't think you can bribe me with sexy times."

"How about pancakes?"

I do a double take. "Come again?"

"I can make us pancakes."

"You don't cook."

Daniel winks. "You're behind the times, Caroline. I added some skills on my résumé over the years."

Mouth open, I stare at him. "Hang on, I need more info. How did this happen? You survived on takeout during college, and Blake's fried eggs."

"Yeah, but takeout is not healthy. Loaded with fats and sugar. Had my nieces and nephews sleep over a few times. Learned to cook the basics for them. Pancakes are everyone's favorites."

Ahem, I'm not melting. Not melting. Not *melting.* Yeah, who am I kidding? I melted already sometime between "nieces" and "favorite." Daniel, the family man. That's something I look forward to seeing. I mean, he's always been close to his parents, overprotective of his siblings, but just the thought of Daniel cooking for his nieces and nephews does *things* to me.

"You look like you just had an entire conversation in your mind just now."

I smile sheepishly. "Yeah, we women tend to do that."

"Walk me through it. Can't read minds. Not part of my skillset, I'm afraid."

"No, I don't think I will."

He levels me with his stare. Stepping closer to me, he brushes a strand of hair out of my face. *Uh-oh.* I can practically feel my determination slipping away. Pulling myself straighter, I try to work in every ounce of severity I can muster in my tone.

"Now, don't go all intense and domineering on me."

"I have other ways of persuading you."

I try to look away from his eyes, or mouth. Unfortunately, the rest of him is just as distracting, if not more so. Why isn't he wearing his shirt? All those hard muscles and defined lines on display is messing with my concentration—not to mention my hormones. In an attempt to put some distance between us, I step back, hitting the counter. Placing my hand on his chest, I shove him gently away. He takes the hint and steps back, but unfortunately, his taut skin simply feels too good under my fingers for me to let go, so instead of retracting my hand, I trace the dents and planes of his abs, the V-shaped lines.

He groans. Oops, lost my head there for a second, and my hands somehow ended up at the rim of his jeans. Flashing him what I hope is a convincing doe-eyed look, I grin, letting my roaming hands drop.

He grips my hips, aligning our bodies. I burn for him at every contact point. Skimming his hands up, up, up the sides of my rib cage, he stops when his thumbs are level with my breasts. Dragging them inward, he flicks my nipples over the fabric until they're tight peaks, until my entire body is wound up.

Then he kisses my forehead and steps aside, biting into his own sandwich, leaving me so hot and bothered I'm entertaining thoughts of an incognito trip to the shower. I need a cold spray.

"By the way, my parents are hosting a Halloween party at their house next week," he says.

"Halloween? That's new."

"Eh, Halloween is a much bigger draw for the

kids than Thanksgiving, I'm telling you. And all the adults are having a kick out of wearing costumes too."

"Wait, what? I can't picture—all adults, really?"

He nods, chuckling. "Yeah. It's a sight, all right. I'd never thought Sebastian or Logan would be up for it, but you wouldn't believe what parents will do for their kids."

"What are you going as?"

"Pirate."

Pressing my lips together, I fight hard not to laugh, but I lose the battle, giggling.

"What's so funny?"

"You, channeling your inner five-year-old. A *pirate*."

Daniel points a finger at me. "Stop laughing or I'll tickle you."

The laughter dies in my throat at once. I take tickling threats seriously. I am the most ticklish person there is, which Daniel knows well.

"You'll need one too."

"One what?" I ask, confused.

"A costume."

Is he saying what I think he's saying?

"You want me to come to the party?"

He winks at me. "Yeah. Come with me. Unless you have plans already?"

My pulse ratchets up, pounding in my ears. *Wow. Wow.*

Daniel doesn't easily invite others to family

events. Summer and Pippa told me that he hasn't brought a date to any event in years. Even after we got together in college, it took a while for him to ask me to join him at family gatherings as *his* date.

"No plans. I'd love to join."

Truth be told, Halloween doesn't even make my top ten list when it comes to favorite holidays, but no way in hell would I miss a chance to spend time with Daniel and the family.

"Great. I know a costume shop. I'll take you there this week." Mercifully, he shrugs into his shirt, buttoning it up. "Let's go or you'll be late."

I stand on my toes, kiss his cheek. Then, feeling feisty, I steal his sandwich.

"Mmm, this is delicious. So, what other skills have you acquired over the years? Just so I'm not gobsmacked again."

Daniel cuffs my wrist in one hand, stealing back the last mouthful of the sandwich. After swallowing it, he leans into me until his breath is on my lips. "I'll allow you the pleasure of *discovering* them. We have ten years' worth of catching up to do."

Chapter Eighteen

Caroline

On Thursday afternoon, I'm speeding through downtown San Francisco like a Tasmanian devil, but I'm going to be late anyway. I'm meeting Daniel to buy a Halloween costume, and I'm supposed to be in front of the store in five minutes.

"I'm so sorry I'm late," I exclaim twenty minutes later. Parking was a nightmare, and I'm not entirely sure I parked legally.

"No problem."

"So, what is this place?" I inspect the display, trying not to let the grizzly masks spook me. The horror aspect of Halloween is why I'm not so crazy about it. But Daniel looks excited, so I don't voice the thought.

"Christopher's wife, Victoria, discovered it some time ago. The entire family buys their costumes from here."

"Why?"

"The owner keeps track of who bought what so no one ends up having the same costume as anyone else."

"Wow, you guys take your costumes seriously."

Daniel grins. "Dead serious. Come on in."

The inside of the shop is much larger than I would have guessed. It's narrow but goes all the way to the back of the building. All around us are costumes, masks, and supplies: everything from fake blood to fake cobwebs—at least I hope they're fake—to vampire teeth that look surprisingly real. Daniel takes my hand, as if it's the most natural thing in the world, and I sigh, relishing the warmth and security his touch gives me.

"Hey, you two!" a woman greets from behind the counter. She has shortly cropped hair streaked with neon pink, and the ends are spiked with gel. She's even more vibrant than the store.

"Hi, Violet," Daniel says. "We're here because Caroline needs a costume."

She nods, tilting her head to one side. "You don't strike me as the type who goes for the spooky costumes."

"You're absolutely right."

"I have just what you need," she says confidently. "I'll take some outfits in the changing room for you. If you see anything you like, grab it and bring it in the changing room too."

I turn to Daniel, sizing him up.

"What?" he inquires.

"Trying to decide what would go with a pirate." I continue to eat him up with my gaze, intending to fully take advantage of the guise of studying him and visualizing him in his pirate costume. He's wearing a simple polo shirt today.

He'd have no problem making a living modeling. The man is a piece of art. I don't think I'll ever tire of drinking him in.

"Found anything you like?" Violet asks, reappearing beside us. "I took Cinderella and Snow White costumes in the back for you."

I perk up at this. "Oh, so princess costumes are allowed?"

"Sure," she answers.

"I'll go right to the changing room and try them on."

Violet leads me to the back with Daniel hot on my heels. Even though he's at least a foot behind us, I can *feel* his presence, his gaze on me.

"Oh, this is beautiful," I exclaim upon seeing the costume. "Let's see how I look in it."

Violet nods. "You'll need help zipping it up in the back—"

"I'll do it," Daniel says. His voice is deceptively neutral, but I don't miss the spark in his eyes. A shiver runs through me, and I inadvertently lick my lips, focusing on the costume.

"Right, you're banned from going anywhere near the changing room, Daniel," Violet exclaims. "No sex in my shop. I mean it. You're looking at her like you want to eat her up."

My cheeks heat up at her bluntness. Daniel merely laughs, shaking his head.

"I'm with Violet," I tell him. "You're not even allowed in the changing room. Sit there, and I'll come out and model for you. I can zip myself up no problem. Plenty of practice."

Daniel's eyes darken, and my resolve nearly melts under his scrutiny, but I stick to my guns. See, it's not just that I like adhering to common standards of public decency, but I love riling Daniel up, teasing him. So I pull the curtain of the changing room *almost* all the way closed. Enough for him to be able to see the peep show, enough to leave him wanting more. *Oh hello, inner vixen, where have you been?*

Once the costume's on, I decide this is the one. I don't need to try on anything else. This just fits right. Smiling, I step outside. Daniel sits in the armchair opposite the changing room, sizing me up with hunger. *Whoops*, I forgot all about the peep show I gave him, and I'm wearing the red lingerie he bought me for my birthday.

"You look fantastic in it," Violet says, startling as the bell rings at the front and the door opens. "Have to go greet the customer. If you need me, shout."

"I love it, and I'm buying it," I announce.

He rises from the armchair, closing the distance to me, taking my hand and twirling me around once. "I'm buying it for you."

"No, you won't. I can afford it."

"It's not a question of affording it. You wouldn't need to buy it if it wasn't required for the party." His voice is low but determined.

"But—"

"If I want to buy my girlfriend a Halloween costume, I damn well will."

Warmth travels through me at his words, and I instinctively squeeze his hand. He frowns slightly, looking down at our interlinked hands, then back up.

"What?"

"You called me your girlfriend." I have no idea why I'm whispering.

He searches my expression. "That a problem?"

I shake my head, hoping he didn't get the wrong idea. "No, I just… it sounds so lovely. I almost can't believe it."

Drawing circles with his thumb on the back of my hand, he says, "Let me get something straight and out of the way. I would have never pursued you again if I didn't want this to be serious."

His expression clouds and I gulp, wanting to kick myself. How on earth did I manage to get him so worried? Biting the inside of my cheek, I debate if I should bring up the fact that I can't have kids now. Isn't it too soon? We've only been back together for a week.

Yeah, but this has been ten years in the making, a tiny voice says at the back of my mind. Telling men about this hasn't worked out so well for me in the past. The first relationship I had after the surgery crumbled the second I told him. He accused me of waiting too long—two months—to tell him, of being dishonest. Learning from my mistakes, I brought the issue up on the third date with the next guy. It didn't go down well.

We haven't even fucked, and you're thinking about

marriage and kids? I'm out of here.

I took a long break from dating afterward. A break which lasted until Daniel. And here's the thing: I know he wouldn't react like the jackasses before, but this still won't be an easy conversation. And one week into a relationship really is too early to bring this up.

"I want this to be serious too, Dan," I say softly. "That's always my problem, isn't it? I jump all in until I'm over my head."

"Then jump all in, love. I'm here to catch you." His lips curl up in a smile, his voice soft but determined. His beautiful words travel straight to my heart.

"I'm swooning a bit," I inform him. Both his hands are cupping my face. He touches the tip of my nose with his.

"If it's just a bit, I'm not doing my job right." He drags the tip of his nose up and down my temple. "Must up my game."

He seals his mouth over mine in a kiss that's as hot as it is sweet. His hands travel down my neck, arms, and then he fits his fingers over my rib cage, his thumbs flicking once over my nipples. Once is all it takes to turn them into hard nubs and to drench my panties. Damn this man and the spell he has on me. Yeah, I'm going to stick to blaming *him* for the way *my* body acts. Sounds like a great plan.

Trailing his mouth to my ear, he says on a growl, "Give me your panties."

"Why?"

"You teased me enough in the changing room. Now I'm going to tease you. Take off your panties and give them to me."

"When will you give them back?" I ask shyly. Thank heavens Violet is busy with the customer in the front.

"When I want to."

Cue lady parts tingling. Every single one of them.

The twinkle in his eyes intensifies. "Still haven't given me your panties."

I back away into the changing room, then slip my hands under the long skirt of the dress and pull the thong down, all under Daniel's intense scrutiny. He holds out his hand, his fingers touching mine as he takes the thong. The contact zings through me.

"Change back, and then we'll grab something to eat."

***

Daniel

"Why aren't you answering?" Caroline asks as I mute my cell phone for the fifth time since we ordered.

"Because this guy always keeps me on the phone for at least half an hour. He'll get the drift eventually."

We're at a Spanish restaurant, and I intend to

enjoy every single moment with her. The rest can wait.

"Is it work stuff?" She sits up straighter, a strand of hair falling across her cheek. She brushes it away, training her eyes on me. "How did the events you told me about on Sunday go?"

"Like I expected. No photos leaked, so I'm gonna need to bait whoever's doing it."

"Meaning?"

"I'm going to talk to them, tell them a story. Some cock and bull about how the company is in trouble."

She takes a sip of her chardonnay and frowns. "I don't get it. Why would tabloids be interested in something like this?"

"They won't, but local business magazines are going to be very interested, and they pay well for exclusive stories. I'm friends with most of them, so I expect them to call me to confirm the story before they publish it."

"And then you'd know who leaked it. Wow, my head is spinning. Can I help in any way?"

"You're sweet, but I'd never drag you into something like this. I'll sort it out."

"It sucks you have to do this at all."

"Yeah. I'm going to cancel all celebrity events until I figure out who's behind this."

"Wow."

"I can't risk any more leaks. It's not just about my reputation, but these people trust me with their privacy. If I can't guarantee it, I'm not going to lie about it."

"But won't this affect your income?"

"Yeah, it will." On a grin, I add, "Why? Will you ditch me if I'm poor?"

She returns my grin. "Aw, I'll gladly take you in if you need a place to live. Purely out of the goodness of my heart. Not because you make tasty sandwiches. Or because you give me great orgasms."

"Very magnanimous of you." Before I get the chance to say anything more, the host of a famous talk show approaches us. She's a regular client of mine. I stand, shaking her hand, focusing on her white hair because every time I look at her long, red, clawlike nails I almost gag.

"Daniel, how great to see you. We need to catch up soon."

"Anytime, Cecilia. May I introduce you to my girlfriend, Caroline?"

Cecilia flashes her a bright smile. "You look familiar. Where have I seen you before? An actress, perhaps?"

Caroline shakes her head good-naturedly. "No chance. I'm a teacher. But maybe I have a famous doppelgänger."

Cecilia's smile falters at the word "teacher." She recovers quickly, but I don't miss the moment, and neither does Caroline. Her shoulders slump a little, even as she juts her chin forward with pride.

"Well, how *nice*."

That just pisses me off. "It is, isn't it? One of the noblest professions, if you ask me. Educating young minds."

"Yes, yes, of course. Well, it was nice seeing you. I wish you both a pleasant evening." Cecilia smiles indulgently before walking away.

"I'm sorry," I tell Caroline as we both sit again.

"Nothing I haven't seen before." She waves her hand, as if saying, "forget it," but I know better. This is a sore spot for her. I liked her mother, but she often—and openly—criticized Caroline's choice of profession, insisting she should have chosen something that paid better. "What you told her was very sweet. But you don't have to defend me."

"Yeah, I do, and I will. I meant what I said to her."

I place my hand palm up on the table, and she gives me hers.

"I don't fit in with your people—"

"Those are not my people. They're just customers. You are my people. You and my family. I don't care about anyone else."

Caroline sighs, shaking her head. "Okay, I have to ask. Did you take any courses on how to make a woman swoon or something? I don't remember you being quite *so* charming last time around."

I give her my most cheeky smile. "Can't give away all my secrets now, can I?" Logan might have given me a piece of advice or ten, and I don't need to take notes to remember it all.

"Well, whatever you did, it's working."

The waiter appears at our table, interrupting the moment as he sets the plates in front of us. I don't realize how hungry I am until I take the first mouthful of paella.

Caroline eats with small bites, a contemplative expression on her face.

"What's on your mind?"

"Our lives seem to belong in different spheres. Don't get me wrong, I love my life, but it's simple compared to yours. After me, you dated models and stars, and I couldn't help wondering that maybe you broke things off because I wasn't enough."

"No! I was young and stupid, and it had nothing to do with you. I wasn't ready for that kind of commitment. I admit I also wanted to experiment more. But the thought of being in it for the long haul scared me." I struggle for words, wanting to make this perfectly clear.

"Dan, it's okay. We were twenty-one. I get it. No one's ready for forever at that age."

"Except our parents."

She grins. "True."

"So, you kept a close eye on me, huh?"

Nodding, she lowers her eyes to the plate, pushing around the food with her fork. "Go ahead, laugh."

"I'm not laughing. I did the same."

"How? My life wasn't under public scrutiny like yours." She frowns, but then her expression blooms into a full smile as she puts two and two together. "Your sisters."

"Exactly. Alice stayed out of it, but Pippa and Summer were relentless. Every time they told me you were dating, I wanted to punch something. Then I felt guilty because I wanted you to be happy. But the thought of you being happy with someone else...."

Narrowing her eyes, she points her fork at me. "You've been sending me negative vibes all these years."

"I wouldn't call it that."

"Hmm, you're right. *Pining* is the word."

"You're enjoying this immensely, aren't you?"

"I've been pining for you this entire time. It's nice to know I wasn't the only one."

She presses her lips together, as if she fears she's said too much. She didn't use to have a filter with me or feel the need to be careful. But right now, she's peeking at me from behind her guard, not quite ready to lower it. I'm not there yet either, but I want to meet her halfway on this one.

"You weren't the only one. Not by a long shot."

She smiles that ridiculously beautiful smile, and fuck if I don't want to get her out of here, take her home, show her all the ways in which I missed her. But she needs to eat first.

"Why aren't you eating?"

She sighs, eying my plate. "Can I take a bite of your paella?"

"Sure."

She takes a spoonful from my plate, chewing

slowly, nodding in satisfaction. "Yours is tastier. I should've ordered the one with chicken too."

"Wanna trade?"

She tilts her head, considering this. "No. Stealing from your plate is more fun."

"That's my line."

"Stole it too."

I laugh, moving the plate out of her reach. "Whatcha gonna do now, Ms. Tease?"

Caroline looks between the plate and me as she taps her fingers on the table. I'm so busy anticipating her next move over the table that I pay no attention to her shenanigans under the table. Right until I feel her bare foot move suggestively up and down my calf. *Fuck me.*

"If I were you, I'd put the plate right back where it was," she says sweetly.

I push the plate even farther away, leaning slightly over the table. "If I were you, I'd stop being a naughty girl. You don't want to turn me on, or I'll forget we're in public. You're not wearing any panties, remember?"

Swallowing hard, she lowers her foot, red splotches appearing on her cheeks.

"I love seeing you blush."

"You don't say."

"Let's go to my house after dinner. Spend the night there." I've been sleeping at her apartment since Sunday, but I want her in my house, in my bed. I want her smell on my sheets, her hair on my pillow.

"You're awfully confident about getting me in

bed tonight," she teases.

Leaning back, I drum my fingers on the table. "Oh, I like my chances. Besides, you'll love my apartment. Lots of windows. It's in Nob Hill, with a direct view over Huntington Park."

"Can you see our faux Notre Dame?" she asks, referring to the Grace Cathedral, which is an exact replica of Notre Dame de Paris.

"Yep. I also have a Jacuzzi."

"Sold."

***

"Wow, your apartment is beautiful, Dan. And the view, my goodness."

She does a full turn, scanning the details of the living room. I don't have much in terms of furniture, just a large white couch, a coffee table, and a recliner in which Alice loves to sit when she visits, but I love my home simple. And I love having Caroline here, in the midst of it all. I can barely keep my hands off her, my self-control dangling from a thin thread. Stepping right behind her, I push her hair to one side, kissing the back of her neck.

"I want to taste you, Caroline. I want to make love to you in every room in this apartment."

"Then get me naked."

Her voice is low, full of lust. I love bringing out this side of her. I make quick work of removing her clothes, and when she's completely naked, I make a confession.

"You're the only woman I've brought here. Except for my family."

I need her to know that, unlike last time, now I understand exactly how special this is between us. Even the doorman was surprised when he saw us come in.

"Oh, Dan!" She peppers my chest with kisses, whispering against my skin. "You're not going to regret it. I'll make you happy." She kisses up my neck, moves to my ear. "You'll see. *So* happy."

One hand around her waist, I hoist her closer to me, tip her chin up with my other hand. The emotion in her eyes brings me to my knees.

I want to be worthy of this look my entire life. Gently I press my mouth against hers. She opens her lips, inviting me in, and I slip my tongue inside. Taking her in my arms, I carry her to my bedroom, laying her on the bed.

She keeps her hands at the side of her head, her hair splayed around the pillow. She looks so perfect in my bed. She belongs here, and I'll be damned if I ever let her leave it. Her round, full breasts beckon to me, her nipples peaking.

I drop my clothes near the bed, taking her panties out of my pocket, then lie next to her. Bracing myself on one forearm, I run my thumb in the valley between her breasts, around one nipple and then the other, until they're both hard.

"Put these on," I instruct, laying the thong on her belly.

"Now you want me to have panties on?"

"Yes. Put them on."

She raises a brow but does what I say, shimmying back in them, looking at me as if asking, "Now what?"

Her chest moves up and down with every breath, the rhythm intensifying as I trace the path of my fingers with my mouth, tasting all that sweetness of hers. I lower my mouth to her navel, then farther on her pubic bone, stopping just above her clit, pressing a chaste kiss there over the fabric.

Pulling back, I run my thumb right over her center, watching the fabric dampen with her arousal, her eyes widening. I blow a breath straight over the darkened patch, and she fists the bedsheet, exhaling sharply.

"Dan, what are you doing?"

"Driving you crazy."

I'm so hard, I can barely hold back, but I want to give her pleasure more than I need to chase my own. Gathering the fabric covering her pussy between my fingers, I rub the lace gently over her clit.

"Oh, oh—this is so good."

The lace is a little rough, so I follow every rub with a lash of my tongue, a succession of soft and coarse. She fists the sheets tighter and tighter, but I know it won't be enough soon. She'll need to touch herself.

When she finally lets go of the sheet, touching her breasts, playing with her own nipples, I nearly come from the sight. Caroline on her back, spread open on my bed, all wild and uninhibited. I love seeing her like this. I stop when she's close to climaxing, pulling her panties down, then lick along her crack.

"Dan. Ooooooh, oh, oh. Can you do that again, please?"

I lick again, and again, feeling her glutes contract in my hands, her cries becoming louder, her arousal dripping on her inner thighs.

When I can't stand not being inside her anymore, I straighten up, balancing on my knees between her open thighs. She lifts her legs, touching my arms with her feet before resting them on my shoulders. I cuff her ankles between my thumb and forefinger, moving her feet until her soles are planted on my chest.

"You'll have better leverage like this," I explain.

She swallows. "Are you sure it's okay for you?"

"Don't worry, baby. I'm strong. Give me your hands."

I reach out, and she meets me halfway. With her hands in mine, I slide inside her, just the tip, rubbing back and forth until she gasps my name.

"Dan, please. I want you inside me all the way."

"Not yet."

I move lower on my knees, changing the angle, but still only giving her the tip. She whimpers, lifting her hips, trying to slide herself onto me, but I pull back.

"Please."

"I love hearing you say please."

"Dan!"

"I'm not giving everything to you. Not yet."

My words send a rush of wetness through her, and her pussy clamps around me, coating me in her arousal. This is torture for me too, but nothing like it is for her. She writhes, thrashing her head around the pillow. But I need to get her soaked and ready, and she's so responsive it damn near kills me. She tries to smuggle her hands out of my grip, but I don't let her go.

"No."

"I need to touch myself."

"You're not allowed to. You'll only receive the pleasure I want to give you. And love? I'll give you so much pleasure, I'm not sure you'll be able to take it."

She exhales sharply, but stops trying to wriggle her hands free. Leverage and control are two reasons I want to hold her here. The third one is that I need the touch. I want to touch her as much as possible, to feel close to her.

When the quiver in her body intensifies, I change the angle again, sliding in deeper, inch by inch, stopping when I reach her G-spot. Her eyes open wide, looking at me wildly, her mouth forming an O.

"Oh, oh, Dan—"

I slide inside her, staying still when I'm all the

way in. When I pull back, then slide back in, her hands tense in mine. I grip them tighter, rubbing my thumbs along her knuckles.

"You're so beautiful."

I need it slow tonight, and I need to look her in the eyes the entire time I'm inside her. She doesn't urge me to go faster, doesn't push herself against me. And she doesn't look away from me. We've always been in sync, but tonight it's like we're reading each other's thoughts, anticipating the other's needs.

Her breasts move up and down on every thrust. Christ, she's a sight. Sweet, sexy, sinful. Nothing is more perfect than getting lost in this woman. I need to touch more of her, so I let go of one hand, holding the other firmly.

I run my palm over her hip, up her waist. Then I bend forward on my knees, changing the angle yet again, and she pinches her eyes shut tightly. I still.

"Open your eyes, Caroline."

"Just a second." Her voice is shaky, her breath uneven. Fuck, I love that I can do this to her. Knock the breath out of her, make her shake with pleasure. When she flutters her eyelids open, I thrust again, moving my free hand up to her breasts, pinching one nipple and then the other. Her inner muscles clench so tight around me that my eyes nearly roll in my head.

When she squeezes me tighter and tighter, I press my palm flat on her pubic bone, driving into her G-spot again.

"Dan!"

Her hips shudder, but I stop their upward swing by pressing my palm harder. She is falling apart beautifully.

"I can't—oh God, this. I can't…too much.…"

"Yes, you can. You'll take all the pleasure I'm giving you. All of it."

She grips the headboard with her free hand, holding on to me tightly with the other one.

"Do you trust me?" I ask.

"Yes."

"Say the words."

"I trust you, Dan. I trust you."

Between her words and her shaky thighs, I nearly explode. My balls tighten, a zing rushing straight to my tip. I drive into her faster, my palm pressing her down as I hit her G-spot again and again. When her back arches up, I rub my thumb over her clit, and she's done for. She goes right over the edge, taking me with her. She spasms around me so hard, she nearly pushes me out. Dropping on top of her, my body still convulsing, I stay inside her, cradling her to me, feeling closer to her than ever but wanting—needing—to be even closer.

"This was incredible," she murmurs on a sigh.

"Mmm, just foreplay. We're not nearly done for tonight."

Her inner muscles clench around me, making me smile. She's as greedy for me as I am for her.

"That Jacuzzi is waiting for us."

Chapter Nineteen

Daniel

"This just isn't for me," Honor says next Wednesday afternoon as we struggle to regain our breaths. We've been testing indoor climbing at a hall near the office, since it's at the top of the list of activities our customers requested. Chelsea's tested it here herself, recommended us to do the same. "What's the point of all this climbing if you don't at least have some gorgeous scenery to enjoy at the end, or some fresh air?"

"I agree. Borderline claustrophobic."

"And it stinks."

"Yeah. But the customer—"

"Is king." She stretches one arm, then the next, looking around at the patrons. "And this place is chock-full. Talked to the instructor earlier, said they're fully booked almost constantly. No denying it's popular."

"Let's have a drink at their juice bar before we leave."

"If the boss buys, I won't say no." We walk side by side, navigating through the climbers and the instructors still on the ground. "So, what's the plan for the gym? Are you already scouting locations?"

Perfect moment to throw her the bone, as casually as possible. "As soon as the bank clears us on more loans, I'll get on it."

"We're in trouble with the bank?"

"Liquidity issues. They're not happy with our cash ratio, but we're still negotiating."

She stiffens, casts her eyes to her hands. "Does anyone else on the team know?"

"I told Marcel and Justin. Colbert too. But don't discuss it with anyone else."

"No, of course not. Wow."

I try to read her body language. Arms folded over her chest, drumming her fingers over her bicep. I hired Honor one year after Justin, about the same time as Marcel. I pay her a generous salary, an even more generous bonus. She has no reason to be tempted by the press.

"I guess it was a little premature to brag about being one of the most successful companies in the Bay, huh?"

Her mention of that article rubs me the wrong way on too many levels, but I do my best to school my expression. We have a quick drink at the juice bar, and then we part ways. She's meeting a group of clients; I'm heading back to the office to sign some papers.

I'm halfway there when my phone rings, Pippa's name appearing on the screen.

"Hey, sister."

A chorus of very loud and very exuberant "Uncle Daniel, it's us" assaults my eardrums. Despite everything, I grin.

"Hi, Mia. Hi, Elena. What's up, girls?"

"Are you coming to the Halloween party?" Mia asks. Despite them being identical twins, their voices differ subtly.

"Yes, I am. I'll be the pirate."

"A pirate isn't scary," Elena says, clearly not impressed by my choice.

"Shhhh, don't be rude," Mia admonishes. "We need to ask him first, and he has to say yes."

"What do you need to ask me?"

"Mom said we're not allowed," Elena clarifies. These girls crack me up every time. They've learned how the world works already. Whenever their parents say no, they turn their charm onto their aunts and uncles. Blake and I are the suckers they can always count on for their shenanigans.

"We need a carriage," Mia goes on. I almost do a double take in the middle of the street. This escalated quickly. No wonder Pippa said no.

"A carriage? With h—horses?"

"Yes, two. And we also—"

A static sound follows, and a yelp.

"Sorry," Pippa says, sounding out of breath. "They hijacked my phone, and I had to chase around the house to find them. You didn't say yes, did you?"

"To a horse-drawn carriage? I was too stunned to answer."

Arriving in front of my office building, I step inside, nodding at the receptionist before heading toward my office.

Pippa chuckles. "They sure take Halloween seriously. By the way, I heard you're bringing Caroline."

"How exactly did you hear?" I ask once I'm inside my office.

"Called Caroline to invite her, thinking you two needed another nudge, and imagine my surprise when she told me you already invited her."

"Let me guess, you already know everything?"

"No, I'm going to need a girls' night out and some alcohol to lure out details. Of course, you could spare me the trouble and just tell me."

"Where would the fun be in that?" I pace up and down the room, taking immense delight in teasing my sister.

"True. Plus, men don't understand the meaning of details. But Daniel? Don't let a good thing go a second time, okay?"

"I don't plan to," I assure her.

"Good. We all work hard, and we're ambitious, but there's nothing like going home to people you love at the end of the day."

"Pippa, are you okay?" I ask in alarm. My sister does love her heart-to-heart talks, but she sounds off.

"Long day at the office. Half the things didn't go my way."

"Ah, I can sympathize."

"And now these two have started bombarding me with their carriage idea. Please promise me I won't find two horses and a carriage on Saturday at

Mom and Dad's house."

"I promise. That's a hard line, even for me."

"Well, it's good to know you have one. I'll keep my phone close. I bet they'll try cornering Blake next."

I laugh. "I'm sure they will."

"I need to go back to watching the little devils. Enjoy your evening, brother."

My mood is considerably better after I click off. Logan once said something similar, that no matter the shit-show going on at work, knowing he'd go home to Nadine and their son put everything into perspective. I grunted and nodded, not really getting it, but now I understand the sentiment.

As I finish signing the stack of papers on my desk, my phone chimes again.

Caroline: I heard back from the preschool closest to the bookstore! They scheduled their first reading next month. Woohoo! And I had an early dinner with Dad. Made him fried chicken. Thought I'd save him (and myself) from his cooking today. There's plenty left over. I can bring you some by if you want. I can make donuts too.

Instead of messaging back, I call her. I need to hear her voice.

She answers right away. "I knew mentioning donuts would earn me a phone call."

"You had me at fried chicken already. How come you're not trying to rope me into coming to your place?"

"Well, I might have bought a bath bomb I'm dying to try in your Jacuzzi."

The thought of Caroline naked in my arms while we're surrounded by bubbles is enough to sell me on anything.

"What smell?"

"Cherries."

I groan. "Don't they have any masculine scents?"

"You're such a man. This is their newest stuff."

"Here's a compromise. You'll try it out. I'll eat the chicken, the donuts, and then I'll have you for dessert. Out of the Jacuzzi."

"Can we sneak in a glass of wine on the terrace too in between?"

"Watch it, or I'll think you only want me for the terrace and Jacuzzi."

"Don't be silly. I want your mad shmexy skills too. I fully expect my mind to be blown tonight."

"I promise I'll up my game. I love exceeding your expectations."

Chapter Twenty

Caroline

On Halloween morning, I decide to kick off the day with an early run and manage to rope Daniel into joining me.

"Whoa, I didn't know your physical condition is this good," Daniel complains. We're both sweating and panting when we enter his apartment, but this was a fantastic run. I love the boost of energy after a thorough cardio training.

I finish stretching in his living room, but Daniel grabs his smartphone, leaning against the bar counter separating the living room from the kitchen area, slipping into what I like to call his "business mode." Despite it being Saturday, he'll be caught up in a meeting the entire day, and we'll meet directly at his parents' house this afternoon.

His expression turns grim the longer he looks at the screen.

"Nope, you're not allowed to frown this early in the morning. What can possibly have gone wrong already?"

He scowls. "Remember I said I'm putting all celebrity events on hold? Well, it's proving to be more difficult than I anticipated. Managed to either cancel or pass on to other companies, but Beatrix won't let me off the hook. She doesn't want someone else handling her bachelorette party. It's in two weekends, in LA."

Sitting on the floor, I pause in the act of stretching one calf, feeling suddenly cold. "Beatrix Mercier? Your *ex*?"

Ouch. Beatrix used to be one of the lead models in the Bennett Show, and she and Daniel had an on-again, off-again relationship for some time, at least if the tabloids are to be believed.

Daniel unhitches himself from the counter, joins me on the floor. "I wouldn't call her that."

I cock a brow. "What would you call her?"

"A friend. We had a one-night stand when we first met, but afterward, we were just friends."

"Really?"

He rubs little circles on the back of my right hand, kissing my shoulder. "Really. The rest of it was the media making things up."

"Probably because the two of you looked incredibly good together in pictures." Fiddling with my thumbs in my lap, I fight the jealousy bug with all my might, but there's no escaping it. Beatrix is the type of beauty that can't be achieved through healthy eating or exercising alone. She has a genetic predisposition to perfection, and she's engaged to one of the hottest A-list actors.

"So, how will you handle this?"

"Depends on you."

My stomach jolts. "What do you mean?"

"I can tell her to bugger off, which is going to cost me some future business. Or I can go forward with the whole thing, but I'd be handling it myself because I don't trust my team at this point."

"Don't cancel on my behalf," I say, still fiddling with thumbs. "I don't want to cost you your business."

Daniel cups the side of my face, tilting my head up until I'm looking at him. "We're building something here. I won't jeopardize what we have for a deal. If you aren't comfortable with this, say the word and I'll cancel."

Oh, this sweet man. My chest rises and falls quickly as I shift on the floor until I'm almost straddling him. "Don't cancel, Dan. Anyway, she's getting married, so I assume she's not going to spend her bachelorette party tempting you."

"Exactly. But Caroline? Even if she would, I wouldn't be tempted." He points with his finger between us. "This, here, is all I want. Us."

"See? No reason to cancel."

He laughs, pulling both of us to our feet, which is when I realize I'm a hot mess. My hair and my clothes cling to me, and there are rings of perspiration under my arms. Yikes. I need to hop in the shower right away. Daniel on the other hand isn't a hot mess, he's just hot. His clothes cling to him, highlighting the strength of his biceps, the defined lines of his abs. I can even make out the V-shaped lines under the fabric of his shirt. It's almost as if he's naked. The operative word being *almost*. Ah, what I wouldn't give for a peek at his sweaty skin. I drink him in as discreetly as possible.

"You're insatiable, aren't you?"

Whoops. I guess I wasn't that discreet after all. I could try to dispute the accusation, but why deny?

"Can't help it. Not when I know what's under your clothes. Makes me want to take them off, jump your bones. It's been a while."

"We made love before our run."

I laugh at how indignant he sounds, almost offended. His hands are in the air, his jaw slack.

"Yeah, but see, I was half asleep when you climbed over me," I explain, stifling yet another laugh because his expression becomes more incredulous by the second. "Now, I am in *no way* complaining about wake-up sex—best way to start a day if you ask me. But it can't count as a full lovemaking session if half my senses are still dormant."

Daniel bursts out laughing, and hot damn, the sound is contagious. Seconds later, I join him and laugh until my belly hurts. Then he pulls me flush against him, tipping my chin up and kissing me. He tastes a little salty from the sweat on his upper lip, but the sheer masculinity rolling off him—*holy hotness*. His irises are dilated with lust when he pulls back.

"Let's take a shower," I suggest.

"Sure, you go first." His eyes twinkle. The bastard. I'm hot for him, and this is how he treats me? Teasing me?

"It'd be more efficient if we showered at the same time. Water conservation and all that."

He focuses his gaze on one of my cheeks and then the other. I'm pretty sure I'm flushing tomato red. His face breaks into a grin.

"That's what we're calling it? Water conservation?"

Before I have a chance to reply, he scoops me up in his arms, carrying me to the bathroom. I can't help myself, and pepper his face and neck with kisses.

"I'm sweaty," he remarks.

"You're mine, sweaty or not, and I plan to take advantage of it every chance I get."

***

I dress at top speed after hopping out of the shower and run off to prepare some toast while Daniel shaves.

"You can leave some of your stuff here," Daniel's voice resounds from the bathroom. "So you don't have to carry that huge bag with you all the time."

"Thanks," I call out, smiling to myself. Warmth spreads through me as I smear the toast with a thick layer of butter, the way he likes it, then put ham and thinly sliced tomatoes over it. I also find olives in the fridge, slice two in half, and add them on top. Stepping back, I assess my work of art. This isn't just a sandwich, it's a *sandwich with love*.

"I'll empty a shelf for you. Or do you need two? For all your lady stuff?"

I freeze. Will he put two and two together when he realizes I don't have any *lady stuff*? Did he realize I haven't gotten my period since we began dating?

He joins me in the kitchen by the time I finish his sandwich, looking harassed.

"Fuck, I'm gonna be late. No time to eat now, I'll take the sandwich and coffee with me." He points to the dark blue cup filled to the brim with coffee. "You can go out whenever you're ready. The doorman will come and lock up."

"Okay."

"What's wrong?"

Damn, how can he tell? Then again, my entire body is tense, which might have tipped him off.

"Nothing," I say evasively, avoiding his gaze.

"Did you change your mind about Beatrix?"

"No, Dan, not at all."

"Was the business with the shelf too much? Too soon?"

I shake my head.

"Something has you out of sorts, I can tell. And you weren't ten minutes ago." His voice is harder now. He won't let it go. "You used to tell me everything."

He's right. I used to talk his ear off about everything. In fact, I often thought I was sharing more than he needed to know, but I wasn't able to stop myself.

Daniel was my opposite, keeping any problems to himself. Eventually, I realized it's a man thing, not wanting to show the weak spots. For me, it was a relief to talk everything out, to hear his opinion, his advice. But in retrospect, I realize that, at twenty-one, I didn't have any real problems. A bad grade or the failure to secure an internship was the worst back then. It was easy to be open when you had no ghosts, nothing to be ashamed of. Ten years later, with some fair baggage under my belt, opening up doesn't come as easy.

"You'll be late for your meeting," I murmur.

"Fuck the meeting. I don't care. I care about you. Tell me."

"I'll tell you tonight."

I turn around, intending to hand him the cup of coffee, when I feel his arms around me, his chest pressed against my back. "I want you to share with me what bothers you, so I fix what I can, commiserate about the rest. I want you to trust me again like you used to."

Oh, he says all the right things, and I feel so safe and warm in his arms that I'm tempted to persuade him to spend the entire day with me. But no matter what he says, I know this meeting is important. I won't let him show up late on my account. It isn't right.

So, I turn around, rise on the tip of my toes, and press my lips to his.

"I do trust you. We'll talk about this tonight, I promise. Now go."

Chapter Twenty-One

Caroline

Jenna and Richard Bennett's home has long been one of my favorite places to hang out. Spanning two stories with a red roof on top, you can always count on having a hell of a lot of fun within its walls, or outside on the enormous property. In spring and summer, it's a sea of green, between the grass and the tall oak trees lining the property. Now the crowns of the trees are a mix of gold and copper, with a tinge of green here and there, though the ground remains a vibrant green. Mercifully, it's been dry today, because the property can turn into quite a muddy affair after a heavy rain.

Jenna Bennett is shuffling around in the white gazebo on the right side of the house, and I head straight there.

She's wearing a fairy godmother costume, complimenting my Cinderella costume just right. The sight cracks me up.

"Jenna, your costume is *fabulous*." A delicious smell reaches me as I step inside the gazebo, and my mouth almost waters when I notice the giant outdoor pizza oven is on.

"Oooh, I didn't know pizza was on the

menu."

Jenna smiles. "Easiest way to feed so many people. And it's a hit with the kids. The first batch should be done in a few minutes. Just waiting to get that crunchy crust."

"I'll help you get them inside."

"Wonderful. I was about to call for reinforcements. By the way, your dad will stop by later too."

"Really? Wow."

"Talked to him a few days ago, wasn't sure I was going to convince him."

"Jenna, when was the last time you failed to convince someone?"

She gives me a wicked smile, which resembles Pippa's very much.

"He's been lonely since Mom passed away. I go to dinner once a week and help him at the bookstore on weekends, but...."

"It's hard to be alone after you've shared your entire adult life with someone. Must feel like half of you is missing. He's always welcome here. I can imagine he gets lonely on Christmas and such, whereas here it's a...."

"Full house," I finish for her.

"Sometimes I think madhouse is the better word, but I love every mad minute." There is a beat of silence, and then Jenna adds, "I'm so happy you and Daniel found your way back to each other again."

"We're having a lot of fun rediscovering each

other. We're taking it slow," I say quickly, hoping this will keep the conversation from spiraling into a heart-to-heart. When Daniel and I first went out together, it wasn't uncommon for Jenna and me to talk about our future as if it was a given. This time, I'm determined to live our love one day at a time.

"As you should," Jenna says. "Even though you have history, it's important to take the time to discover the people you are now, build a foundation. You never fall in love the same way twice, not even with the same person."

"That's excellent advice."

Jenna is a wise woman. I've always been close to her, almost as close as to my mother. In some instances, I even shared more with her than with my own mom, because I didn't want to worry Mom, and because Jenna isn't as judgmental.

When the timer of the oven buzzes, Jenna opens the door, pulling one pizza to her, inspecting it. Oh God, it smells delicious. I hope Jenna is happy with the level of crunchiness, or I might have to resort to underhanded tactics to convince her to let me have a slice right now.

"They're perfect," she announces, taking out the two pizzas and shoving in two more, setting the timer again. We each carry one inside. Predictably, they're gone within minutes, and everyone is still hungry.

Daniel arrives when the second batch is ready. He's drop-dead sexy. I mean, he generally has an air of rebellion about him, even when he wears a suit, but with the cotton shirt, sleeves rolled to his elbows, and belt with a large skull in the center, he's downright delicious. I'm about to shower him with compliments when a distraction arrives in the form of Will, Sebastian's son, and Elena, Pippa's daughter.

"Uncle Daniel, Will says there are no fairies, that I'm *stupid*."

Will nods and grins.

"Will, you're not allowed to call your cousin— or anyone else—stupid. It's rude," Daniel admonishes.

"But there are no fairies," Will says stubbornly, stomping his foot.

Elena's eyes widen. "Yes there are. Uncle Daniel told me so. Tell him, Uncle Daniel. Tell him."

I mask my laughter with a fake fit of coughing. Ah, my imagination will have a field day trying to visualize how that conversation went between him and Elena. Daniel looks at me for help, but I'm quite curious how he'll find his way out of this on his own. Both Elena and Will are looking at him expectantly. Elena folds her arms over her chest in a Pippa-like fashion. Will copies her stance a few seconds later.

Daniel lowers himself on his haunches, until he's at their level, and then he wraps his right arm around Elena, his left one around Will. Warmth flashes through me as I watch him. Goodness, there is so much tenderness and love in the way he holds and talks to them. I've never seen this side of him, and I'm surprised at how strongly it impacts me. No matter how much I tell myself, or Jenna, that we're taking it slow, I can't help imagining our future.

Belatedly, I realize I've been so lost in my thoughts that I missed Daniel's explanation, and it must have been a good one because both Will and Elena are smiling ear to ear, already moved on to the next topic.

"Uncle Daniel, can you bring me more fairy dust? Pleaaaaaaase." Elena's body language is spot-on. Wide, pleading eyes, hands joined in prayer, not to mention the way she says, "Uncle Daniel," with the sweetest inflection.

"Sure thing."

Elena smiles, taking Will's hand, their feud clearly forgotten as they walk to her twin.

"That went well," Daniel says with the air of someone who just avoided D-day. Damn it, I really wanted to hear him explain about the fairies. But I can't ask him again without giving away that I've been daydreaming.

Daniel touches my face, sliding his hand in my hair, and I realize my lack of teasing him probably made him suspicious. But he doesn't ask, doesn't press. Instead, we catch each other looking after Will and Elena, and I'm certain he knows exactly what I've been thinking about.

"Come on. Let's go bring some extra fairy dust. Mom said she's keeping all the supplies in the storage room upstairs."

"What exactly is fairy dust?" I ask as Daniel takes my hand, leading me upstairs.

"Glitter."

He opens the door of a small storage room, turning on the light. The tiny cubicle is chock-full of supplies.

"We're never going to find it," he says on a groan, surveying the mountain of random supplies.

I chuckle. "Daniel on the search for glitter that he's trying to pass off as fairy dust to his nieces. Never thought I'd say this sentence. I love this side of you."

"Yeah?"

I nod, suddenly feeling warm all over. It's silly, but I feel as if I just confessed a deep secret. Vulnerability grips me, and I break eye contact, afraid I'll give myself away.

A loud bang sounds from below, startling both of us, but we relax as the unmistakable sound of kids laughing follows.

"These little devils," he murmurs. "They raise hell whenever they're all together. But the more, the merrier. The Bennett genes need to be carried on."

A ball of tension settles in my chest.

"Yours too. I can imagine how pretty a girl would look with your hair, or your eyes. Lovely. Even though I'd have to spend half my life fending off suitors."

I laugh nervously, my stomach contracting now too. The implication in his words is clear, and part of me is melting into a puddle. But the other realizes this is it. I've got to tell him I can't have kids, so he can cut his losses. Back in college, he hadn't been crazy about kids, but then again, not many college-aged boys are. If the adoring way he treats his nieces and nephews wasn't a dead giveaway that he wants his own kids, his proclamation just did. He'll make a great dad.

This isn't the right time, no. But there will never be a *right* time, and he deserves the truth. Gathering my courage, I say, "Dan, remember this morning?"

"When you promised to tell me tonight whatever was bothering you? Yeah." He leans against the wall next to the open door to the supply room.

I suddenly feel exposed, dressed up in a Halloween costume. Some serious clothes would have been good for this conversation. But I'm not backing out.

"It wasn't the shelf talk that had me out of sorts, but you mentioning my lady stuff."

I'm not looking at him, instead fixating on a box inside the room.

"I don't have any supplies. I don't need them anymore. A few years ago, I got pregnant. Unexpected, but that's beside the point. Anyway, it was ectopic. Baby was growing outside the uterus, in the fallopian tube. Not viable. Found out too late, when it grew very large and ruptured. It caused a lot of damage, a hemorrhage, and they had to do a hysterectomy."

I pause to catch my breath, still not looking at him. "So, I can't have kids. I'm sorry I didn't tell you sooner. I didn't know how or when. This is a lot to put up with. And if you want to cut your losses, I understand."

It'll break my heart, but I'll understand.

I'm still stubbornly looking at the box. My eyes are stinging with unshed tears. He shifts closer to me, brings one hand to my face.

"I'm sorry this happened to you. I can't imagine how hard it was."

"It *was* hard. Mom was with me at the hospital, but I still felt so alone and empty."

"How about the baby's father?"

"Oh, he hadn't been happy about it in the first place. As I said, accidental. We'd split up anyway, and he was relieved." That phone call had been a low. Hearing his relief while I felt like a fundamental part of me didn't exist anymore.

"Dan, say something," I whisper, chancing a glance at him. The set of his jaw is firm, his eyes hard.

"I've never regretted letting you go more than now."

I cringe, biting the inside of my cheek. "Wouldn't have changed the outcome. The doctors said I had a rare genetic problem, so a normal pregnancy wouldn't have been possible. I had faulty equipment to begin with."

"Not what I meant. But I'd never have let you go through that alone. I'd have been there, right next to you."

"Oh."

"What did you mean with cutting my losses?"

"You want kids, and I can't give you any."

"There are other ways to have kids, like adoption."

The first tendrils of hope grip me, but I have to ask. I have to be sure. "What about the Bennett genes?"

He smiles. "It's a fun thing to say, but I don't need a kid to be blood-related to me to love it. Do you?"

"Of course not. Dan, do you mean this? Do you really mean it?"

"I'm dead serious."

"I wanted to tell you right when you called me after my birthday. But it would have sounded like I assumed too much. I'm still not assuming, by the way. Nothing about the future. Just taking it one day at a time, rediscovering each other." I kiss his jaw, his earlobe, shuddering lightly. "You're the best man, Daniel. The best man in the whole world."

He wraps his arms around me, keeping me close to him, stroking my hair. "Caroline, stop kissing me like this."

I startle because I wasn't kissing him in a particularly sexy or seductive way, but he has one hand in my hair, the other on my hip. Maybe he can feel the shift between us too, the incredible closeness. Instead of heeding his request, I continue to kiss down his neck.

"Stop kissing me," he repeats, his voice rougher.

"I can't help it. You're the sexiest pirate I've

ever seen," I joke. I need to feel close to him right now. I can't explain it, but I want to feel as much of his skin as possible. So, I slide my hands under his shirt, my fingertips tracing the ridges of his abdominal muscles, pressing against the tightness. It's still not enough.

He fists my hair with the hand at the back of my head. He walks me backward, then unhitches the hand from my waist, and I hear the sound of a handle being pressed down, a door opening. He backs me into one of the rooms, closes the door behind him. Then I hear the unmistakable sound of him locking the door. The room is empty, save for a vanity table and a large mirror hanging over it. Daniel's intent becomes clear when he looks at me. The lust and determination in his eyes nearly make my knees buckle.

"Here?" I whisper. By way of answering, Daniel tilts my head up, kissing me hard and hot, walking me backward again until my ass presses against the vanity table. Daniel aligns our bodies, pressing our hips together. His erection is straining against his pants. I feel it from my pubic bone right up to my navel.

"Won't anyone—" I begin when he breaks off the kiss.

"No one will even notice we're missing. I need to be inside you. I need it, do you understand?"

"I do. Because I need it too."

He spins me around. "Hold on to the vanity table."

I don't even think of disobeying him.

"I need you to be quiet," he says. He's behind me but looks me straight in the eyes through the mirror above the table. I nod, anticipation coursing through me.

"No matter how hard you come, you have to stay quiet."

Oh my. That's a delicious promise if I ever heard one. While I grip the table, he drops the hand from my waist to my outer thigh, cinching up the fabric of my dress until he reaches my skin. I break out in goose bumps.

He feathers his fingers from the side of my thigh to the back of my legs, then up, up, up to my buttock. Pushing my thong to one side, he swipes one finger in the crease between my ass cheeks. Heat rushes low in my body. He groans, burying his nose in my hair, breathing in deeply.

Spreading my thighs wide with his knee, he brings his fingers right to the rim of my opening, moving them in a circular motion from one fold, up to my clit, down the other fold. The first wave of pleasure spreads like wildfire through me. I clench the muscles in my ass to steady myself. My fingers spasm.

Daniel slips two fingers at once inside me, and my vision clouds. I grip the table so tightly that my knuckles turn white. He moves his fingers in and out of me in a maddening rhythm until I'm so turned on I can barely see straight. He pushes my dress up my waist. A second later, the *rrrrip* of a zipper being lowered reaches my ears. Another second later, he buries himself against me so deep that his pubic bone is pressing against my ass.

He stills for a few seconds, wrapping both arms around my middle in a tender hug, staring me straight in the eyes in the mirror.

"I want everything to go right between us this time," he says in a low, careful voice. "I don't want us to go too fast, but I've waited for so long...."

"That nothing feels fast enough," I finish for him.

He nods, tightening the hold of his arms, starting to slide in and out of me. "Yes. Exactly."

I rest my head back on his shoulder. Keeping me close to him like this, he whispers sweet and dirty nothings in my ear.

Tension builds inside me, making my inner muscles clench. Daniel digs his nails in my waist, lowering one hand until he reaches my clit. My thighs quiver and I bite down on my lip to keep from making any noise.

But then he pinches my clit between two fingers and I buck over the table. I'm almost blind from the sudden burst of pleasure.

"Dan," I say, voice shaky. Straightening up, I feel him spasm inside me, his hand applying more pressure on my clit.

"Dan, oh—"

I take his hand away from my waist and bring it to my mouth. Daniel understands my wish at once and claps his hand around my lips. Any sound I'll make will be muffled, but I still try with all my might to internalize the pleasure.

The problem with internalizing the pleasure is that it increases the intensity. My nerve endings feel like hot needles. The muscles in my tummy contract, as do those in my ass and thighs. My entire body braces itself for the orgasm. I've never come so fast in my life.

"Oh fuck, this feels good," Daniel whispers. "You're so tight, baby. So tight, it's driving me insane."

I squeeze him so hard with my inner muscles, I nearly come again just from feeling every inch of him filling me up. Heat flashes through me, and it takes me a second to realize why I'm not coming down from the high of the orgasm. Daniel is still touching my clit. Has he no mercy? I attempt to push his hand away, but he shakes his head.

"Shh, trust me."

"I'm too sensitive," I protest, even as pleasure pinches me, feeling like hot needles again.

"I know. But you're so close. Trust me on this. The second one will be more intense."

He drives inside me harder than before, his thighs slapping against my ass, his fingers turning me insane. When I feel him widen inside me, I cover my mouth with his hand again.

"Fuuuuuuuuck." He presses his mouth in the crook of my neck to muffle his own sounds, and it sends me over the edge. I explode all around him for a second time.

Maybe it's because I finally laid myself bare before him, but even though we're hiding in a room, dressed up as a pirate and Cinderella, and our lovemaking was rough and hard, I feel closer to him than ever before.

"I feel it too, Caroline." We make eye contact in the mirror, and I'm surprised at the vulnerability in his gaze. "Everything you feel in this moment, I'm right there with you."

***

We clean up quickly in the bathroom next door, find the damn glitter, and try not to look too guilty as we head back downstairs. No one seems to have noticed our absence, but maybe that's because things escalated quickly. Mia and Elena are now fighting over which one has the better costume— they're identical—and Will ran smack-dab into a cup with orange juice, so he's now soaked and crying. Sebastian's trying to cheer him up while Ava changes him.

Their daughter, Audrey, watches them with her lower lip trembling, clearly not impressed that her brother is getting all her parents' attention. *Uh-oh, I sense danger.*

I motion Daniel with my head. "Let's go distract Audrey."

He grins, holding out his hand in front of me. "Ladies first. After you."

I pinch the bridge of my nose, feigning

disgust. "Coward. Sending me to the wolves first."

He steps right next to me, bringing his lips to my ear. "Hey, you're better with kids than me. Besides, I love hanging in the back. I get a perfect view of you swinging your ass from side to side."

"You can't even make out any shape under all these layers."

"I've got the sight of it naked imprinted on my retinas."

"Daniel!" I admonish in a whisper. "We're surrounded by your family."

"Makes this so much more fun. Seeing you turn red to the roots of your hair."

"Stop that. Unless you don't want to get laid for three days straight."

He throws his head back, laughing. *Laughing!* Yeah, my admonishing skills need a lot of work.

"Sweetest challenge I ever heard."

We calm Audrey down by distracting her with a game of trick or treat. Before long, Will joins us too. Dad arrives shortly after seven, looking around incredulously.

"What is your costume, mister?" Mia asks him as soon as I introduce her to him.

Dad glances at me for help. He's wearing regular clothes, a shirt and cotton trousers.

"He's a librarian," I say with as much seriousness as I muster.

Mia frowns. "Which story had a librarian?"

"Bet all of them did. All castles had a library. They needed a librarian."

Mia ponders this for a few seconds before nodding. "Do you want to treat or trick, Mr. Librarian?"

Dad smiles and Mia takes his hand, leading him to the other kids. The party lasts late into the evening, and between seeing Dad smiling more than he's done in ages and feeling Daniel's gaze on me, the warmth of his family surrounding us, I can't help hoping there will be many more evenings like this one.

Chapter Twenty-Two

Caroline

"You're a life saver. Thank you so much," Linda exclaims, taking the plate with quiche out of my hands.

"Only half is for you, by the way. The other is for Bing."

Upon hearing his name, the golden retriever pokes his head through the open door.

"Bing, stay inside," Linda commands. "You're the best friend ever."

Well, not so much. I feel like I've sort of abandoned Linda lately.

"Are you sure you don't want to join our girls' night in? At least for a bit?"

"Nah. I'm just gonna curl up in bed and sleep. Working on a Saturday sucks. How do you still have so much energy? You've been helping your dad all day and look at you. You're practically radiant. You changed your skin toner? Or is it all the sexy time you're getting lately?"

I tap my chin, pretending I'm thinking hard. "The vote goes unabashedly to sexy time."

Even though I am getting none tonight because Daniel is out of town, running the bachelorette event for Beatrix. But I'm looking forward to the estrogen-filled evening and catching up with Summer and Pippa. We didn't get to talk too much on Halloween, so I'm expecting this to last until late in the night.

"Heard from Daniel today?"

"Nah, he's busy. He'll call if he has time."

Linda runs a hand through her hair, messing up her lovely curls. "Girl, if my man would spend the night with an ex, especially one who looks like that Beatrix chick, I'd be biting my nails, texting him every fifteen minutes."

I sigh, not at all willing to open this can of worms with her. "She's getting married—"

"How about the friends attending the party? I bet they're single, and just as hot. Hot people are always surrounded by hot people."

Damn! I hadn't even given one thought to the other women there. Palms suddenly a little sweaty, I shift my weight from one leg to the other.

"For the love of all that is holy, Linda! You've got to stop being so pessimistic."

She shrugs. "Maybe you're too trusting. You've been back together what, a month? Men will be men, just saying. You flaunt so much perfection and beauty in their noses, they'll fall for it."

Isn't she a ray of sunshine? To her defense, she does have chronic bad luck in the dating department. But maybe her expectation that all men are assholes actually attracts assholes.

As I move around my kitchen some ten minutes later, checking on the quiche, my insecurities kick in. Maybe I shouldn't eat the quiche, but opt for a low-fat, tasteless alternative instead. And the wine is a bad idea. Alcohol has so many calories....

I wonder what models eat to stay so thin, to maintain that flawless beauty. Bet quiche isn't on their approved meals list. Damn it, this is all Linda's pessimism getting to me. I swear pessimism should be on the list of infectious diseases. It spreads like wildfire, sticks like a pest.

My heart grows a little heavy. Should I be more cautious? Is it too soon to be this trusting? Jesus, I'll drive myself crazy if I keep on like this. As if on cue, I receive a text from Daniel.

Daniel: The girls started with the cocktails at lunch. Half can't walk in a straight line already. Feel like a babysitter. Hope your day is better.

I laugh nervously, my heart growing heavier still. Damn it, I've got to stop this. Before I know it, I'll be fearing an apocalypse coming.

Caroline: Pippa and Summer will be here soon. I suspect in a few hours we'll be needing a sitter too. Have fun!

By the time my doorbell rings, I've managed to push some of my worries to the back of my mind. A little quiche and a lot of wine should help push them *out* of my mind.

"Oooh, you didn't have to bring anything," I

say, welcoming them inside. The Bennett sisters each carry a bag.

"This is the first proper girls' evening in a long time," Pippa says. "I'm not cutting corners. When you said quiche, I thought, you know what goes with so much fat? More fat. So I bought ice cream."

Summer nods, holds up her bag. "I was in the mood for chips. But I also brought avocado and tomatoes to make guacamole. That should balance it out, right?"

I laugh. "Not really, but girls' night isn't for balance. It's for fun."

"That's our girl." Pippa shoves the ice cream in my freezer as I take the quiche out of the oven. The crème fraiche is the perfect shade of cream, and the crust is dark brown.

"Besides, isn't it officially the cold season? The body needs more fat," Pippa muses. Well, mid-November doesn't quite qualify as the cold season, but I can see her point.

Both girls are wearing jeans and casual shirts. Pippa's blonde hair is braided, while Summer wears hers in a messy bun at the base of her head. Neither wears makeup. One thing I love about girls' nights in? How casual we all are.

Summer finishes preparing the guacamole at the same time the quiche is cool enough to eat. Let the feast begin.

We carry the food and the wine to the living room, and the girls make themselves comfortable on the couch. I sit on the ottoman so I can look at them. An hour later and three glasses of wine down each, we sit on the floor, scooping guacamole with the chips, reminiscing about that one time six years ago when we wanted to have an extended girls' weekend in LA where their cousin, Valentina Connor, lives, but the car's navigation system wasn't working, and we ended up getting lost.

"Lesson learned: we never let Pippa drive again," Summer exclaims.

Her sister elbows her playfully.

"Oy! You could've pointed out I was heading to the Pampas *before* I drove a hundred miles in the wrong direction."

Summer grins. "True, but I was too busy gossiping with Caroline."

We're soul sisters, Summer and I. Gossiping with the girls is one of my favorite activities to relax, along with discovering a great TV show and binge-watching it, lying in a hot bath, and spoiling Daniel. Not necessarily in that order. The three of us burst into giggles, and I laugh until every limb in my body feels lighter.

Once we've calmed down somewhat, we all talk about our jobs. I always had a secret crush on Pippa's job as designer at Bennett Enterprises. The jewelry she makes is just breathtaking. I might lead a low-key lifestyle, but a girl can feast her eyes.

Summer works at an art gallery and paints as well. I have one of her paintings hanging in my bedroom—sunlight reflecting on a tranquil sea. It's a brilliant sight to wake up to.

As we down the last of the chips and the quiche—which goes amazingly with guacamole, as it turns out—Summer says, "Caroline, we haven't officially talked about you and Daniel at Halloween, but this means you've got two more weeks of information to share. We're all ears."

Pippa holds up a finger. "I'll bring the ice cream first."

"And teaspoons. They're in the drawer to the left of the oven," I instruct.

Once we're armed with teaspoons, we eat the ice cream directly out of the carton, and I launch into a detailed account.

"Damn girl," Pippa exclaims when I stop to catch my breath. "You're on a roll."

I'm basking in this moment. Ah, how I have wished for this day—when Dan and I would be together again, and his sisters would poke their noses into our business, dissecting every little thing.

"Well, how can you overanalyze everything with me if you don't know all the details? So, I demand honest honesty—"

"Honest honesty? This wine is strong," Summer interjects, inspecting the label on the empty bottle.

"Shh, don't interrupt or I'll lose my nerve. Do you think Linda's right and I'm too trusting? I keep saying that I'm taking this one day at a time, but I'm doing the opposite. I'm jumping in with both feet. But I've wanted Daniel to be mine again so badly for so long that I'm not even sure *how* to do things differently."

Ugh, now I've done it. I hadn't meant to say the last part out loud.

"Wow. This is the first time you admit you've wanted to be back with him all along," Summer says, absently moving her teaspoon around in the ice cream carton.

I could try to downplay it, but they'd see right through me. "I didn't want to admit it even to myself. I knew how pathetic I'd sound."

"Wanting to be back with someone you love doesn't make you pathetic. It makes you human." Pippa straightens up, crossing her legs in a yoga pose. "And back to your question, no, you're not too trusting. You know better than anyone what you have with Daniel. Linda is your friend, but I don't like how she talks about men. I bet even if she had a perfect partner, she'd still find something to complain about. Daniel's not an asshole. And I'm not saying this just because he's my brother."

Summer snickers. "Yeah, you are. Admit it, you're biased."

"Of course, I'm biased. But my bias comes from thirty years of studying my brother. It's rooted in observation."

"Because poking your nose in someone else's business is foolproof scientific evidence," Summer says.

Pippa clumsily climbs back on the couch, rubbing her hip. "Floor's too hard. I can't feel my ass anymore."

"That might be the wine's doing," I inform her solemnly.

Pippa tilts her head, as if considering this. "You're such a great friend. And you make my brother happy. You should be a Bennett already."

Oh man, oh man, that sounds so good. So, so good.

"I dreamed about this the first time around," I admit. "Caroline Bennett has such a nice ring to it."

"Speaking of rings, I already have the one for you in my mind." She wiggles her eyebrows, rubbing her hands excitedly. "Just need the word."

This escalated quickly.

"No more talk of rings. I said I dreamed about this the *last* time. Now—"

"You're taking it one step at a time." Summer winks, taking the carton of ice cream in her lap, monopolizing it.

"I'm usually a happy drunk. What's wrong with me?" I'm disgusted with my own negativity.

"Nothing wrong. Doubts and fears are normal. You're in love with a man you lost once, and you're afraid of losing him again," Pippa says.

I pull my knees to my chest, suddenly feeling exposed. "I didn't say anything about love."

The girls smile, exchanging glances.

"We can read between the lines," Summer informs me.

Chapter Twenty-Three

Daniel

"Come on, sleepyhead. One kiss. I know you're awake. You peeked when I was getting dressed."

In response, Caroline hugs the pillow tighter under her head, blinks open an eye, closes it again. "I like you better naked."

"I aim to please, but I have an early Monday today."

"Mmm... bad words."

"If you're not giving me that kiss, I'm going to take it."

She wiggles her sexy bare ass, eyes still closed. "What's stopping you, Bennett? Take what's yours."

Cheeky woman.

Putting one knee on the bed, I lounge over her, kissing up her spine, giving her ass a little smack. She moans softly, reaching back with her hand when I'm kissing the side of her neck, tugging at my hair.

She's usually an early bird, but I kept her up late last night. The weekend was a shit-show of epic proportions. It's the last bachelor or bachelorette event I'm organizing, no matter how high profile the customer requiring one is. Drove right here yesterday afternoon, needing to see Caroline, to get my fill of her—which I still haven't. I hover over her, just feeling her warmth and sweetness, all the good things she brings in my life. As if sensing how much I need her, she takes out a hand from under her pillow, caressing my neck, pulling me closer.

Staying here with her sounds like the best use of the day, but duty calls. And if there's one thing I can't persuade Caroline to do, it's to call in sick. Her work ethic is killing me.

She falls back to sleep just like that in my arms, and I move away, careful not to wake her. She's taking her group to the circus today, so she starts later.

The day goes downhill the second I climb into my car. My phone rings, a familiar name appearing on the screen: Jake Wensworth, owner of the *San Francisco Business Report*, the most successful local business magazine.

"Hi, Jake!"

"Daniel. Not too early, I hope?"

"Not at all. You've got news for me?"

"Yeah. You were right. Someone from your team *is* out to get you. We got a call from a guy named Hamel—"

My body goes cold. "Justin Hamel?"

"Yes. He went into some detail about liquidity-to-asset ratio and so on."

"And you're sure it was Hamel? Not

Colbert?"

"One hundred percent. He didn't give us his name, but we searched his number online, found an old CV with his name and number listed."

After a long pause, I finally say, "This isn't what I expected."

"I'm sorry."

"I'll deal with this today. At least this circus is ending. Thanks, Jake."

"No problem."

After we hang up, I grip the wheel tighter, pressing the gas pedal and speeding through the city, my mind stuck somewhere between numbness and anger. Why would my mentor turn against me?

I summon Justin in my office the second I arrive and cut to the chase as soon as he sits in front of me.

"I received a phone call from Jake Wensworth today. The name ring a bell?"

Justin nods, his expression betraying nothing, setting me even more on edge.

"He had some rather disturbing news for me. It appears you called him to report the company is in trouble."

A vein twitches in his temple. "That's not true."

"I only told this to a few people."

"One of the others must have—"

"Cut the crap. Your phone number is listed online. It was you. Just like the leaked photos to the tabloids. Why?"

Tired of doing this the polite way, I rise to my feet, pace the space behind the desk, stopping in front of the window. Justin's narrowed eyes follow my every move. I can practically hear him calculating the chances of convincing me that someone else is to blame.

"I trusted you. You've been with me since I started this company—"

"Yes, all that trust and the hard work didn't keep you from promoting others over me, did it?" he sputters between gritted teeth.

"What?"

"You built this company with my help. I hired Marcel, and you promoted him over me. You even promoted that bitch, Honor—"

"Don't call her—"

"I don't give two shits about what you want."

He rises to his feet, and I cross the room until I'm right in front of him. "This is exactly why I didn't promote you. Your leadership skills are nonexistent. You can't lead or give feedback. You make at least one person uncomfortable during our weekly meetings."

"I know how to do my job. I don't need pretty rich boys talking about leadership skills, feedback loops, and all those fancy words you learn in business school."

I stare at him. He was my first employee. Sometimes high-maintenance, sometimes even rude, but I learned a lot from him, except for said leadership skills.

"So, this is all out of spite?"

He juts his chin forward, jamming a hand on the desk. "The extra money wasn't bad either."

"I could've given you more money. All you had to do was ask."

"Someone had to take you down a notch or two from your high horse. I figured a few lawsuits would do the trick. But people like you always come out on top, right? All that Ivy League education and money shooting out your ass, all those *connections*."

"Right. Wensworth is one of those connections. You have one hour to clean out your desk and hand in your resignation."

"No, no. I won't make this easy for you. You want me out, you do the work."

"Don't think I won't."

Words I never thought I'd tell someone I considered my mentor. I looked up to him despite his faults. How did I let this get here?

"Your star will fade eventually, boy. Mark my words. Yours and your family's."

"Leave my family out of this," I warn, curling my palms to fists.

"I kept hoping to have something on them. Almost had my chance when your little sister was all over that drummer at the beginning of the year. Summer Bennett flashing—"

"You talk like that about my family, you won't be able to walk tomorrow, forget coming to the office. Out. Now."

I curl my fists tighter, fighting to keep my

anger under control. He's deliberately provoking me. If I hit him, I'll have a lawsuit on my hands. I only unclench my fists when he leaves my sight.

I remember the drummer he's talking about. We planned a New Year's event for a local rock band, and my sister joined us. She and their drummer hit it off right away. I kept an eye on them the entire night, ready to play the big brother card if it came to it—read: if he'd tried to rope her into a one-night stand. Would've pissed off my sister, but the guy was an asshole. Nothing came out of that night, but the thought of Summer's life splashed in the tabloids because of this idiot—and because of me—is enough to make my blood boil.

***

Caroline

By the time five o'clock in the afternoon rolls around, I'm *so* ready to call this a day. Most days I love my job, but today isn't one of those. Taking the kids to the circus turned into a circus all on its own.

"Thank God that was the last one," Karla says, sounding as exhausted as I feel. We're in the park facing the circus, and the last kid was just picked up.

"My feelings exactly."

"I'm out of here too."

"Have a nice evening, Karla. Any plans?"

"Does collapsing on my couch with a glass of

wine count as a plan?"

"Absolutely."

"There's my plan, then. How about you? Are you dating Daniel Bennett? When he picked you up last week, you looked *cozy*."

I will kill Daniel. Yes, I will. By cozy, she probably means she saw Daniel pulling me behind his car and kissing the living daylights out of me.

"No one will see," he said.

"We're well hidden here," he said.

"We're dating, yes."

She beams as she motions to a cabbie to stop. "Well, if he picks you up again, by all means, tell him to come inside. He's a sight for sore eyes."

I decide on the spot that shall not happen. Daniel's six feet of deliciousness are for me and me alone. Yeah, I'm possessive.

"See you tomorrow, Karla."

After she slides into the cab, I head to my car, already excited about my trip to the thrift store near my building. The owner emailed the pic of a gorgeous scarf she received today and said she's putting it aside for me until this evening. I can't wait to put my hands on the pretty thing.

While driving, I thumb off a message to Daniel. We made no plans to meet, but lately we've been playing a game I love. He asks me to come over to his place, and I pretend I don't want to, just so he can make full use of his extensive—and delicious— persuasion skills. As if I really need to be persuaded. I love being in his home and walking around Nob

Hill. Between the vintage barbershops, the cable cars, and the old-luxury vibes coming from buildings such as the famous Fairmont Hotel, it's a pleasure to be there.

Caroline: Everything okay?

My phone buzzes with an incoming call the next second. I immediately answer.

"Hey, how was your day?" I ask.

"I've had better."

"What happened?"

"Long story." The defeat in his tone startles me. "I'd really like to hold you tonight."

Instantly I sense this isn't the time to play our little game.

"How's a bubble bath in your Jacuzzi sound? No girly bath bomb, I promise."

He laughs, but it doesn't sound wholehearted. Not like he means it.

"Sounds great. I'll be at my place in about an hour, but the doorman can let you in if you arrive earlier."

"I'll be there in forty minutes, and I'll prepare everything."

I'll have to forego the trip to the thrift shop, but it doesn't matter. Someone else can have the pretty scarf. Daniel comes first. Whatever he needs, I'm there.

To my utter shock, I realize ninety-nine percent of the bath bomb offerings are targeting women. The best I can find is a marine-scented one, but I'll double-check with Daniel *before* dropping it in the water.

When he arrives, he's giving off every single vibe of *broody Daniel.*

"I have the bath ready. Well, the Jacuzzi's full. The verdict's still out there on whether the bath bomb is masculine enough. 'Marine scent,' it says, but that's open to interpretation. Don't want you smelling like a mermaid."

This earns me a small smile. *Hmm… we can do better.* Taking his hand, I lead him to the bathroom.

"I'm taking care of you tonight," I announce when we arrive at the Jacuzzi. I turn around, raising my hands to undo his shirt buttons, but Daniel catches both my wrists, cuffing them in one big hand. Then he pulls me into a long, deep kiss, bringing his other hand to the back of my head.

Oh boy.

This is his manly way of saying, "Yes, yes I need you to take care of me."

One day, I'll write a book aimed at men, explaining in great detail how admitting out loud that they have their vulnerable moments won't kill them. Right now, I have more important things to do— namely, taking care of *this* particular man.

First, I need to get him naked. Now, I'm not one to take advantage of a vulnerable man for my own pleasure, but getting him inside the tub requires me to take his clothes off.

If I prolong the process, taking my sweet time… well, no one can blame me. Daniel's body is a piece of art. It deserves all the stroking and worshiping. I run my fingers over every inch of skin I uncover, and when that isn't enough anymore, I use my mouth too. Down his chest, tracing the ridges of his six-pack with the tip of my tongue until I feel the bulge in his pants press against my throat. Lowering myself on my knees, I undo the button and the zipper, pushing his pants and boxers down.

I take his erection in my mouth, looking him straight in the eyes. He exhales sharply, bringing his hand to cup the side of my face, sliding it to the back of my head, the pads of his fingers pressing on my scalp, as if he's barely refraining himself from fisting my hair. Oh, I love it when I bring him this close to losing control. I don't want him to keep his rough side in check tonight, so I'm going to tempt the hell out of him, right until he loses it. Watching his eyes, I slide my mouth lower onto him, and then lower still, until I feel his tip at the back of my throat. Daniel feels it too if the low, husky groan is any indication. Heat zings through me at the sound. Just like that, I'm burning for him.

Damn it. This whole thing is backfiring. My grand seduction plan is supposed to drive him so crazy that he pushes all his troubles to the back of his mind. It isn't supposed to turn *me* on so much that I feel like throwing my plan away and jumping his bones right now. No, no, I'll stay put. Tonight is all about him.

As if sensing my need, he says, "Touch yourself."

I don't need to be told twice. I move my

hand, but splay it wide on my stomach instead of doing anything naughty, because I just got an idea. I want him to tell me what to do. I want his instructions, every step of the way. Daniel loves giving me commands when we're intimate, but not more than I love following them. I shrug, opening my eyes wide, hoping he'll get my point. I can't talk with him filling my mouth.

Oh, he does.

"Run your finger over your panties, from your clit down to your opening."

Slowly, I push my pants down, kicking them away, then run my hand over the silk of my panties, just the way he told me to. A rush of arousal dampens my panties. I press my thighs together. Daniel's eyes become hooded. He draws in a deep breath, and when his lips part, I see his teeth are clenched. He pulses in my mouth, and I clamp my lips tighter around him.

"You're driving me crazy, woman. Touch yourself again. Run your fingers up one fold, then down the other. Don't touch your clit this time."

I nearly bite him when I press the drenched fabric against my sensitive folds. A tremor shakes my entire body, but I move my mouth slowly over him while I touch myself. I'm getting the hang of this multitasking thing, even though I'm so turned on, I can barely think.

"You're making yourself wet. And you're driving me crazy. Slide your hand inside your panties. Touch your pussy."

I dive my hand right in and hear a small *splat* as my fingers slip through my arousal. Daniel tugs at my hair in a wild gesture. Then he pulls out of me.

"Get inside that tub, Caroline. I need to fuck you right now."

He helps me up to my feet, pushes my panties down in an instant, and once we're both naked, we lower ourselves into the tub.

"I'll sit. You climb on top of me. The tub floor is too hard for you."

I climb on top, lowering myself onto him, taking him in all at once.

"Ah!" I gasp, but barely have time to draw in a deep breath when Daniel starts pounding me so hard, I clasp the edges of the tub to ground myself. He's leveling himself on his palms and foot soles, driving into me like a man determined to chase the last drop of pleasure tonight. It's relentless fucking, but also lovemaking. I watch him lose himself in me, taking me higher with every thrust and then higher still until we're in that heightened state of mind where no thoughts exist, just sensation. I shatter around him when he rasps out my name, chasing his climax.

I feel more than see him lean back, resting his head at the edge of the tub, pulling me flush against him so I'm lying with my head on his shoulder, the water reaching up to my chin. My back is completely out of the hot water, and I feel a little cold.

Slowly, I become aware of Daniel splashing water over my back, warming me up. I snuggle closely up to his neck, peppering his skin with kisses.

"So, where's that bath bomb you keep threatening me with?"

I reach out to the edge of the tub, bring it up for his inspection. He sniffs it.

"Doesn't smell like your usual stuff."

Chuckling, I pull back, sitting so I can look at him. "I don't attack a man when he's down. I'll force my vanilla and lavender bath bomb on you another time. What's the verdict on this one?"

"Bring it on."

I drop it in the water, then reach for his shower gel. "I'm going to rub this into you, like a massage."

"You're going all out tonight."

"Told you I'd take care of you."

Something flickers in his eyes, but he doesn't say anything. I rub gel on my palms, then get to work, massaging his chest, his arms, the front of his shoulders.

"Found out who leaked those photos."

"Oh! By your disgruntled look, I'm going to take a guess that it wasn't the intern."

"It was Justin. I promoted Marcel and Honor over him, and apparently it was enough to turn him against me."

"I'm sorry. That's terrible. But now it's all over, right? It's all good?"

"Firing the man I considered my mentor doesn't exactly feel like winning."

"I bet not."

"He actually said he'd hoped to have something to leak about my family. Nearly got a shot at Summer at the New Year's Eve party last year."

I lower my hands from his shoulders to his chest, feeling his heart beat frantically, and I know he's playing in his mind what could have happened. I'm imagining some worst-case scenarios too, but I'll keep that to myself. It's the last thing he needs to hear right now. He needs my strength, and to be comforted.

"Some brother I am, eh? And a fantastic boss too." His voice dripping with sarcasm, he rests his head back on the edge of the tub.

"Dan, stop beating yourself up about everything. You are a great brother, *and* a great boss. Karla told me that on the trip, Marcel and Honor were only saying positive things about you."

"They won't trash me in front of customers. Doesn't mean they really think that. When I started this company, I wanted to build something I could be proud of. Make my family proud."

"You should be proud of what you built. And your family is proud too. If you don't believe me, just ask them."

"You're so beautiful, sitting here, listening to me." He takes my hands to his lips, kisses my knuckles. He's never showed me this side of him before, never let me see him vulnerable and emotional. "I'm so happy I have you."

"I'm happy to be here, Dan."

He's still in *brooding mode*, though. Still

vulnerable and unhappy. I bite the inside of my cheek, pondering what to say next. Reassuring him it's all good won't help. Sometimes we don't need to hear "everything will be okay." We already know that, but we still feel like we could have done better, like we're not enough. The feeling is all too familiar for me, and while I avoid talking about it, maybe sharing this will help him—at least make him understand it's normal to feel like this from time to time. Not pleasant, but normal.

"I have these moments too," I say softly. "When I don't feel like I'm enough."

Daniel straightens up, fixing me with his gaze.

"When Mom boasted to everyone that my brother is a neurosurgeon, told me I could have done better than being an elementary school teacher." This was the easy part to confess. Swallowing, I trace a random pattern on his chest with my forefinger. "Then, after the miscarriage and the surgery, the few times I told men I couldn't have kids, it didn't go well at all. They kind of made me feel like I'm not woman enough."

The muscles in his arms and shoulders tense. He pulls me closer until I'm lying on top of him. "That's why you were afraid of telling me."

"Yeah."

"Is being around kids hard for you? At school or with my family?"

"Not at all. I've always loved kids. After the diagnosis, I immediately started thinking about adoption, and it felt right. But not everyone thinks this way."

"*They* were not men enough for you. No big loss for you."

"You've got a knack for turning this around to make me look like a prize."

"You *are* a prize. You're a smart, funny, and loving woman. You're everything. My everything."

I curl in his arms like a kitten, soaking in his words. His admission beckons me to counter with one of my own, to open up.

"You're my everything too, Dan. You're the best thing that happened to me. The best."

This right here—each of us baring our souls to each other, sharing our fears—feels more intimate than anything we've done before. We never laid ourselves bare this way the first time. Maybe because at that age we didn't have many skeletons, or maybe we just weren't ready to trust the other with the less-than-perfect stuff.

"Even when I'm a mess?" he asks.

I'm flat against his chest, so I can't see his expression, but I spy the way his hand tightens on the edge of the tub. My answer is important to him. I'd argue he's far from being a mess, but it's not what he needs.

"Even then. Especially then. You're human. My human. Here's a little secret. I know you're not perfect. No one is."

"Damn, all that hard work and I still can't fool you into thinking I'm perfect."

"Nope. The jig is up, I'm afraid. But I'll be

here no matter what, ready to listen to you, with a bath and anything else you need. I promise."

"I don't need the bath, or anything else. I just need you." He threads his fingers through my hair, his breath caressing the side of my head. "Listening without judging, trusting me."

I nibble at the base of his neck, which might possibly lead to a hickey, but I need to kiss him, touch him. I need to feel closer to him. No clue if he's ready for sexy time again, though.

"Lying naked on top of me is also a big bonus," he adds in a naughty whisper. I giggle against his neck, happy we can find the light and humor in any situation. The joke's on me, it appears. He's always ready for sexy time. *Men.*

"I knew it. It all comes down to sex. Watch it, or I *will* treat you to my vanilla bath bomb."

He slips one hand between us, teasing a nipple. "They're awake already."

"Keep going like that and I'll upgrade to a cherry and honey bath bomb. You'll smell like dessert for a week."

Chapter Twenty-Four

Daniel

Turns out firing someone for attempted sabotage requires more paperwork than setting up a damn company.

By the time Thursday rolls around, I'm ready to forget this week altogether, pretend it didn't exist. Solving everything this week is imperative because I have a tour on Monday, and I'm flying out to Sydney next Tuesday, where I'll be closing a business deal. I have a hearing tomorrow morning for Justin's case, but as I pull my car in my parents' driveway, I'm determined to let loose, enjoy Thanksgiving dinner.

A flurry of voices echo in the house when I step inside. Everyone is sitting on the various armchairs and couches in the enormous living room, a drink in hand. After greeting my parents and Martin, I head straight to Caroline, who is sitting on a sofa, talking to Landon Connor, a cousin from my mom's side of the family.

"Landon, good to see you, man." I shake his hand, kissing Caroline on the forehead, then sitting on the armrest. "I didn't know you were coming tonight."

"Wanted to head out to LA, but didn't work

out time wise."

The Connor clan resides in LA, but Landon moved to San Jose years ago with his wife, Rachel. Unfortunately, since she passed away, my cousin seems to be spending every waking moment working.

"Ouch, I bet Valentina has put a ransom on your head," I say, referring to his twin sister who likes to organize family events as much as Mom.

"I'm waiting for 'Wanted' signs to pop up any second now," Landon replies. Caroline grins, wrapping an arm around mine.

"Val needs to come to San Francisco more often. I need someone to teach me how to properly perform Irish dances. I can't believe she's so much better at it than I am. You lot are only half-Irish!" she says.

"Ah, my dad took his dancing seriously," Landon says. His father emigrated from Ireland to America around the same time Caroline's parents did. "And Val's the only one who can dance out of the lot of us."

Caroline sighs wistfully. "I'll be happy if I can evolve to the point where I'm not stepping on my own toes anymore."

"Or mine," I supply.

She jabs me playfully with her elbow. "I did not step on yours."

Landon winks. "I can confidently say you step on your dancing partner's toes too. Had a black toe or two myself after Blake's wedding."

Caroline folds her arms, glancing from

Landon to me. "You're banding against me. That's unfair."

Landon holds up his hands in defense. "Just presenting evidence."

"Sorry to interrupt," Summer calls, approaching us. "I need to steal my favorite cousin for a bit."

As Landon rises from the couch, I warn him. "Don't believe her. She plays the favorites game with all of us."

Landon laughs, lacing an arm around Summer's shoulders. "I'm the only cousin here tonight. I'm the favorite by default."

"He still looks so sad even though it's been a while since Rachel passed away," Caroline says in a low, wistful voice. To me, Landon looks just fine, but I'll admit I don't pick up on these things like my sisters or Caroline do.

"She was his wife," I say simply. If something happened to Caroline, I don't think I'd ever recover.

"I know, but I was hoping he'd catch the Bennettitis virus too. He *is* related to you, after all."

"Blake's been giving you ideas, huh?" I ask with a grin. Ever since our eldest siblings fell in love one after the other, Blake declared the Bennettitis virus is ravaging our family.

"He has. And by the way, Blake was saying something about a guy's night out tomorrow evening."

Just then, Mom announces the turkey's ready, and we can all head to the dining table. Taking

Caroline's hand, I lead the way.

"Speaking of brothers, I talked to Niall today," I say, pulling out the chair for her.

Caroline groans. "He gave you the talk, didn't he?"

"Yeah, but he was more laid-back about it than I expected."

She cocks a brow as I sit next to her. "Define laid-back."

"He didn't tell me anything I wouldn't tell someone dating Summer," I say truthfully.

"Wow, you've had quite a day, between dealing with the stuff with Justin and my brother semi-threatening you." Leaning in, she adds in a conspiratorial whisper. "I'll take care of you tonight, I promise."

"I'll hold you to that."

Predictably, Thanksgiving dinner stretches for hours, right until Will falls asleep with his head on the table, and we decide to call it a night.

***

The next evening, I'm the last to arrive at Blake's bar, where I decided with my brothers plus Pippa's husband to have our men's night out.

Everyone's sitting around two high bar tables pushed together: Sebastian, Logan next to him, then Eric. Blake, Christopher, and Max are on the other side.

"How did it go?" Logan inquires. "Blake told us."

I groan, staring at Blake. He was supposed to keep his mouth shut. I haven't told any of my other siblings about the issue with Justin because I saw no point worrying them, but when I called Blake at lunch to tell him I'd be late this evening, he insisted I tell him why.

Blake grins. "Blame the beer."

"You've just had half a glass."

"Blame my big mouth. Thought they should know. They usually have good ideas."

"If you need lawyers, we have a whole lot of them on payroll already," Sebastian offers.

"Nah, I'm good. A competent team is handling it. Just want to get it over with. Forget it happened."

Logan drums his fingers on the table. "Might happen again, so look out. Corporate sabotage isn't that uncommon."

"It isn't?" I raise a skeptical brow.

"Nah. You get frustrated employees everywhere. Pay attention to vengeful ex-employees. We had one once who tried to stop a transport to Europe. Was a bit of a nightmare."

Max chimes in. "Competitors sometimes get nasty too. Stir up legal trouble, or send the feds over."

"Low chances, I'd say. Not a big fish like Bennett Enterprises. No big fish in my industry at all. Doubt any of the others would waste their time with something like this. I wouldn't."

Sebastian scratches his chin, downs a

mouthful of beer. "Because you're decent. Not everyone plays fair. If your lawyers don't come through, we can help. Ours have handled just about everything."

Surprisingly, the news that my brothers have gone through something similar calms me somewhat. It's good to know this is at least in the realms of normalcy.

Blake looks at me smugly. His first reaction when I told him was "Why the hell aren't you telling the others? I bet they've seen it all at Bennett Enterprises. They'll have some advice."

Unlike me, Blake's never had any issues asking my brothers for help or advice.

"Say it," he demands.

"You were right."

Blake pumps his fist in the air, opens his mouth. I hold up a hand to placate him. "No more gloating. I need a beer."

Several beers in, the conversation focuses on Bennett Enterprises. Since everyone except Eric, Blake, and me works in the company, this happens often. My brothers are smart as a whip, and I like to listen to them mastermind. More than once during casual nights out, I picked up valuable management or operational ideas that I implemented in my own business.

"Enough with the Bennett Enterprises babble," Blake says eventually. "It's all good and interesting, but this is not the boardroom. If I'd known you're using this night out to draw out strategies, I would've taken Clara out instead."

Logan grins. "Feel free to dump us for your wife anytime. She might not be too keen on you tonight. As far as I heard, the girls are having a blast. First time Clara's out with them since the baby came, right?"

"Yeah," Blake confirms. "She was nervous about it, but she needs some time for herself."

"Pretty crazy that Mom and Dad take the kids in overnight," Logan says. "Suppose raising the bunch of us was practice enough."

"No idea how they did it," Sebastian says.

Logan claps his shoulder. "You're on your way to find out, with two more coming in a few months."

He and Ava shared the news yesterday. Is it my imagination, or does Sebastian look tense?

He takes a long swig of his beer, nods. "My worst fear—not being able to provide for or protect my wife and kids. Either because I die, or worse, become incapacitated and they have me as a burden."

Everyone at the table falls into a stunned silence. I can't even count the instances in which Sebastian voiced fears on one hand. This must be weighing very hard on him.

"Your wife is a strong woman," I say eventually. Everyone else seems still too stunned to react. "She'd manage no matter what life throws her. And you have us. No matter what happens, we'd take care of Ava and the kids. You can count on me, on all of us."

Sebastian nods, but still looks out of his depths. Logan seems to snap out of his stupor, backing me up immediately. The others chime in too, reassuring my oldest brother.

"Never seen him like this," I comment to Christopher ten minutes later when we line up at the bar to bring more beers.

"I did," he says quietly. "When he found out Ava was pregnant the first time. Alice and I were with him. He was wondering if he'd be a good dad, things like that. Gave us a bit of a shock, to be honest. But I understand where he's coming from. When Victoria got pregnant, I had some of those thoughts myself. She read up about it, said they happen. Never thought they'd happen to Sebastian because he's always in control, always sure of himself. And why the hell is it taking so long to get some beers?"

It takes us five more minutes to finally return to the table. I turn to my twin.

"Blake, honest feedback: your bartenders are slow as fuck. Took them forever to take our order."

"Oh, shit," Blake says. "That's not on the bartenders. It's on me. Told them to go slower after our third round. We still have to get the girls. Better be able to walk in a straight line while we're at it."

Logan gapes at him. "Never thought I'd live to see the day when Blake's the most responsible of the bunch. Fatherhood's done wonders for you, baby bro. Now, make sure this one follows in your footsteps. Settles down and everything." He hooks one thumb in my direction.

"Oy, I'm right here. I can hear you," I say in mock offense. It's been too long since Logan rode my ass. Used to do it far more often in my early twenties. In all honesty, I did need that then. Nothing like a big brother breathing down your neck to motivate you to get your shit together.

"You were meant to hear it," Logan informs me. "You pull a stunt on Caroline like you did last time, it's not going to be pretty."

One thing I can always count on: my brothers won't hold back punches. Literally *or* figuratively.

Blake jerks his head back. "Logan, if you want my help cornering Daniel, I'm gonna need more heads-up than this."

Perfect. Blake will have my back. Twin bond and all that.

Pointing a finger at me, he says, "I'm with Logan. Any funny business and I'm decking you."

Twin bond's worth shit tonight, apparently.

"Whose side are you on?"

He doesn't hesitate. "Caroline's."

"So am I." I raise my glass to them. "And guys? Leave the cornering to our sisters. They're so much better at it."

Chapter Twenty-Five

Caroline

For a variety of reasons, Monday isn't my favorite day of the week, but today I'm borderline panicking. Ever since I arrived this morning, I've had the impression that Karla and Helen are talking about me. Am I being paranoid? Have I done something wrong? Surely the principal would have told me.

During the afternoon break, I head straight to the staff room.

I find Karla and Helen with their heads together, stopping dead when they see me, straightening up.

"What's going on?" I inquire. "You two have been acting odd all day."

They exchange uneasy glances. Right, not my imagination, then.

"Did I do something? The principal didn't tell me—"

Karla shakes her head. "Nah. It's something else. You didn't see. I thought it might be that. You were too calm the entire day."

Panic flares inside me now. "See what?" Did something happen to Dad? Daniel?

With an apologetic look, she stands up, takes

her phone out of the front pocket of her jeans, taps it a few times, then hands it to me. Ice-cold dread sweeps over me. Now I understand the whispers, the furtive looks. On the tiny screen is a photo of Daniel and someone who is definitely *not* me. By the rich blonde mane and the article's title, I know it's Beatrix.

And though the picture is badly lit and unclear, things are not looking good. I can't be sure, because the angle's bad, but there seems to be lip-locking involved. I don't want to think too closely about that the tangle of arms. I scroll down, reading the article. A glance up at the browser tells me it's a trashy gossip magazine. Wasn't expecting anything less.

Back to the article. I fight the knot in my throat, blink a few times to clear the haze in my eyes.

Why on earth is this such news? Probably because Beatrix is engaged to an A-list actor. Swallowing hard and squaring my shoulders, I hand the phone back to Karla.

"Isn't this the guy you're seeing? Daniel Bennett? We thought it was him," Helen says uncertainly.

"Yes. So?" I ask harshly.

"Oh," Karla says, clearly misinterpreting my stoicism for indifference. "We didn't realize you two were *casual, no strings*."

Thankfully, they don't get to pry much longer because the principal walks in, asking us about the trip we're planning with the kids to the zoo next week. I answer almost robotically, my mind spinning, focusing on a few words. *Casual, no strings.*

Once the principal's out of the staff room, I excuse myself too, telling everyone I'm heading outside to prepare the yard for the afternoon after-school activities—which is true, but I also need to be alone with my thoughts.

I sway a little, unsteady on my feet as I make my way around the yard, my mind spinning and spinning until the vortex of thoughts is mirrored in my stomach, and I feel like I'm going to throw up.

Time to sit down a bit, draw in a few deep breaths, revisit the facts. One: the picture was unclear. Two: he came straight to me after the party, slipped in my bed.

But Daniel did break up with me once because he wanted to *experiment* and wasn't ready to commit. This was ten years ago, though. And this time, it's all been so different. So much sweetness underneath the passion, so many honest moments where we both let our guards down. It wasn't all in my head, was it? It wasn't just me building it up in my mind? Assuming there was more?

But the picture, that damn picture. Fuzzy and badly lit as it is, it's still enough to raise my doubts. He didn't tell me anything about the weekend except that he won't organize other bachelorette parties. I didn't read anything into it. Should I have? But he wouldn't have slipped right back in my bed if anything had happened.

By the time I head back inside, I feel like a

zombie, tired from fighting with myself, from measuring pros and cons in my mind. I'm going through the motions, willing this day to finally be over so I can get out of here. Helen and Karla keep glancing furtively at me, and I want to tell them to mind their own business. Except when your personal life is online, it's everyone's business. From time to time, I check my phone, but there's no message from Daniel. No surprise there. He said he'd keep his phone shut off today so he can concentrate on the group instead of dealing with calls related to the employee he fired.

He's on a day trip with a group, on a boat tour around the bay with a three-hour stop at Alcatraz. But he did tell me he'll go to his office after the tour, at around six o'clock.

So, the second the last kid is picked up, I head straight for his office, my mind made up.

***

Daniel

Lena is still at reception when I step inside my office building.

"Daniel, you're here. Finally. I need to—"

"Give me five minutes, Lena. Five minutes."

She nods, lips pressed together.

Inside my office, I finally turn on my phone. Jesus. Notifications keep popping up on my screen like mad. I have missed calls from my entire family.

Shit, did something happen to any of them? Or Caroline?

Then I see the dozen missed calls from my employees too. I've got about two dozen messages too. From Beatrix as well. What does she want from me? Speak of the devil, she's calling right now.

"Finally, you pick up," she exclaims.

"What's going on? Been on a tour all day, my phone was turned off."

"Great. I take it you haven't seen the photo? The article?"

"What photo? What article?"

She talks so fast, it's hard to keep up, but I do my best, swearing in between.

"I don't get it. They've got a photo of what? Nothing happened."

"Oh, for God's sake, Daniel. You're a veteran at this. The press spins everything around. They've got a picture of me hanging around your neck when you were bringing me back to the hotel, half passed out. Light's crappy, so is the angle. Looks like we're kissing."

I groan, dragging a hand down my face. How the hell did this happen? My stomach sinks. Has Caroline seen this? Did she believe it? Fuck.

"Beatrix, I got to go. Need to make an important call."

"Grant and I will be making a statement about this. You might get a bit of hate email from his fans, but—"

"I'll deal with it. But I need to go right now. I

have something important to do."

As soon as the call disconnects, I look up the article online. My entire body tenses, then relaxes again. The photo doesn't look too damning to me, but that might be because I was there and know what happened. Will Caroline believe me? I don't have much in my defense except my word.

Rumors about myself never bothered me, unless they could hurt my family. I've always focused on killing fake stories about my brothers. Since Logan and Sebastian are something close to golden boys, the made-up rumors about them are especially vicious. Just last month, a local trashy magazine was about to publish a "story" about Logan having another family. Blake and I called in about one hundred favors so it would never come out. Sebastian says fighting these things is futile. Maybe he's right. The family would know the truth anyway. But here's the thing: their kids aren't old enough to understand. They'd just get confused, maybe hero-worship their fathers less.

And when enough shit gets written about you, people eventually start believing that at least some of it has to be true. Since my eldest siblings have always been a more interesting target, I never cared much what was written about me. Now, though, I have a big reason to care, and her name is Caroline.

Sitting at the edge of my desk, I hover with my thumb over the screen of my phone. Nah, this conversation needs to be face-to-face. If my word is all she'll have, I best deliver it in person.

Lena pokes her head through my door. "There's someone here to see you, Daniel."

When the door opens wide, Caroline comes into view. She gives Lena a small smile, comes inside, and closes the door.

"You saw." Lamest opening if there ever was one.

Caroline nods, chewing on her lower lip, avoiding eye contact. "Just after lunch. The girls at work showed me." She takes a deep breath, snaps her gaze up. "And I decided I don't believe a word of it. That picture? Might look like a kiss, but I'm sure it was not."

I cross the room to her, wrap my arms around her waist, and kiss her hard. Fuck, I didn't even know how much I needed this. Her full trust. Her blind trust. She pushes her sweet body against mine, sighs against my mouth. As long as she trusts me, I don't care about anything else.

"You decided, hmm?" I murmur when we pause for a breath, keeping my arms where they are. I'm not letting her go. Not yet.

She nods, sighing quietly. "I panicked at first, but you've been so... I mean, everything between us has felt so real, I thought there's no way you'd do that." Uncertainty flickers in her eyes, her body tensing. "Would you?"

"No, love, I wouldn't." She relaxes in my arms. "Before you came, I was just thinking about how to build my defense when all I have is my word."

"Your word is enough for me," she says almost breathlessly, smiling up at me—best damn thing I've seen all day. I pull her even closer to me. Caroline is one of a kind. I knew that nine years ago too, but was too stupid to fully appreciate it. Now I'm going to show her how much I appreciate her, every day. I kiss the tip of her nose, her forehead, dust my lips to her temple.

"Here is the entire story: Beatrix was drunk, I carried her back to the hotel. Her friends helped her to her room. There's nothing more to it."

"I believe you."

Just like that. She believes me.

"Thank you for trusting me."

"This feels different than before." Her eyes widen, and she immediately casts her glance away, shaking her head as if chastising herself for saying out loud something she wasn't supposed to. She's adorable when she has entire conversations in her head, but I want to be part of this particular one.

"Different how?" I nudge.

"Never mind." She tries to wiggle out of my arms, but I just keep her more firmly in place.

"I want to know."

"No, you do not. These are things better kept for girls' night out. Women dissect these topics for hours at a time. Men are more straightforward, and feelings talk sends them running for the hills, and—"

"Give me more credit." I kiss the tip of her nose again. "Come on, try me. How is it different?"

"It feels deeper. More real."

"Thank God I'm not the only one feeling this way."

***

Caroline

Did he just say that?

"Dan," I whisper, but don't say more because he seems to want to continue talking, and I want to soak up every word.

"Back in college, I cared about you, but not like this. I liked how much fun we had together. Liked undressing you every chance I got. I like those things now too, but also our quiet nights together, asking you about your day, telling you about mine. These last couple of weeks haven't been the easiest, but knowing you're mine, all sweet and wild. I like building a life together with you, Caroline."

"So, what you mean is, before you used to enjoy the sun with me, and now you also like holding an umbrella over me when it rains."

He furrows his brow, looking confused. "What?"

I smile sheepishly. "Sorry, my mom used to say that: love isn't just about enjoying the sunny days together, but holding an umbrella for each other when it rains."

"Ah, I get it."

He seals his mouth over mine, kissing me hard. His hands move around my back, slide down my ass, groping me shamelessly. Then he kisses down my neck, my shoulder. Feeling his lips and frantic breath on my bare skin sends sparks all over my nerve endings. His mouth becomes greedier still, descending on my collarbone.

"What are you doing?" I whisper.

"I need you."

"Ri—right now?"

"Right now. I'm not going to allow you to leave this office until you come."

I let out a sound of exasperation mixed with excitement, but don't make a single attempt to wiggle out of his arms, or to stop him. I want this, his unrestrained passion.

He kisses me again, harder, as if he hasn't kissed me in weeks. When he unhitches his lips, he directs his attention to my chest. I'm wearing a knee-length wool dress, and thick stockings that reach my upper thighs. I'm also wearing a push-up bra, so my girls are squished together nicely. Daniel clearly appreciates this, dragging his lips on the tops of my breasts.

"You drive me crazy," he murmurs. "We're going to have to be quiet."

A thrill runs through me, jolting my cells alive. This is going to be fun.

I lean into him, kissing his lips, his jaw. He has a light scruff I adore. It grazes my lips, but just barely. It's a little rough, a lot masculine. Like Daniel.

I want to kiss every inch of him, but one look at Daniel makes it clear he has other plans. Those sinful dark eyes are trained on me, so full of lust and determination it makes my stomach flutter. He towers over me, skimming his hands over my shoulders, down my arms. His mouth is everywhere, nipping at my neck, grazing my shoulder. I'm shuddering in anticipation, not knowing where he'll put his lips next. Will it be my chest, my shoulders again? He does neither, instead whirling me around, pushing my hair to one side, and kissing the back of my neck until I'm trembling in his arms. I decide to stop trying to anticipate his every move and just allow myself to be surprised. And holy hell, does he ever surprise me by cinching the dress up at my sides, lifting it up, up, up. Then he pushes the thong to one side, driving a finger inside me. I buckle forward, a gasp escaping my lips.

"Quiet," he growls.

"How do you expect me to be quiet when you do this?"

Daniel moves the finger in and out of me, sliding a second one inside.

"I love that you're so wet for me, Caroline." His voice is a low, sinful whisper. When he slides his fingers out, moving to my clit, I nearly bite my tongue with the effort of staying quiet. I won't be able to do it. He circles my bundle of nerves until my entire body tightens up.

With a sharp exhale, I push his hand away, turning to face him. Time to give him some of his own medicine. Before he can do anything, I lower myself onto my knees, work on his belt, freeing him, and *holy shit*. The sight of him in his clothes with just his cock hanging out is surreal. I want to eat all of him up, one lick at a time. But that's too ambitious a project for right now, so I settle for licking all over his erection. Up to the base, back to the crown, dipping my tongue in the crevice right under the tip. Daniel lets out a low, guttural groan.

"On my desk, Caroline."

Holy bananas, his tone is doing wicked things to me. So of course, instead of doing that, I take him deeper in my mouth. Daniel gasps, the veins on his neck cording briefly. Then he pulls out and helps me to my feet.

"I said on my desk." He swipes his tongue over my lips before claiming my mouth. I feel myself walk backward and then the edge of the desk presses against my ass. Daniel hoists me up onto it. I let my flats drop to the floor.

"On your elbows."

I do just that, perching my feet on the edge of the desk.

"You look sexy in these stockings," he says as I gather my dress around me, and I make a mental note to wear them with garters next time. He pushes my panties to one side. But just when I think he's going to drive inside me, he bends down, kissing me right on my folds. My hips lift off the desk, pressing against his face.

He slides his tongue inside me, his thumb pressing on my clit. Oh God, this is all too much. Tension strums through me, intensifying quickly.

Too quickly.

I'm right on the cusp of an orgasm, but Daniel stops, instead sliding inside me, covering my mouth with his hand. I explode the moment he enters me, spasming around him, my groans muffled by his palm. Then he brings his hands under my ass, lifting it a little. Fingers pressed deep into my glutes, he starts loving me in earnest, hard, fast, and desperate.

"Come closer," he rasps in between thrusts, and I understand what he means, because I feel the same way too. I want—need—to be closer to him. Touching isn't really possible in this position, but I want to be as close to him as possible.

I push myself up, almost in a sitting position, leveling myself on my palms, changing the angle between us. Daniel thrusts against a point so deep inside me that my tongue sticks to the roof of my mouth. He leans over slightly and our mouths clash halfway in a frantic kiss. I can taste both of us in this kiss, and it is the damned sexiest thing. We kiss each other's sounds of pleasure. The muscles in my arms scream in protest, the edge of the desk cutting into the soles of my feet as I meet his desperation with equal fervor.

"Fuck, I need to touch you," he said hoarsely. "I need your skin."

He doesn't finish the sentence. Instead, he lifts me off the desk, laying me down on the carpet. And then he unbuttons his shirt faster than I've ever seen him. My work is easier; I just lift my dress over my head, unclasp my bra and throw it somewhere in the room. Then Daniel lies on top of me, every inch of my torso touching his front. The skin-on-skin contact is like a breath of fresh air.

"I needed to be close to you like this," he whispers in my ear as he slides inside me.

"So did I. But I didn't know how to ask."

"I have a confession to make." He touches my cheek with the tip of his nose tenderly. "I don't know if I'm falling for you all over again, or if I never stopped loving you."

My eyes well with emotion. "I never stopped."

He looks straight down at me, smiling before covering my mouth with his. We rock against each other, a tangle of limbs, caresses, and kisses until we both shatter from the sensations.

Limp with pleasure, we remain sprawled on the floor, drawing our breaths. Right until a knock at the door startles us. Jumping to our feet, we arrange our clothes as quickly as possible. Daniel opens the door, and Lena hovers in front of it.

"Sorry, Daniel, but it's late, and I'm having dinner with some friends. Is there anything you need me to do before I leave? How do you want to handle the Beatrix issue?"

"Don't worry about it. She and Grant will make a statement. There's not much else to do except wait for it to die down."

"Do you think this has anything to do with Justin?"

Daniel narrows his eyes, considering this. "I bet he paid someone at the LA hotel to take pictures for him. Go to your dinner. Sorry I kept you waiting."

She glances at me, hides a small smile. My entire face feels on fire.

"No problem. Have a good night."

When he closes the door, I cover my cheeks with my hands. "She knows."

"Nah."

"She *knows*."

"She suspects. Different things. But since she's leaving anyway...." He wiggles his eyebrows. "We could pick up where we left."

"Daniel Bennett, are you propositioning me again?"

"Yes."

I narrow my eyes, planting my hands on my hips. Right, this is supposed to be the "stern woman look"—something Mom and Jenna Bennett always pulled off to perfection. I have a hunch I look ridiculous, but persistence leads to mastery.

"I will have you know that was cheap." It also made all my lady parts tingle, because I'm just as cheap, but I'll keep that to myself.

"Caroline, don't play the proper card with me. I know you too well." Stepping closer, he adds in a lower octave, "And I just had you on my desk and the floor of my office."

"It was worth a try, though," I say with a shrug. Then I have a wicked thought, and well, since we just established *proper* isn't cutting it for us, why not voice it? "I won't mind if you take advantage of me some more once we get out of here, though."

His eyes widen, and he exhales sharply. One of his hands twitches as if he wants to touch me right here and now, and is barely restraining himself.

"You're a little wicked thing," he murmurs.

"All your fault. You stand there, all hard muscle, full lips, and sexy eyes, what's a girl to do?"

I'm enumerating all this on my fingers, looking down at them. When I raise my gaze to him, I startle at the vulnerability etched on his expression.

"What do you feel when you're with me, Caroline?"

"I feel that I belong in your arms."

He exhales, and for a brief second, I wonder if he really thought I feel anything less. He takes one of my hands, kisses my palm, then moves my hand up his cheek, leans into my touch. He looks so vulnerable, I don't know what to make of it. So I follow my instinct, stepping closer and rising on my toes to kiss him. He responds with so much tenderness, it makes my insides melt. I lace my arms around his neck and put as much heart as I can in the kiss. We only part when we both need a mouthful of air.

He still looks out of sorts, almost nervous. I wish I knew what has him so on edge. That would make softening said edge so much easier.

Before I have a chance to ask, Daniel moves around to the back of his desk, picks something up in his fist from the top drawer, and returns to me, holding it up.

"I want you to have this," he says.

"A key?"

"To my apartment."

"Oh, sure. Want me to water your plants while you're gone to Sydney?" I make a mental inventory of them. There are only three pots.

He shakes his head. "No, I want you to have it. For good."

Oh. Oh!

Now I understand why he was nervous. If I'm honest, I've become jittery myself in the two seconds since his meaning clicked into my mind. Then my heart swells with emotion.

"Wow, are you sure?" I ask. Wrong approach, because his expression hardens a bit.

"If you don't want—"

"I do want it," I assure him. "But I don't want you to regret it."

He's smiling now, and some of my anxiety bleeds away. "It's a little fast, but it also feels like I've been waiting ten years to do this."

I take the key, and if I were alone, I'd hug the tiny scrap of metal to my chest. Well, on second thought, why shouldn't I? I've never been shy about expressing myself, and Daniel is intimately aware of my little displays of craziness. So, I hug it to my chest, and shimmy my hips in a small dance too. He's giving me a piece of his heart, and I make a silent promise to cherish it, take care of it. Yes, this feels like it's moving faster than the wind, but I can learn to fly at his speed.

He laughs, cups my face, and kisses me again. "I love seeing you so happy. Making you happy."

"Back at you. Just giving you heads-up, but I'm so happy right now, I'd do anything you ask me."

"See, now giving me carte blanche like this is dangerous."

"No, it's not. I trust you."

"You do?"

"Yeah. I trust you to take advantage of me thoroughly and completely."

Daniel steps closer, leans into my private space until he's so close, we're breathing the same air. His eyes have a dangerous glint, and heat rushes through me. How can he do this? How can he still take my breath away? Still make me weak in the knees with nothing more than a look? In all these years, I haven't grown immune to his charms in the least. If anything, I've become more susceptible.

Right now, I feel particularly close to him. I tighten my grip on the key and can't help smiling from ear to ear. I'm going to make a copy of the key to my apartment for him when he returns from Sydney.

Chapter Twenty-Six

Caroline

We spend the night at his apartment but don't sleep at all, what with his early flight. Plus, we need to get our fill of each other before he leaves on his trip. He'll be gone for the rest of the week. Call it advance lovemaking.

"Can you check the airport website for any delays while I shower?" he asks from the bathroom.

"Sure."

I check the airport's website, and the flight is still on schedule. Then I make the mistake of opening his Facebook app. It's a habit, because I do that almost every morning. And I freeze. The app opened on the page for his business, and he has a flood of messages. Some private, some for everyone to see.

How dare you break up that couple! Grant finally found himself a nice woman to settle down with. You should be ashamed.

Wow, I never knew Beatrix and Grant were America's new *it*-couple, but it's not like I'm up to date with celebrity gossip, and judging by the number of hate messages Daniel received, they have quite the fans. Some public messages are even worse, insinuating the photo looks as if Daniel's taking advantage of her.

What the hell? How can people just throw around accusations like this? It's insane. I barely stave off the urge of replying to every single one of them, give them a piece of my mind. By the time Daniel comes back from the shower, I've worked myself into a frenzy, pacing the room.

"What's wrong?" he asks. I shove the phone in front of him.

"These people. How can they say all this?"

Daniel frowns at the screen, shakes his head. "Things will settle down after Grant and Beatrix make their statement, but I'll have my PR team on this anyway."

He dresses, checks his luggage with supreme calm.

"How can you be so calm about it?" I ask, putting on yesterday's dress and the tights, but foregoing the panties. "Doesn't it bother you? To read all those things?"

"No. I know you don't believe them, and my family certainly doesn't. Anyone else can have a field day for all I care. It'll die down."

"But—but won't it affect your business?"

He grins, pulling me into a hug. "Don't worry, if the business goes bust, I'll retrain. Think I'll be good at anything else? I can always be a stay-at-home dad to that entire brood we're going to adopt."

Wow, wow, wow. Every fiber in my body melts.

"You joker," I whisper, my voice thick with emotion. "I can't believe you'll be gone for the entire week. And I hate the time zone difference."

"Me too, but we'll work around it. Come on. Time to go or I'll be late. If I miss the plane, I'll never hear the end of it from Christopher for not using the private jet."

"Why aren't you?"

"Jet's engine's small, Australia's far. Would've had to stop for fuel a few times. Not worth it. Trip's long enough as it is. Ready to go?"

I'm going with him to the airport since I'll be driving his car back. "Yeah, but I'm hungry. How about I buy both of us a sandwich and coffee while you get the car out of the garage?"

"Sounds good."

We ride the elevator down together and I step out on the ground floor, crossing the large lobby area. The doorman isn't here. Weird. In all the times I've been here, I've never seen the entrance area unsupervised. When I step outside the building, I realize why the doorman isn't in his usual spot: he's out here, talking sternly to a young man, camera hanging from his neck. A reporter, clearly. My stomach constricts when I hear him utter the name "Daniel Bennett."

"He'll want to give his side of the story to the press, with everything they're saying out there. This is for his own good," the reporter says.

"You're not going inside this building. If you barge in again, I'll call the police," the doorman says.

"Tell him I'm down here, then. He'll want to say something in his defense. Unless what they're saying about him *is* true, and that's why he's taking the coward's way out, ignoring everything. I can write about that too if I don't get anything. Won't reflect well on him at all."

Something snaps inside me. Maybe it's because I was already so worked up on Daniel's behalf since I saw those comments, or because the idea of people trashing him even more makes me see red, but this is the last straw. I stride toward the pair of them with determination.

"Don't you dare write more lies," I tell him, fighting to keep my temper under control. "Daniel is a good man, and all those things are just that—lies."

"And you are?" he asks, brow raised.

"We're dating. And I know Daniel hasn't cheated."

Loud honking startles me. Daniel's car is right at the end of the ramp coming out from the underground garage. He gestures to me in a "come here" motion with his head, and I don't hesitate. Without another glance at the reporter or the doorman, I practically run toward the car, hearing the reporter fire off question after question behind me.

By the time I climb in the car, I realize I'm shaking. Daniel drives off right away.

"Caroline, what happened? Was that a reporter?"

I nod, trying to speak past the lump in my throat.

"You didn't tell him anything, I hope?"

Swallowing hard, I fiddle with my thumbs, then tell him exactly what happened.

"Are you mad at me?" I ask quietly.

"For jumping to my defense? No. But this might make things hard for you, Caroline. They might try to contact you again."

"I'll just ignore them."

"Not so easy sometimes."

My stomach grumbles loudly as I sink lower into my seat, enjoying the soft, welcoming leather. "Crap, I forgot about the sandwiches and the coffee."

Daniel puts a hand over my laced fingers, which are still slightly shaky.

"I'll get some food into you right away." True to his word, he pulls in the parking lot of a diner a few minutes later. "Be right back. Wait here."

He returns with coffee, sandwiches, donuts, and muffins.

"What's all this?" I ask, pointing to the sweet stuff.

"I have three sisters. Sugar's the answer to everything."

"That's a gross generalization of the female population."

"Subjective, I admit. But I'm taking my chances."

As he drives away, speeding in the direction of the airport, I down a sandwich and a muffin.

"You're right. I do feel a bit better. I don't

know why I got so worked up."

"It's normal, don't fret about it. But since you feel better, I want you to listen to me."

"Oh no, you're going to admonish me. Can I go back to pretending I'm still scared?"

He laughs. "I told you I'm not mad. I'm not going to admonish you, just give you some advice. Don't talk to the press again, at all. You see a reporter, you walk the other way around. Promise?"

"Sure."

"I mean it. You don't want to become their target. It's exhausting." He takes one hand from my lap, bringing it to his mouth and kissing my knuckles.

"Keep your eyes on the road," I say.

"They are. Don't need them to do this." He turns my hand around, kisses my palm. "That was a sweet thing you did. I thought I was an expert at loving you, but you make me fall in love more every day."

I smile, shimmying in my seat. "See? I don't need sugar. All I need is you sweet-talking and I'm walking on sunshine."

We reach the airport far too soon for my taste, but just in the nick of time for him to catch his plane. He gives me a hurried kiss and a "take care," and then he's gone.

***

The day drudges on slower than ever, leaving me too much time to think, to worry. About what in particular, I don't know, but there is a nasty feeling in my stomach, and it won't go away. By noon, a statement from Daniel's company is published, and by the end of the day, Beatrix and her fiancé release one too, assuring everyone it was just a nasty rumor and their wedding plans are continuing without a hitch.

I'm not mentioned anywhere, which gives me some peace of mind. When I get home, I decide my funk is just about Daniel leaving, the prospect of being one week without him, and the lack of sleep from last night catching up with me.

After a quick dinner, I head straight to my bedroom. I'm about to change into my pajamas when I notice one of Daniel's T-shirts by the bed. He must have forgotten it here. Smiling, I pick it up, sniff it tentatively. Smells worn, but in a pleasant way. It smells like Daniel, so I wear it to bed, feeling a little closer to him this way.

I wake up with a start before my alarm rings. Light is streaming from outside, so it's morning already. Did I sleep in? Forget to set my alarm? Confused, I blink, look around the room, then realize the source of the disturbance. My phone is ringing; the caller is a number I don't recognize.

Briefly, I consider not answering. What if it's a reporter? Well, if it is, I can just hang up. This could be important. Keeping my fingers crossed, I answer.

"Hello?"

"Is this Miss Caroline Dunne?"

"Who's asking?"

"I'm calling from the San Francisco General Hospital. Your father was just brought in, and you're listed as his emergency contact."

I jump out of bed so fast I nearly sprain my ankle. "Is he all right? What happened to him?"

"We don't know what happened, but he suffered a fall."

"How—how is he?" I hold my breath, my throat clogging up.

"Nothing certain yet. We're going to take him up for a scan shortly, do some more tests. Do you want to keep him company in between tests?"

"Yes, of course. I'll be out the door in ten minutes. Five. Tell my dad I'll be there, okay? I'll be there. What floor?"

I commit all the details to memory, then end the call. I'm out the door in four minutes.

At the hospital, it's not so easy to find my dad. Turns out the details she gave me on the phone weren't correct. Or maybe my mind's so scattered that I memorized it wrong. That's a possibility.

"Please check your records," I beg the receptionist.

"Miss, our computer system is down at the moment," she repeats for the third time. "I'll tell you as soon as they start back up. It shouldn't be more than a few minutes."

I can barely hold back my frustration.

"Have you tried calling your father?"

I nearly want to slap myself because of course I *haven't* thought about calling him. What an idiot I am. He'll tell me where he is. Except if he's too weak, or too sick, but I refuse to consider that possibility. Drawing in a deep breath, I step away from the reception desk, into a quieter corner, and dial his number. It rings, and rings, and rings, then goes to voice mail. Panic flares through me, but I dial again. This time, he answers.

"Hey, baby girl." His voice is so weak it scares me.

"Hi, Dad. I'm at the hospital. Where are you exactly?"

"Eighth floor, don't know the room number."

"Doesn't matter, I'll find you. I'll be there in a few minutes. I'll find you."

Don't panic, Caroline. Don't panic. I repeat this mantra from the second I end the conversation as I head to the elevator. I try to concentrate on the positive aspect: he answered. It means he's not in surgery or in a coma. Both very good things. But why did he sound so weak, then?

Stepping out of the elevator, my eyes sweep around to identify whoever is part of the personnel. Scrubs. The first two I ask aren't any more helpful than the lady on the ground floor, but the third time's the charm.

"Oh, Martin Dunne. Yes, follow me. He wasn't brought in too long ago."

I follow the nurse through the labyrinth of corridors until we reach a small room with two beds.

Only one is occupied, by my dad. I bite my tongue to keep from gasping. A scratch runs at the side of his head, from his cheek right up to his temple, and he's white as a sheet. Somehow, he looks tiny in that bed, white linen up to his chest.

"Hey, baby girl."

"What happened?" I look at the nurse, who holds up her hands to indicate she doesn't know.

"I'm going to leave the two of you and take him up for a scan in about twenty minutes."

As she leaves, I sit on the edge of Dad's bed. He brings out a hand from under the sheet, and I grasp it reassuringly. Leaning in close, I inspect his scratch. Up close, I can see they smeared a yellowish substance along it. Okay, at least they took care of this.

"I'm okay, baby girl. Don't you worry about me."

He sounds and looks weak, and nothing at all like my dad, so worrying doesn't even begin to cover it. I'm now actively fighting to keep the panic at bay. Little kids fall all the time, but a fall at his age is no joke.

"Did you hurt anything else besides your head?" I ask.

"Nah. Just a scratch. Doctor said I might have a concussion too."

Oh, dear God. Again, at his age, that's no small thing.

"What happened? You fell?"

He lifts his head, motioning to the glass of

water on the small bedside table. Grabbing it, I hold it for him to drink. As he sips, I notice scratches on his left hand too, running up to his elbow. He fell on his entire left side, then?

"It was a weird morning," he says after he's done drinking. "Woke up earlier than usual because I had a delivery at the store. When I arrived, there were three guys out front. Never seen them in the neighborhood." He pauses, frowns, as if he forgot his train of thought. As much as I want to know the whole story, I don't push. "Didn't look like they'd come to rob anything, were too relaxed. Too out in the open. One had a camera around his neck."

I stiffen at the mention of the camera.

"They started asking me questions about Daniel. About you. Personal questions. I figured they were reporters, tried to shake them off. Kept following me around, pestering me with questions. They didn't leave even when the delivery truck came, insisted I give them your home address." He pauses again, this time for a longer time span. "When I didn't, they became even pushier. Couldn't shake them off at all, tried harder, somehow ended up on the pavement. Knocked my head hard. One of them called an ambulance. I figured it had something to do with that article about Daniel yesterday," he continues.

"You saw it?" I ask in surprise.

"Yeah. Any truth in it?"

I shake my head, in no mood to talk about that. All I want is for a doctor to come in and tell me my daddy will be fine.

The nurse returns a few minutes later with the doctor. I immediately spring to my feet, anxious to question the hell out of him, wring out every detail. Briefly I wonder if I can take the doctor to one side, ask him without my dad overhearing. But that's silly. Dad is not a baby, and this is *his* health we're talking about.

Can't help wanting to protect him from bad news, though. It's a habit I formed back when Momma was sick. I used to talk to the doctors when Dad wasn't around, because he burst into tears whenever there was bad news. She had advanced carcinoma. There was always bad news.

"Can you please walk us through everything?" I ask the doctor.

"Of course. We did a physical exam when he arrived. All signs point to a concussion, but a CT scan will remove any doubt of anything more serious, like a brain bleed or a subdural hematoma. We're keeping him the entire day, anyway. At this age, it'll be a big risk sending him home. A bleed can develop slowly in patients of a certain age, and it's best if he's here if it happens."

"Now wait a minute," Dad exclaims. "I just hit the pavement. What's all that talk about staying the entire day?"

"It's standard procedure," the nurse says good-naturedly.

"We'll know more after the scan," the doctor continues. "I don't want to alarm you if there's nothing to be alarmed about."

Yeah, *that* sounds reassuring. I bite back the retort, not wanting to worry my dad, not wanting to look worried for his sake. I have plenty of time to freak out on my own, once they take him away. For now, I square my shoulders and paste a smile on my face.

"It's all standard procedure, Dad. Don't worry."

He protests while the nurse and I help him out of bed. He's not steady on his feet, which is why she puts him in a wheelchair, and I swear to God, the sight of him in it breaks my heart. He looks so scared and defeated, sitting in the wheelchair in that huge hospital gown. An irrational fear grips me, and all I can think about when they wheel him away is my mom.

Please, please, please, Momma, don't take Daddy to you just yet.

Chapter Twenty-Seven

Caroline

Filled with too much energy to sit, I pace up and down the corridor, worry eating at me. Gathering my wits, I call the principal to let him know I won't make it today. To be on the safe side, I take off tomorrow too, so I can dote on Dad. He's very understanding. The man will have a batch of his favorite donuts on his desk on my first day back. What I really want to do is call Niall, but I'll wait until they return with Dad so I can give him all the details.

God, how I wish Niall was here. I need to be next to someone who loves Dad just as much as I do. I can't get the image of him in that wheelchair out of my mind. But I have to. Panicking would do no one any good. He'll be back any minute now, and I can't be in the midst of a panic attack when he does.

Fifteen minutes later, the nurse is back with Dad, a doctor on their heels.

"There are no signs of bleeding on the brain," the doctor informs me. "But we still want to keep him under observation for a few hours, because he lost consciousness during the fall."

Dad falls asleep almost as soon as they bring

him back, so I head back to the corridor and call Niall. He doesn't pick up, but after I text him **Need to talk to you as soon as possible**, he calls me right back. I tell him everything, starting with the article about Daniel and ending with Dad's trip to the hospital.

"Jesus, how is he feeling?" Niall asks. "Is he coherent?"

"Yeah, just tired."

"Can I talk to him?"

"He's sleeping right now. He looks so small and vulnerable in the hospital gown, Niall."

"Everyone does," he says gently. "I'm going to try to talk to a doctor I know there. Maybe they can send me the scans over, so I can look at them too."

"You—you think they might have missed something?"

"No, but it never hurts to have a second opinion. And well, I'll feel more at ease if I look at them myself."

I understand the sentiment perfectly. If I could read CT scans, I'd want to see them too.

"How are you feeling?" he continues.

"Scared… guilty."

There is a short pause, and Niall says, "You shouldn't have talked to the reporter."

I swallow hard. "He was there, spewing nonsense about Daniel. Trust me, if you'd been there, you wouldn't have been able to keep your mouth shut either."

"Is there any truth in the article about Daniel?"

"No," I say without hesitation. "Look, this will all blow over soon, and Dad is all right. No harm done."

"What if it happens again? Daniel's company is a revolving door for celebrities. Only a matter of time before he gets caught in the crossfire again."

I press my lips together. I have no comeback because it's something I fear too.

"We'll cross that bridge when we come to it," I say firmly.

"How about Dad? He's not getting any younger. What if he gets caught in the crossfire too, and next time he isn't so lucky?"

I ball my hands into fists. "That is a low blow, Niall."

"I'm worried for Dad, okay? For you too." he says angrily, then exhales sharply. "Do you want me to fly to San Francisco? I can catch the next plane."

Despite his harsh words, I appreciate the offer. "It would mean a lot of trouble for you, though, right?"

"It would, but I'll come if you need me. If Dad needs me."

"It's okay, Niall. I'm handling this. Dad's okay. Don't worry."

"Okay. I'm going to hang up now and try to reach my contact at the San Francisco hospital, ask for the CT scans. Call me if anything changes."

"I will."

I'm seething after our conversation, alone with my thoughts, which are even darker after the fallout with Niall. At first, I'm mad at myself for allowing him to get to me like this. But then I have to be honest with myself: his words got to me because I've had those same thoughts too, the same fears.

I play with my phone in my hands, itching to talk to Daniel, to hear his voice. But the time difference to Australia is seventeen hours. It's still nighttime there. So I call Blake instead and tell him everything.

"The fucking media. Don't worry. Daniel and I will sort this out. Best not to take your dad back to his house today. It's too close to the store and there's a slight chance one of the reporters hung back."

"Sure, I'll take him to my apartment. They don't seem to have my address yet."

"Perfect. What did Daniel say?"

"Haven't talked to him."

"Why?"

"It's the middle of the night in Sydney."

"So what? He'll get wrinkles if you wake him up from his beauty sleep? I'll talk to him as soon as I hang up. Call if you need anything else."

"Sure. Thanks, Blake."

Far from easing my mind, the conversation with Blake only sets me on edge more. Now Dad can't even go home because of me. I go back inside his room, sit next to his bed. I brought this on Dad, no questions about that. I look at his figure huddled under the sheets, struck again by how frail and old he

46 refining

looks, and somehow even smaller than before. What if this does happen again? Niall *is* right. Daniel's company is a revolving door for celebrities.

Damn it, this is not the time to have a "dark night of the soul." I read about that once, and didn't quite understand what it meant. Well, now I do. I feel as if I'm literally lost in the dark, with no idea which direction is the right one, what would lead me to safety.

Not that there is ever a good time to have a breakdown, but if I have one, I would have preferred to at least have chocolate on hand. Not the type I can find in a vending machine either, but homemade chocolate cake, the kind Mom used to bake. Yeah, I'm picky even when I'm having a breakdown.

I jump in my uncomfortable seat when my phone chimes and rush straight out of the room so it doesn't wake Dad. Then I glance at the screen, and my throat closes up a bit. Daniel is calling. Clearly Blake wasted no time.

"Hi!" I say.

"Blake told me everything. How's your dad?"

"Sleeping. Nothing came up on the scan, but they want to keep him under observation today because he was unconscious for a few seconds after he fell."

"I'm so sorry. Is there anything I can do? Is he comfortable there? Do you want him to be transferred to a private hospital? Are you comfortable?"

I can't help the wave of warmth spreading all

the way to my fingertips. I love that he cares so much.

"No, we're fine, but thank you."

"When are they discharging him?"

"In the evening, I suppose. I'll take him to my apartment, for tonight at least. Blake said it would be better if he didn't go back to his house, because it's too close to the store, and some reporters might be lingering there."

"I'm sorry about that."

"Not your fault. No one to blame but me and my big mouth." I drop my flats to the floor with a thud and curl my legs under me.

"I'm sorting everything out, okay? Tomorrow he'll be able to go back home."

"Dan, what if all this happens again? I'm scared."

"I can't promise it won't, but we'll be better prepared. I'll coach you about what to say to the press. It'll be easier dealing with them if you have some standard lines."

I laugh out loud. "Oh, Dan, I think you forget who you're talking to. When have I ever been able to stick to my lines? Wrong girlfriend for that."

The laughter dies on my lips. I have no idea where those words came from, but now that they're out in the open, I have to consider them. Maybe he really does need another girlfriend. One who can be coached into what to say, who wouldn't just say what she felt, what was on her mind. One who can not only keep up with his lifestyle but also help him thrive instead of making life more complicated for him. My heart breaks a little at the mere thought that I'm not enough. "I don't really fit into this part of your life, do I?"

"Don't be ridiculous. If it's necessary, I'll work less with public personas, or not at all."

Now I'm panicking. "You will not do such a thing. You run a successful business, and you won't change a profitable strategy because of me."

"We'll figure it out, okay?" When I say nothing, he adds, "Why didn't you call me, Caroline?"

"I knew you were asleep." For the first time, though, I realize there's more to it. I didn't call because I didn't want him to sense the fear and hesitation in my voice. The doubts.

"I'm getting on a plane in the morning, and—"

"No, no, no. We're fine. Sealing the deal in Sydney is important. Look, Dad's doctor is heading this way. We'll talk later, okay? I have to go now."

"Okay."

***

Daniel

"Do you have all that down?" I bark.

"Yes, Daniel, I'm not hearing impaired," my assistant says, displaying the first sign of impatience. I was wondering when she'd start picking on me.

Truthfully, I *want* to pick a fight with someone. Maybe that way I'll lose some of the frustration suffocating me.

"Okay. Keep me posted."

"Sure thing. Want me to call Coleson and Stanhill?"

"No, I'll call them myself."

The skyline in Sydney is still pitch dark, but I feel wide awake. Partly because I'm still functioning on San Francisco time. My body usually needs two days to beat the jet lag. But I've been on high alert since talking to Blake. After talking to Caroline, my mind started to spin. My priority, for now, is to make sure no reporter dickhead bothers her *or her family* any longer. The never-ending to-do list I'm dictating for my assistant is the start. Then I'll have to go through my own to-do list, call the right people, starting with Coleson and Stanhill.

"Are you getting any sleep?" she inquires.

"Got in a few hours. They'll have to do."

"So, you're going to be working in both timezones?"

"Looks like it."

"Well, have fun. I'm gonna start on the mile-long to-do list you just dictated to me. Bye, Daniel."

"Bye."

I'm going to call Stanhill first, then plow through the list of people I have to talk to. That should prevent me from replaying the conversation with Caroline in my mind over and over again.

Damn it, I can't stay in my room anymore. I'll

go to the hotel's gym, make all the calls while running on the treadmill. I need to move. Dressing in running gear, I head to the gym and am surprised to see a young woman behind the welcome desk. When I read the gym was open twenty-four hours a day, I assumed it was entirely self-service. First-class service, I suppose.

"Good evening." She smiles, hands me two towels. "Jet lag?"

"Yeah."

"We get that a lot. There are refreshments in the bar area inside the gym."

"Thanks."

There are three other hotel guests inside the gym, but I find a treadmill far enough away that I can make my calls without disturbing them.

I'm in the middle of my third call when Blake's name appears on the screen. I politely tell my conversation partner I'll call him back, then answer my brother.

"Did you find out which publication he was from?" I ask without further ado.

"Yes. *A-Lister Laundry.*"

"Okay, just got off the phone with Stanhill. He's drafting up all the cease and desist papers."

"I also talked to an insider from *Hollywood Gossip*," he says, referring to the tabloid that first published the picture. "You were right. They did get the picture from Justin Hamel."

"The idiot just signed his sentence. I'm going to sue the crap out of him."

"Did you talk to Caroline? Tell her this won't happen again? That it'll be easier to deal with the press once she knows what to tell them?"

"Yeah, I did. The conversation didn't go the way I hoped."

"So talk to her again."

"I will. She said she'll call me back. I'm still waiting."

"For fuck's sake, don't wait too long. Our sisters insist women need time to mull over things, but all my evidence points to the contrary."

"Thanks for the advice, Blake. I need to call Stanhill back. I'll talk to you later."

"Sure. But I'm serious. Don't wait too long."

After clicking off, I rewind the conversation with Caroline in my mind for the millionth time. I felt her slip away from me during our conversation, and I didn't know what to say to win her back. For that matter, I still have no clue what to say, or I'd call her back right this instant. The fear and worry in her voice paralyzed me.

I need a damn good plan before I talk to her, but my mind seems to be filled with fog thanks to the jet lag.

No matter how I spin it, this is all my fault, and the worst of it is I can't guarantee it won't happen in the future. What if something worse happens next time? What if Caroline herself gets in an accident? Just the thought of something bad happening to her gives me heartburn.

In the past few weeks, I looked up a few

adoption agencies, familiarized myself with the process. I want to spend the rest of my life with Caroline. I can see us together, in our home, complete with a white picket fence and a brood of kids. I want to hear her laughter every day, hear her soft breathing at night sleeping next to me, warming my bed and my life. I need her.

I love this woman. I want her safe and happy, always.

Chapter Twenty-Eight

Caroline

"You don't need to babysit me."

The conversation isn't going the way I hoped, though it's nothing less than I expected. Dad hasn't been upset by the news that he can't spend the night in his own house right until I made the mistake of saying the new arrangement means I can keep an eye on him.

"Dad, you had a serious fall. If you don't want me keeping an eye on you, I'll talk to the doctor, ask him to keep you overnight."

"You got your stubborn streak from your mother."

I barely suppress a grin. Dad can be such a child when it comes to hospitals. I have no power to convince a doctor to keep him for longer than necessary, but Dad hates hospitals enough that he doesn't want to risk me asking. Niall managed to get hold of the CT scans too, and his opinion mirrored the doctor's here.

I'm waiting for Dad to change in the bathroom when I hear two familiar voices coming through the open door.

"They said room 23B, right?" Summer asks.

"Yes. Oh look, it's this one. The B is a little faded."

The second voice belongs to Jenna Bennett. I smile for what feels like the first time today when the two women step inside the room.

"What are you doing here?"

"We just found out about the whole incident." Jenna glances around the room worriedly. "Where's Martin?"

I motion toward the bathroom. "Changing. They discharged him a few hours early, so we're going home."

Summer smiles, holding up one forefinger. "We have a proposition. Since you can't go back to Martin's house tonight, why don't we all go over to Mom and Dad's? Plenty of space, and more people to look after Martin."

I look from one woman to the other and barely bite back the impulse to hug them both. It isn't just the space I'm grateful for, but the company.

"That would be great, but let's see what Dad says. Whatever you do, don't mention the part about looking after him."

"Men." Jenna shakes her head, waves a hand. "Leave this to me."

Dad steps out the next second, his eyes widening. "Quite a welcome party, eh?"

Jenna smiles sweetly. "We would've been here earlier, but we just found out. Lucky you were still here. You're in excellent shape, I see."

"Thank you," Dad says, with an air that

indicates he's thinking, *Finally, someone sees things my way.*

I'm taking mental notes. First step, buttering up.

"Can I tempt you with a homemade dinner at our house? Maybe even spend the night? We had the grandkids over the weekend, and since they left, the house is so empty. Richard and I could use the company."

I stare at her. Forget taking notes. That level of mastery cannot be achieved by simply following a set of instructions. Even Summer looks at her mother in appreciation.

"She even plans to make chocolate mousse," Summer adds. Man, what a low blow. Chocolate mousse is Dad's favorite.

"Well, I had a concussion, not a heart attack, so I'd better eat as much sugar and butter while I can get away with it."

And the matter is settled.

Dinner lasts well into the night. Since Dad slept plenty during the day, he isn't in a hurry to go to bed. I stay with him out in the gazebo after Richard, Jenna, and Summer turn in.

"Great people, the Bennetts," Dad says.

"They are."

"What's on your mind, child? You've been sad the whole day, and it's not just about me."

I never could hide my feelings from Dad, so I tell him about the conversation with Daniel, my doubts, my fears. I even let a few tears slip. It's dark, and I'm sitting on the opposite side of the table from him. No one can see.

"Don't you worry about me. Next time an idiot shows up, I'll hose him. See how he follows me around soaking wet. I was just unprepared this time."

"But—"

"Caroline, you've loved this man for almost ten years."

I open my mouth, close it again. Can't argue there, and in any case, Dad didn't frame it like a question.

"Now you're telling me that you think you're not right for him because... what? Your lives are not one hundred percent compatible? Because you think a schoolteacher isn't glamorous enough for him? Good enough for him?"

I haven't actually uttered any of those words, but obviously Dad can make more sense of my jumbled words than I can.

"Let me tell you something. You're worth everything, and Daniel knows this. And another thing? Compatibility is overrated. Your mother and I agreed right out of the gate on maybe ten things during our entire marriage. Why do you think you kids each have two names?"

The corners of my mouth twitch. My middle name is Siobhan. "Which one was your idea?"

"Siobhan."

"Thank heavens Mom stuck to her guns, then."

Dad laughs, then goes serious again. "If I said black, she said white. If there was only one option available, she'd make up the second one just so we could disagree about it. And I don't regret any of those moments. She was the love of my life. I'd give a limb to have her back. And if it was the other way around, if it was your mother here in front of you, she'd say the same."

The tears are falling in earnest now, and I'm not even bothering to wipe them away. And Dad isn't done.

"Nothing came easy for us. Moving all the way from Ireland, away from our parents. Starting a family here with no one to rely on. Every couple has their challenges. Everyone has problems. That's life. One challenge after the next. And the best thing by far is to have someone you can love and trust by your side to take on those challenges."

I wipe my eyes and cheeks dry.

"Daniel is a successful man, and success comes with its own set of challenges. As I said, challenges come in many forms. With patience and compromise, you'll get far. You'll both make mistakes, but if you're willing to work on them together, they're halfway solved already."

"Wow," I say finally, moving to Dad's side of the table. I don't hesitate to lean into his open arms.

"Still my baby girl, eh."

"Yeah."

"Sleep on this, baby girl, and tomorrow give him a call. Talk to him. You'd be surprised how everything seems doable once you talk it through."

We make our way back to the house, but once I'm on my own, I dial Daniel's number. I can't afford sleeping on it. Thanks to the time zone difference, he'll be asleep after I wake up, and I want to hear his voice, talk to him now. Except the call goes directly to voice mail. Maybe he's in a meeting. I pace around the house, go to the kitchen. There is still some chocolate mousse left, and Jenna insisted so much for me to eat it at dinner that she won't mind if I eat it now, right? I need some sustenance.

I concentrate on the sweet treat, and after half an hour dial his number anew, but I get voice mail again. I have a sour taste in my mouth, despite having just swallowed the last of the mousse. Energy strums through me and I head outside, take a long walk on the property. An hour and a half long. Whatever meeting he's in, there have to be breaks. I try him again to no avail.

My heart seems to weigh double as I return to the house and climb in bed. When I talked to him today, I felt him put up some walls of his own. Will I be able to get through them? To reach him?

***

Since I go to bed at four o'clock, I wake up feeling hungover the next morning. I might have done a bit of crying in my pillow too. I'm still clasping my phone. That's how I fell asleep. I look at the screen and my stomach plummets. I have no messages, nothing. Thank God I took the day off today as well. I wouldn't have the energy to deal with a group of kids.

After dressing, I go down to the kitchen, only to find Dad already there and looking much better than I feel. Jenna is trying to feed him the contents of her entire fridge. I smell bacon and eggs, and my stomach rumbles. How I can still be hungry after all the mousse I had last night, I don't know. But hungry I am.

"Morning," Jenna greets. Dad merely waves, chewing on his breakfast.

"Where are Richard and Summer?" I ask.

"Summer's at the gallery. Richard is in the gazebo, repairing a loose board."

We make small talk over breakfast, and I do my best to assess Dad's health status without seeming overprotective. He truly does look much better than yesterday. He's no longer pale, and it helps that he isn't wearing the hospital gown anymore. He looks like my strong father again, not the sick man he seemed yesterday.

After breakfast, Dad goes out to help Richard, despite mine and Jenna's protests.

"I'm not a sick man." He shuts us down and strolls out of the room.

While I help Jenna clean up, my mind races to Daniel. Even if he had back-to-back meetings, he could at least have texted. Now I'm worrying not only that he might have dumped me cold turkey, but that something bad actually happened to him. For the tenth time this morning, I wonder if I should ask Jenna if she heard from him, but I don't want to worry her.

"Someone ate up all the chocolate mousse last night," Jenna comments with a smile.

"Was hard to resist it, knowing it was in there."

Jenna looks straight at me, and I have the distinct impression the woman can read my every thought.

"I was going to make apricot jam today," Jenna says.

"Oh, I'd love to help."

Working side by side with Jenna is pure bliss. She radiates calmness, relaxing me, making me feel safe, loved.

"It'll pass by quickly," Jenna says out of the blue.

I snap my head up from the table where I'm slicing apricots. "What?"

"This media attention. The good thing about gossip magazines is that by the time a new day rolls around, no one cares about yesterday's gossip."

"I suppose you're right."

"This happened to us too." Jenna takes the apricots I sliced and pours them into the large pot on the stove. She's now with her back to me, so I can't see her expression. "In the beginning, when Bennett Enterprises was on the rise, getting a lot of media attention, Richard and I had our share of run-ins with overeager reporters. It wasn't always easy. We weren't used to that kind of life. We had to be careful who we spoke to, what we said."

I strongly suspect Jenna hasn't told this to any of her kids, for fear she might sound ungrateful. "But rough patches come and go. Can't all be smooth sailing, can it?"

"No, it can't. But you've done a brilliant job with all of it, if you don't mind me saying." I join her at the stove and put a hand on her arm. Jenna is right. It's exactly what Dad said too, and I make up my mind on the spot.

I need to see Daniel. Forget calling him. I mean, the man isn't answering anyway. But I want to talk to him face-to-face. Once I was young and stupid, let him slip away from me. I'm definitely not that young anymore, and I like to think I got smarter over the years.

I will head to Sydney on the next flight. I thought about this the entire morning. What held me back was the fear Daniel wouldn't want me there, and the price of the airfare. Buying a ticket on such short notice comes with an astronomic cost—about a month's worth of rent. It would make a dent in my already depleted savings, but I don't care. It will be worth it. As to Daniel, well… I just won't let him push me away. I allowed it once, won't do so again.

There's also the small fact that I'm supposed to be working for the rest of the week. I'm not so sure the principal will be so understanding, no matter how good my cocoa cookies and donuts are. But I just have to take the risk. There's no way around it. I'm all in, and I want Daniel to know this. I've been all in from the beginning but was afraid to admit it, even to myself. Not anymore.

"Jenna, do you mind if I leave in about an hour?"

"Oh. Why?" Jenna stops in the act of stirring the pot.

"I want to fly out to Daniel. The next plane to Sydney leaves in a few hours. Need to go home to get my passport and pack a bag."

Jenna chuckles and raises both hands, sending a few drops of marmalade flying around the kitchen.

"Ah, I can't let you do that, my child."

I blink. "Why?"

Jenna checks the time on the grandfather clock on the wall. "Because Daniel will be landing in about four hours."

Chapter Twenty-Nine

Daniel

By the time I step out of the plane, my legs are stiff. My entire body is protesting. A trip to Australia is always exhausting. Reversing the trip within forty-eight hours is insane.

I was afraid I'd fall asleep during the cab ride to my parents' house, but I needn't have worried. The cabbie's murderous driving skills have me on high alert.

When he slows to a stop, I tip him anyway, out of sheer joy that I survived the ride. I walk the long path from the gate to the house, my spirit lifting with every step. I called Mom as soon as I had any semblance of a plan. I could've called any of my siblings, but when the going gets rough, no one's better at being on top of things and calming the waters than Mom. I also knew Caroline needed Mom's soothing presence after the entire incident.

I can't wait to see the look of surprise on her face when she sees me. As I approach the front door, I see my father and Martin on the far end of the property. From here, I can't assess Martin's appearance, but I assume the man is recovering well if he can traipse the distance.

I follow the sound of Caroline's and Mom's voices to the kitchen. Caroline is laughing, and I let the sound wash over me, melt away some of my worries. As soon as I step in the kitchen, I feel like I'm literally going to melt. There are about a million degrees inside, but I forget all about it at the fantastic sight in front of me.

Mom and Caroline are huddled around three large pots at the stove, tasting the contents. Caroline looks relaxed. She's also sexy as hell, wearing some shorts I've never seen on her and a washed-out tank top. Her hair is up on top of her head, messy strands hanging out.

Catching sight of me, she lets out a little shriek, then covers her mouth.

"What are you doing here already?" she asks through her fingers.

I look at my mother in defeat. "You told her." I should have seen this coming. Keeping secrets isn't her forte.

She shrugs.

"Told her you'd be here in four hours. Kept an element of surprise."

Oh, how helpful.

"With that said, I'm out of here," she continues. "Martin, Richard, and I are going out for dinner."

"It's early afternoon," Caroline points out.

Mom winks. "Early dinner. The house is all yours."

The second she leaves the kitchen, Caroline

goes into a frenzy. "I need to shower. And change clothes. I was going to before you came. I'm wearing Summer's old clothes, and I'm sweaty. Stinky too, I think." She sniffs the air a bit, then drops her face into her hands. "I can't believe I sniffed myself in front of you."

Adorable as it is to see her this flustered, I have to put a stop to this before she works herself into even more of a frenzy. I roll my suitcase against a wall, then head to her.

"Stop driving yourself crazy."

If I thought my words would calm her, I was dead wrong. She's shaking like a leaf, and a strand of her hair is clinging to her cheek. After several attempts to push it away, I realize there is marmalade in it. I clean her up with tap water and can't help myself. I kiss her. I wanted to say a million things first, but I need this more. I need it desperately. I tease my tongue over her lower lip until she parts her mouth, granting me access. She tastes like apricots and sugar, and I wrap my arms around her, pull her flush against me, greedy for her warm body, her soft skin. Even lost in her as I am, I can still feel her shuddering, and not in a good way.

"Why are you so nervous?" I ask, pulling back. I'm nervous too, but she seems downright scared.

She takes a deep breath and stares at a point on my chin, clearly avoiding my eyes. "You didn't fly over from Australia to break up with me, right? For my own good or something?"

Ah, I understand her worry perfectly now, given our past. "No. Absolutely not."

"Okay." Tension bleeds away from her limbs. She nods, smiles up at me. "Okay. But if you had flown in for that, I wasn't going to let you do it. Not without putting up a fight first."

"Will you look at that? My little tigress."

"I'm sorry about how I handled things on the phone. I was scared and the stupid came out."

"You had all the reasons to be scared, don't apologize." I take her hands in mine, steeling myself. *Here goes nothing.* "I can't promise something like this won't happen again. I'm going to do my best, but I can't guarantee it. I'll make whatever changes are necessary in my business to minimize the risk, cut out all the celebrity outings, but I can't guarantee it won't happen again. Can you live with that? Can you love me despite that?"

***

Caroline

The strain in his voice cuts through me.

"I don't need you to promise me anything, Dan. And you will not change your business for me. I'll learn to deal with it. You can teach me. Coach me, as you put it. I can learn. I want to. Anything you need, I'll be there. And I love you no matter what."

He presses his forehead to mine. "God, it feels good to hear that. I love you too. So much. It's always been you. Always will be you."

No, no, no. Calm down, silly heart. I need my wits about me, and my ears free of the relentless thumping that makes discerning his words rather difficult. He seems to have more to say, and I don't want to miss one word.

"I want us to build a life together. I want a family with you. Tell me you want the same," he whispers.

"You know I do."

"I need to hear it."

"I want a family with you. I want to spend the rest of my life making you happy. I'm all in, Dan. I'm all in."

He lets out a sharp exhale, releases my hands, and cups my face instead. Then he kisses me, and it's like I'm breathing again for the first time since I dropped him off at the airport. I've been too stressed out to fully enjoy the first kiss, but I'm determined to enjoy every single second of this one.

I slide my arms under his, encircling his torso, pulling him to me. He brings our bodies flush against one another, sinking against me as if he needs to feel every inch of my body against him, as if he needs me as much as I need him.

I give myself to him the way I always do: wholeheartedly. Only this time, I try to put every feeling and emotion into the kiss.

When we pull apart, I notice I'm trapped between the counter behind me and Daniel in front. Talk about being between a rock and a hard place.

Such a sweet hardship. I'll take it any day of the week. Dan kisses my forehead, my temple, then the tip of my nose. I'm shaking lightly. Maybe from the relief of being back in his arms and knowing he wants me in his life forever, just as I want him. Maybe it's because every cell in my body is clamoring for skin-on-skin contact, for him to be inside me. I want us to be united in every way.

As if reading my mind, he takes me in his arms, carries me up the stairs.

"I'm staying in your old room," I inform him, a thrill of anticipation running through me. He carries me straight to the en-suite bathroom. While we're ridding each other of clothes, I search his face. I'll never tire of looking at him, of trying to read him and anticipate what he needs to be happy.

We step in the shower together, and as the warm water sprays down on us, Daniel pours shower gel on his palms, then lowers himself, running his soapy hand along my leg, up one thigh. He brushes his thumb over my clit, luring a moan out of me, right before he moves his hands on my other leg, starting to soap it from my ankle, making his way up slowly. I'm shuddering with anticipation, my center burning. When his hands reach the apex of my thighs again, I need his fingers inside me so badly I nearly beg for it. Looking straight up at me, he slides his hands over the outside of my thighs to my ass, cupping it. One swipe of his tongue against my clit is all it takes for me to cry out for him, fisting his hair. He licks me again and again, until I'm unsteady on my legs. Then he kisses up to my navel, moves to my breasts, sucking one nipple into his mouth.

"Dan, oh!"

I feel him lift my legs, propping me back against the tiled wall. Instinctively, I wrap my legs around him and he lowers me onto him, filling me inch by inch. He groans my name as I clench around him and kiss his neck. His hands are holding my ass cheeks, his fingers digging into my skin. He fits me so perfectly. We simply stay like this, not moving or attempting to, simply *being* with each other. This moment is so intimate I'm trembling from the intensity of it.

He presses his thumb at the corners of my mouth, then kisses me again. When I part my lips and his tongue slips inside my mouth, I feel more tenderness and heat than ever before. I pulse around him, push my hips forward, seeking friction. He kisses down the side of my neck, then back up before finally unhitching his lips from my skin and looking me in the eyes.

"I still can't believe I'm lucky enough to have your love," I whisper.

"Then I'll do my best to prove it every day."

Chapter Thirty

Caroline

"I am so proud of myself. So proud." I smile as we step out of the hotel lobby and into the pleasantly cool Vegas morning.

Daniel cocks a brow. "You're worse than Summer."

"What are you talking about? I only fangirled about five times."

Batting my eyelashes, I flash him a grin. What was he expecting? He just introduced me to one of my *favorite* TV stars, Nina. When Daniel told me he was organizing her birthday party in Vegas and asked me if I wanted to join him, it took me all of five seconds to say yes. He patiently coached me how to deal with paparazzi in case any show up. He also gave me advice about how to act when I meet Nina. I'm still working on implementing it.

"What do you want to do?" he asks. "We have the whole day to ourselves."

"Well, since you're the Vegas expert, and I've never been, I want a private tour."

"Your wish is my command. Mid-December isn't the best month to be in Vegas, but at least we won't cook. Our last stop will be the Bellagio fountains. There's a water show every thirty minutes."

We're staying at a hotel on the Strip, so we're right in the middle of the hustle and bustle. I've visited quite a few cities, and they each have their own pulse, something that sets it aside from any other place—something beyond architecture or language or history. Vegas is colorful and vibrant, holding a sense of wonder and danger, and I can't wait to explore it with Daniel.

Some five hours later, I feel like my feet are about to fall off. We've visited all the major casinos—my favorite is hands down the Venetian, with its picturesque bridges, and the High Roller, the giant ferris wheel. As we watch the water show at the Bellagio fountains, I understand why Daniel kept it until the end. It's truly breathtaking, the best way to end the tour.

"You're truly a Vegas pro," I compliment him once the show is over and the tourists scatter. "Is there anything you haven't done in Vegas? Actually, don't answer. Some things I don't need to know."

Daniel chuckles, tucking me into him, kissing my cheek. "I have no secrets."

I unzip his jacket, snaking my arms inside it, holding onto him. He's grown suddenly quiet, a contemplative expression on his face.

"There is one thing I haven't done here," he says.

Is it my imagination, or does he sound a tad

uneven?

"What?"

He takes my hands out of his jacket, leading me through the streets once again. I have no idea where we're heading, but I trust him.

We enter one of the lower, inconspicuous buildings on a side street. I don't realize what we've walked into at first. There are many couples around us, some not entirely sober.

I only put two and two together when I spot the couple at the far end of the room, and the wedding officiant behind them.

"Oh my God." My mouth goes dry. We're in a chapel. Daniel's eyes are trained on me, waiting.

"That's one thing I haven't done. Anything you want to change about that?" he asks, voice rough, full of emotion.

"You planned this?"

"No. If I had, there would be no one else here, and I'd be wearing a suit. I'm not a cufflink man, but for such an occasion...."

I'm not dressed for the occasion either, obviously. I'm wearing jeans, a pink sweater under my jacket, and pink ballerina shoes with oversized bows.

"Oh, Dan! I—yes, let's do this. But wait... our families won't be too happy. But I also don't want to wait."

This might be a little surprising, a lot reckless, but oh my goodness, it feels so right. So perfect.

"It's up to you. We can wait and do

everything in San Francisco. Or we can do it now. Or we can have both. We can get married here, throw a party home."

"Sounds great." I'm so excited I can barely get the words out.

"Which part?"

"The last one. Wedding now, party home."

Dan doesn't answer. He simply pulls me in and kisses me hard. The sound of hands clapping fills the room. I blink open one eye and see that everyone is watching us.

"I love you so much," I whisper. He smiles, keeping me close, and I lose myself in him, in this moment.

I watch the couples in front get married as if through a haze. My senses seem to be completely consumed by Daniel. Our hands are clasped together as we wait.

When our turn comes, Daniel talks to the officiant in a low, hushed voice before the ceremony begins. As we stay next to each other, and the minister presents us with rings—simple gold bands—I can't help but wonder why everyone doesn't do this. Sometimes I think weddings are more for the benefit of the guests than the bride and groom, who often stress themselves out to please the guests at their own expense. This is perfect for us.

When the ceremony starts, I feel my entire body tense, excitement and adrenaline coursing through me. No nerves or hesitation grips me. This feels more right than anything ever has.

I can't believe this moment is here, that Daniel is standing next to me, about to become my husband. I'll make him the happiest man on earth; that's a vow I'm making to myself, and I intend to remind myself of it every day.

"Have you prepared any vows?" the officiant asks.

"No, but I want to say a few words anyway," Daniel says, turning to face me. "Caroline, we met when we were just becoming adults. You were my friend, then my lover. Then I let you go. I promise I'll never let you go again. You're my everything. And you'll be my everything for the rest of our days."

I smile, tears prickling at the corners of my eyes. We needed these years apart to become the people we are now, to grow and learn how to be there for each other in all ways.

"I love you, Dan. No matter what life will throw at us, I'll be there for you. I'll love you through all of it, until my last breath. And whatever comes after that, I'll love you then too."

Chapter Thirty-One

Caroline

I twirl once, watching the fabric float around me. The light pink chiffon swirls in waves. I love it. The bodice is tight around my torso, V-shaped, with broad straps across my shoulders. The skirt reaches down to the floor and is so voluminous, I'm afraid I'll get lost in it. Yet for all the fru-fru and seven layers of veil and whatnot, it's remarkably easy to move around in it.

When Dan and I touched down from Las Vegas, our wedding bands caused quite a stir, which is why we decided to have a second ceremony too, not just a party. So here we are, one week after Christmas, having a winter wedding.

I have to admit, I can't wait for the ceremony. There is something about making promises in front of everyone I love that beckons to me. It's the part I look forward to the most. And giving Dad the opportunity to walk me to the altar.

I admire my engagement ring again. The double infinity knots are all elegant curves and shiny diamonds. When Daniel gave it to me, I asked why infinity knots, and he answered, "Because we are forever."

I only received the ring yesterday. Daniel asked Pippa for a custom-made engagement ring, and Pippa confided in me that Daniel turned out to be her most demanding customer. They spent the two weeks since we returned from Vegas working on it.

"On the bright side, spending weeks overworking my creative juices gave me an idea for a new line of engagement rings: unusual designs. More than the princess, prong, and usual cuts and settings."

The sound of the door opening snaps me out of my daydreaming. Dad walks in, teary-eyed, and I can feel the emotions coming off him in waves. *Oh no!* At this rate, I'm going to turn misty-eyed in no time.

"Dad, I must say, you look dashing in a tuxedo." This is the first time I've seen him wearing one.

"Your mother would never have let me go to my daughter's wedding without one."

He opens his arms, and I walk right into them. I never missed Mom more than today, and this has to be just as hard for Dad. When we pull apart, he takes something out of his pocket.

"This belonged to your mother. I kept it with me, but it's a shame not to be worn."

He opens his fist to reveal Mom's old silver butterfly pendant.

"I don't know if it goes with your dress. It's not so fancy."

"Of course I'll wear it. It's perfect." My voice

wavers, loaded with emotion. I turn so he can clasp it around my neck, and we both sniffle lightly.

"Thank you, Dad." I feel a bit as if Mom is with us too, right this very moment.

We head out of the bedroom, down to the living room. I chose to get dressed here in my childhood home. Niall should arrive any minute now to drive us to the church.

"Fathers usually say no one is good enough for their daughters, but I don't feel that way. Daniel is a great man, and he loves you."

"Thank you, Dad."

"When I saw your mother, I knew."

"Really?" I've never heard their story. Too personal, I suppose, and I haven't asked.

"Yes. Took some time convincing her, though. She was always the practical one. Wanted to be sure we weren't being hasty."

"Sounds like her, yeah." I laugh, touching the pendant. Just then, a honk from outside tells us Niall is here.

The church is full to capacity with our family and friends, and I do my best not to let any nerves show as I slowly walk to the altar, my father's arm steadying me. When we come to a stop in front of my man, Daniel looks Dad straight in the eyes and says,

"I promise to take care of your daughter, love her, and respect her."

"I know you will."

After the ceremony, we head on foot to the restaurant, which is just across from the church. It's a lovely venue, large enough for the three hundred guests attending. Only about fifty were at the church; the rest will come directly to the restaurant. Daniel and I are leading the group of fifty, crossing the street. It rained this morning, so I have to keep my dress up to keep the hem from getting dirty. My satin shoes will probably be a mess, but no one will see them under the dress.

The restaurant is surrounded by a beautiful garden, and vines loop around the black iron entrance gate. Past that, a path of cobblestones leads to the front door of the restaurant. It was easy enough to walk on the uneven cobbles wearing flats, but in heels it's hell. I don't even voice that thought before Daniel hooks an arm around my waist, steadying my every step.

He only lets go inside the restaurant, where servers are waiting with trays of champagne. As the guests help themselves to a glass, I notice Summer is firing off instructions to the wedding planner. I barely suppress a grin. Between the wedding planner and Summer, Daniel and I didn't have to do much in terms of organizing.

We take two glasses for ourselves, then welcome every guest. We finish the greeting round by clinking glasses with Pippa and Summer.

"No more weddings to organize now," Summer says wistfully.

"What are you talking about?" Pippa asks. "We have more single cousins than I can count. Look at all those Connors. And there's you, of course."

"Of course. I'm sure the right one's out there somewhere. He just needs a map to find me. Or a compass. Better yet, a GPS. Mine's definitely not working. Keeps sending me into dead ends."

Boy, do I love Summer's optimism and energy.

"By the way, you have five minutes until your dance begins," she informs Daniel and me. Right, for all her sweetness, she does bossy well.

"Yes, boss," I say, trying to swallow my anxiety at the thought of dancing in front of everyone. Dan and I decided we're just going to dance to one of our favorite slow songs, without any fancy choreography.

By the time Daniel pulls me onto the dance floor, I've worked myself into a frenzy. But as soon as the song starts and he wraps an arm around my waist, taking my hand in his, some of that tension bleeds away. Dear God, how he holds me, how he looks at me, as if I'm the most precious thing in the world.

"I love you, Dan," I whisper.

He smiles, kissing the corner of my lips. "I love you too."

I melt against him, feeling safe and loved in his arms. Once the song is over, others join us on the dance floor.

The very best thing about the wedding dress? It's so long and voluminous, no one can see my feet. As long as I manage not to step on my own toes, I'm golden.

Between the food and the dancing, the night is a hit. The most memorable parts are the speeches. They start out humorous and relatively safe while our dads hold the mic, but the whole affair quickly spirals into wild and inappropriate when Blake's turn comes.

By the time the party is over, part of me wishes we could go on, even though I also desperately want our wedding night to begin.

After the last of the guests leave, and the family is carrying our presents to the car, Jenna hugs us both goodbye.

"Any words of wisdom?" I ask as I pull away from her arms. She looks from Dan to me, beaming.

"Laugh often. Don't go to bed mad. Learn to let go. Things are never as bad as they look like. Don't say hurtful things. You don't mean them, and you can't take them back. Don't forget to say 'I love you,' even after many years pass. Always look for the best in each other. Always love each other. And when there's a lot of love, you can work everything else out. Together."

Epilogue

Daniel

Two months later

"Caroline?" I set my keys in the yellow, fish-shaped bowl in the foyer, my hand shaking slightly around the envelope. I was supposed to be home in two hours, but once I got the news, I couldn't resist. She isn't in the living room. Upstairs, then.

I jog up the flight of stairs and smile. She added even more books to the bookcase on the upper floor of our house.

Martin's store is doing just fine since he and Caroline are arranging readings and games with nearby schools almost every second day. She also seems to be returning with new books almost weekly.

We moved into the new house three weeks ago. Four bedrooms is too much space for the two of us. But soon, it won't be just the two of us.

She's singing in the bathroom. Through the cracked door, I see her lying in the tub, bubbly water up to her chest.

Her hair is piled up in a bun, and pedicured toes peek out from the edge of the tub. The smell of vanilla assaults my senses. Any day now, I'll man up and jump in with her even if she's using one of those sickly sweet bath bombs. Approaching the edge of the tub, I notice the headphones, and the phone lying on the floor next to the tub. As gently as I can, I pull out an earbud. She startles anyway, splashing water and foam everywhere.

"So sorry," she mumbles, clearing the foam that landed on my shirt. She stops moving when I hold up the envelope. "Is this what I think it is?"

I nod, emotion clogging my throat. "Arrived at my office half an hour ago. I couldn't wait."

"Can you take the papers out so I can see them? My hands are wet."

I waste no time pulling the papers out. There it is, black on white. We are now officially the parents of seven-year-old Hugo and his sister, three-year-old Elisabeth. We had to wait until after the business with Justin Hamel was sorted because having an open case with the courts wouldn't have worked in our favor with the adoption agency. We decided to settle out of court, and he won't be bothering anyone I love ever again. Caroline and I filed our adoption petition the next day.

When our social worker told us that older children who are already in the system have less chance of being adopted because couples always want babies, Caroline and I decided on the spot to opt for such cases. One month later, she told us about Hugo and Elisabeth, and we said yes and filed all the papers.

Caroline stands on her knees on the floor of

the tub, reading the words again and again.

"We can pick them up in two weeks. Our kids. They're ours, Dan."

"Yeah, they are." I set the papers aside on a dry spot, then cup her face, kissing her cheek, her temple. She's trembling slightly in my arms, emotion pouring off her. "And we're going to love them so much. So much."

She rises to her feet, reaching out for a towel. I get it for her, drying her off, then lift her in my arms, carrying her to our bedroom, kissing her the entire way.

When I lay her on our bed, she looks up at me with so much tenderness and adoration, she brings me to my knees.

"Promise me you'll always kiss me like this," I say. "That you'll always look at me like this, as if I'm everything to you."

"I promise. I don't know how to love you any other way, Dan."

"Good, because I will love you more every day."

THE END

Other Books by Layla Hagen

The Bennett Family Series

Book 1: Your Irresistible Love (Sebastian & Ava)

Sebastian Bennett is a determined man. It's the secret behind the business empire he built from scratch. Under his rule, Bennett Enterprises dominates the jewelry industry. Despite being ruthless in his work, family comes first for him, and he'd do anything for his parents and eight siblings—even if they drive him crazy sometimes. . . like when they keep nagging him to get married already.

Sebastian doesn't believe in love, until he brings in external marketing consultant Ava to oversee the next collection launch. She's beautiful, funny, and just as stubborn as he is. Not only is he obsessed with her delicious curves, but he also finds himself willing to do anything to make her smile. He's determined to have Ava, even if she's completely off limits.

Ava Lindt has one job to do at Bennett Enterprises: make the next collection launch unforgettable. Daydreaming about the hot CEO is definitely not on her to-do list. Neither is doing said

CEO. The consultancy she works for has a strict policy—no fraternizing with clients. She won't risk her job. Besides, Ava knows better than to trust men with her heart.

But their sizzling chemistry spirals into a deep connection that takes both of them by surprise. Sebastian blows through her defenses one sweet kiss and sinful touch at a time. When Ava's time as a consultant in his company comes to an end, will Sebastian fight for the woman he loves or will he end up losing her?

AVAILABLE ON ALL RETAILERS.

Book 2: Your Captivating Love (Logan & Nadine)
Book 3: Your Forever Love (Eric & Pippa)
Book 4: Your Inescapable Love (Max & Emilia)
Book 5: Your Tempting Love (Christopher & Victoria)
Book 6: Your Alluring Love (Alice & Nate)
Book 7: Your Fierce Love (Blake & Clara)

The Lost Series

***

Book 1: Lost in Us (James & Serena)
Book 2: Found in Us (Jessica & Parker)
Book 3: Caught in Us (Dani & Damon)

***

Standalone USA TODAY BESTSELLER

Withering Hope

Aimee's wedding is supposed to turn out perfect. Her dress, her fiancé and the location—the idyllic holiday ranch in Brazil—are perfect.

But all Aimee's plans come crashing down when the private jet that's taking her from the U.S. to the ranch—where her fiancé awaits her—defects mid-flight and the pilot is forced to perform an emergency landing in the heart of the Amazon rainforest.

With no way to reach civilization, being rescued is Aimee and Tristan's—the pilot—only hope. A slim one that slowly withers away, desperation taking its place. Because death wanders in the jungle under many forms: starvation, diseases. Beasts.

As Aimee and Tristan fight to find ways to survive, they grow closer. Together they discover that facing old, inner agonies carved by painful pasts takes just as much courage, if not even more, than facing the rainforest.

Despite her devotion to her fiancé, Aimee can't hide her feelings for Tristan—the man for whom she's slowly becoming everything. You can hide many things in the rainforest. But not lies. Or love.

Withering Hope is the story of a man who desperately needs forgiveness and the woman who brings him hope. It is a story in which hope births wings and blooms into a love that is as beautiful and intense as it is forbidden.

AVAILABLE ON ALL RETAILERS.

***

Published: Layla Hagen 2017
Cover: http://designs.romanticbookaffairs.com/

***

Acknowledgements

Publishing a book takes a village! A big THANK YOU to everyone accompanying me on this journey. To my family, thank you for supporting me, believing in me, and being there for me every single day. I could not have done this without you.

<<<<>>>>

YOUR ONE TRUE LOVE

Printed in Great Britain
by Amazon

80060738R00187